INTIMACY
ISSUES

Claudia Whitsitt

CLAUDIA WHITSITT

ACKNOWLEDGEMENTS

My team of supporters is so vast; it's hard to know where to begin. My husband, Don, reads countless drafts of my work, offers me solid advice, and prepares gourmet meals so that I can write. Best of all, he knows when to serve me a glass of wine! My children, Noah, Melissa, and Jenna provide me with hugs, laughter, and boundless love. My parents, Pat and Larry Teal, share their interest and pride. My friends and family provide me with an endless cheering section!

My gratitude also pours out to my Southern California Writers Conference family. In particular, I'd like to thank Michael Steven Gregory and Wes Albers for supporting and promoting my work. To my editor and multi-talented friend, Laura Taylor, I'd be lost without you. Jennifer Silva Redmond, Bob Yehling, Jean Jenkins, and Matt Pallamary—you guys are the best! Thanks also to Jeremy Lee James, whom I can always count on for his truthfulness, humor, and friendship.

To my writing group and home team: Barbara Stark-Nemon, Kathy York, and Patty Hoffman. Hugs all around!

Yes, Jeff Daniels, I wrote the book!

Last but not least, to my publisher, Patricia Maas—to you my heartfelt appreciation for pushing me to produce suspenseful and gripping reads!

Thanks, I love you all!

This book is dedicated with love and gratitude to Lori LaBoe. Your constant encouragement, honest feedback, friendship, and devotion are unequaled. Not only do you foster my writing life, but you bring light and laughter to all of my days. I am so blessed to have you in my life, and I thank God for you each day. We're soul mates, girlfriend, and I love you more than words can say!

CHAPTER ONE

MY NAME IS Samantha Stitsill — mother of five, special education teacher, and as of eleven months ago, widow. Oh, one more thing. The day after my husband died, the man who'd stolen his identity broke into my home. I had no choice but to shoot him dead on my basement stairs. Bastard.

Around the time I lost my husband, my teaching buddy, the fiercely Italian bombshell, Diane Rossi Harris, married, got pregnant on her honeymoon, and moved to our small town. Her close proximity kept me grounded, and her husband's history as a confirmed bachelor provided me with plenty of light-hearted amusement. Chris had definite ideas about what constituted an intimate relationship. Very different ideas from Di's.

Spring had arrived in our quaint little town of Dubois, and at last the sidewalks were clear of snow. I even detected a tinge of green on the landscape. In an effort to keep our aging bodies tuned, Di and I forged a pact to walk 4.6 miles a day. For a precious sixty-five minutes each afternoon, we talked as fast as we walked — therapy and exercise. It was all the time we could spare. My kids could only be trusted alone for so long, and the sitter Diane employed for her infant could only be available until 5:30 p.m.

As we angled past the Dairy Queen and crossed the main drag that separated the north end of town from the south, Di began chattering. "Last night I put my foot down and insisted Chris and I try to sleep together. Really sleep together. You know, my head on his chest, his arm around my shoulder."

I laughed. "He's never been a cuddler. How'd that work out?"

Di shook her head. "Not well. Within an hour, Chris shook me awake and told me to move. He felt hot and needed to stretch."

"He's high maintenance, Di. Don't take it personally."

Di shook her head, barely stopping for air. "I grabbed my damn body pillow, positioned it in the center of the bed, rolled over, and closed my eyes. Then, he said his back hurt, and begged for a back rub so I had to reach over the stupid pillow and massage his shoulders."

I grabbed her elbow and saved her from rushing into traffic. "You knew this before you married him, and you also know how easy it is to change a man."

Di nodded, rolling her eyes.

"Don't get me wrong. I get it."

"I'm adamant he try cuddling every couple of nights. I'll wean him into it, just like I'll wean Ava off my breast when she turns one." Her pace quickened and she giggled. "That's eleven months off. I'm guessing it'll take at least that long."

Rivulets of sweat streamed down my temples, and I swiped at them as I remembered my late husband. "Jon loved to cuddle. There were times his arm weighed so heavy around my middle, I ached when I woke up, or I'd have to move his hand off my boob during the night just so I could go to the bathroom."

"Sorry." Di shot me a sympathetic gaze. "I didn't mean to bring up painful memories."

"It's okay. It's getting easier. Most of the time, I'm so busy with the kids, I don't have time to think about him. And I take care of long nights with a sleeping pill."

"Whatever works."

I glanced at Di and grinned. "Busy works."

"They say the first year is the hardest."

"I'd guess they're right," I agreed. "I'm closing in on the first anniversary, and life seems a bit more normal."

"Normal," Di huffed. "Whatever the hell that is."

"Seriously," I agreed. "And now that Marie and Annie have their learner's permits and fight to drive me all over town, I don't have time to let my thoughts wander. Driving with those girls is nerve-wracking."

"Are they bad drivers?"

"Not at all, but they both have attitude. Typical teenagers. Can't tell them anything. They require practice, I require patience."

We rounded the corner near the middle school and headed down the long straightaway toward the elementary schools on the north end of the campus. The afternoon sun beat down on us and not a single tree lined our path. All this talk of the girls driving caused beads of sweat to trickle down my back like a waterfall, so I increased my stride, anxious to reach the next sliver of shade, a short half-mile away.

"It's because Jon died in a car accident, don't you think?" Di pumped her arms to keep up.

"Probably has something to do with it. I can't even bring myself to think about the girls driving on their own."

"It's a while away. You'll be fine by then."

"I hope you're right."

"You're tough. You've survived this tragedy. It'll work out."

I nodded. I already knew I could handle anything. I'd pretty much proven it.

"Since we're talking about uncomfortable issues today, can I ask you about Detective McGrath? I thought he might be a possibility. I sort of remember him from our canoeing accident last summer." Di peered at me. "He's cute, right?"

I nodded as I pictured McGrath. "Very."

Jim McGrath, the detective who'd helped me to figure out who'd stolen my husband's identity, had become a friend. Then, after Jon's impostor invaded my home and I'd killed him in self-defense, McGrath helped me mop up the mess so the cops, the FBI, and the other alphabet government agencies would leave me the hell alone. But I'd felt guilty continuing our relationship. I was married, but I felt a serious growing attraction to him. Then my husband died. That's enough to mess with anybody's mind.

Up until now, I'd hesitated to reveal the totality of my feelings for McGrath to Di. I didn't want to be judged. I guessed it was time. "I only met him a short while before Jon's death, remember? We kept it professional. Granted, we both felt a strong attraction, and if Jon hadn't died, well, I can't guarantee what would have happened. But I asked McGrath for time and space. He's been respectful of that. To be honest, I miss him. Or at least the idea of him."

"Enough time has passed, even by Emily Post's standards. Why the heck don't you let yourself go?"

"It's been forever. I don't even know if he's single anymore."

"Call him. Meet him for dinner or..." Di paused. "Remember after I divorced? You made me go out with Chris."

"Coffee. I can see a coffee date." I thought about more than coffee, though.

"There you go." Di flashed me a look of supreme satisfaction.

"What?" I squinted at her.

"I think you're going to wind up together someday." Di had feelings about everything. Especially relationships. She drove me crazy with her cockamamie hunches. But, in this particular case, I sort of hoped she was right.

"Doesn't seem possible."

"You're wrong." Di shot me another all-knowing look.

When we ended our walk at Di's driveway, I waved a

kiss goodbye before covering the driver's seat with a clean towel, starting the van, and heading home.

How would I manage a date? I thought about it. My father-in-law, Ed Stitsill, had moved down the road after his wife, Betty, had died six months ago. Ed helped me to shuttle the kids back and forth, lent a hand with homework, cooked the occasional meal, and even whistled while he performed simple home repairs. He loved his grandkids and pitched in at my house to help bridge the gap until he found a new life. I knew he'd babysit if I decided to go for coffee with McGrath.

Ed had encouraged me to get back in the game just a few days ago. "I know you loved my son. And I understand your need to devote yourself to the kids this past year. But I also know three things. You're young. You have a lifetime ahead of you, and Jon wouldn't want you to be alone."

I wasn't so sure about that. If I'd died and left Jon behind with five kids, would I have been that magnanimous? From a rational view, yes, but my heart broke at the thought of him being with another woman, even though I'd had to deal with that very real possibility around the time of his death. This was going to be complicated.

"You need to put yourself out there," Ed encouraged.

I flipped my thoughts to practical matters. "Who wants a woman with five children?"

"The right man, Sam."

"Seems like a lot to ask," I'd retorted. Not that Jim McGrath didn't fit the bill. Hell, I'd bet serious money that he'd seize the opportunity if I gave him half a chance. If he hadn't found someone else in the meantime, that is.

McGrath, all man, punched responsibility in the face like a boxer in pursuit of a prize. But five kids? McGrath had been married once, a long time ago, but he didn't have kids of his own. Nor did he have nieces or nephews he spent time with on a regular basis. As I pondered the situation, I wondered if he could adjust to the commotion of kids rushing around, arguing with each other, raising a constant ruckus.

"The kids aren't going to be home forever," Ed reminded me. "They'll grow up."

While I recognized the truth of his words, I also felt an obligation to raise my children to adulthood without disrupting their lives any more than necessary. Before Jon and I had married, the older kids had already weathered tough divorces. My kids' dad disappeared with a bottle of whiskey. Jon's kids' mom preferred drugs over her relationship with them.

Due to his ex-wife's love affair with heroine, Jon had been granted full custody of Will and Marie two years after we married, and their supervised visits with their mother since then had been spotty. In the brief patch when she'd gotten herself clean, they'd enjoyed a few special moments, but that deteriorated the instant she allowed her pusher to move in with her. That was shortly after Jon died. I'd had to juggle that troubling, dangerous situation on top of everything else.

I couldn't allow Will and Marie to spend time in that environment; they'd become my kids too. So I withdrew a chunk of change from Jon's life insurance policy and hired an attorney. After an ugly investigation on the part of Child Protective Services and a draining series of court hearings, the judge awarded me guardianship of the two of them. It was worth every cent to have the assurance that they would live safely and soundly under my roof.

I'd had to agree to a supervised visitation schedule, but their biological mom rarely showed up for her designated visits, and we'd weathered that emotional scarring for the most part. There were tears and meltdowns a few times, but Nick and Annie would remind Will and Marie that they could always count on us. On occasion, I'd considered contacting a shrink and asking for a group rate, but for the time being, we were holding our own.

Also as a result of the court proceedings, I'd been promised adoption if Will and Marie's mother tested positive for drugs, missed her court-ordered parenting classes, or continued to cohabitate with the former convict within the next year. In my mind, it was just a matter of time before the kids were mine. Thank you, God.

On second thought, coffee with McGrath might be more than I could take on right now. I pulled into the driveway and parked in the garage. The house still stood.

Through the garage window, I spotted Nick and Will, now twelve years old, as they tossed a football back and forth in the yard. Then Lizzie, who'd just turned seven, threw open the screen door as I stepped out of the car. I shut the van door and as I approached her, she flung her arms around my middle. "Where are Annie and Marie?"

"Upstairs, fixing each other's hair." Lizzie gazed up at me with a toothless grin. "What's for supper?"

"Soup," I said. "I'm going to warm it up right away and pop biscuits in the oven. Be a good girl and set the table."

I noticed the blinking light on the answering machine and shook my head. For the life of me, I couldn't understand why the kids never listened to the voice mail. On the other hand, it meant that messages didn't get discarded without my knowledge. Good news or bad, I'd deal with it later. I pulled the soup pot from the fridge, set the burner on low, and rushed upstairs for a five minute shower.

Forty-five minutes later, the kids fed and the dishes cleaned up, I poured a glass of cabernet and snuck out onto the front porch to catch my breath while the kids started their homework. The air had chilled in the typical Midwestern spring evening, and I shivered. As I settled back and rocked in the wicker chair, I felt a familiar tug on my heartstrings. I missed Jon. Part of our usual routine had been to grab a glass of wine and escape from the kids after the evening meal. Even if just for a quick trip to the living room, we'd always taken the time to catch up with each other.

I swallowed hard. Thinking about the possibility of letting McGrath back into my life scared me half to death. Part of me still ached for Jon, but another part of me longed to feel whole and normal again. When Lizzie turns eighteen, I'll only be fifty, I realized. There would be plenty of time for me then, right? Then again, did I really want to wait that long?

Lizzie peeked out the door. "Mom," she whined. "Multiplication tables."

I nodded and headed back inside. The light on the answering machine still flashed. While Lizzie ran upstairs to retrieve her books and flash cards, I punched the play button.

"Hi, Sam," he said. "It's me. Been thinking about you. If you feel like it, give me a call."

My heart stuttered. Jim McGrath.

CHAPTER TWO

BY THE TIME I ushered the kids to bed, exhaustion wormed its way through me. I remembered when they were small and I could actually stay awake after they'd fallen asleep and have some time to myself or alone with Jon. As I closed the door to my bedroom, set my wine on the nightstand and fell into bed, I thought again about Jim McGrath. What did his call mean?

It was unrealistic of me to have expected him to wait while I grieved for Jon. But it had almost been a year, and he'd phoned. A shiver sliced down my spine. I'd hoped that he'd waited. Still, I couldn't bring myself to call him back. Not yet.

I tossed and turned for ninety minutes. Finally, I opened my eyes and peered at the clock. Midnight. Too late to call anyone. I picked up the phone anyway and dialed McGrath's cell, a number I had committed to memory long ago. As the phone rang, my stomach knotted.

"Hello?" he answered, sounding more than a little sexy.

"It's me, Sam." Electricity zipped through me.

"It's great to hear your voice."

I stared into the dark, propped on my elbow with the phone nuzzled against my ear. My heartbeat quickened and a smile crossed my face. "Yours, too," I admitted. "How've you been?"

He chuckled. "Lonely, to tell you the truth."

"What, no one's taken you off the market yet?" I joked, unsure how to interpret McGrath's remark. The thought of being with him again made me weak, or perhaps it was the thought of not being with him that turned my legs to jelly.

"Hardly," he answered.

"What's new?"

"Hoping you'll consider going out with me."

I stayed quiet for a full sixty seconds. "I don't know if I'm ready."

"What's holding you back?" he asked.

I rolled onto my back, settling against the pillows. "So many things," I admitted. "The kids. I don't want to disrupt their world. My public persona. I don't want anyone thinking I'm moving too fast."

"Not to be disrespectful, but it's been almost a year."

"I guess I hoped by now I'd feel more..." I paused, "closure."

"I get it," McGrath replied. "Jon died a world away. You didn't see his body after his death," he continued, "and then not being able to put a set of logical events together leading up to his accident. The lack of clear answers from the government..."

"You've always been quick to figure me out." I smiled.

"Detective-think," he said. "I've mastered the nuances."

I shook my head. "It's scary. I admit things to you that I barely admit to myself."

"It's one of my charms," McGrath said as he softened his tone.

"Amazingly, you're right." I agreed, then grew quiet for a long moment. "Did I wake you?"

"Trying to change the subject?"

"Maybe," I confessed.

"Rouse me any time. But if you'd prefer, we could talk during the day. We could even meet for coffee. Better yet, a drink."

"Can I think about it?" I asked.

"Boy, you're tough. It's just a drink. I promise. Think of it this way, you'd be giving a lonely guy a boost."

"Well," I said, "if you insist."

"When?"

"Can I check with Ed and call you back?"

"Ed? You're seeing someone?"

"My father-in-law." I laughed. "He's also my sitter."

"You about stopped my heart," McGrath said.

"Right." I chuckled. "There's a long line of men knocking down the door." So he's that interested. Inside cartwheel. "Most times, Ed's available, but I hesitate to make plans without checking with him first."

"How long are you going to make me wait?"

"I'll call you soon. I promise." I stole a moment to think. "We could meet tomorrow evening or Saturday, if he's free."

"Okay. I'll count on it. I've missed you."

I placed the phone back into its cradle, surprised at the ease with which I'd given in. I rolled over and fell sound asleep — without the aid of a sleeping pill for the first time in almost a year.

When I awoke the next morning at 4:15 a.m., I popped out of bed with renewed energy and plowed through my morning routine. I buzzed downstairs, dressed and enjoying my first cup of coffee by 5 a.m. By the time I woke the kids for school, I'd cycled two loads of laundry and straightened the family room. The older four grabbed a quick breakfast before they rushed out the door. I called up to Lizzie, whose elementary school started an hour later. "C'mon, girl, the mom bus is leaving." I lobbed my purse over my shoulder.

Lizzie ran downstairs, hair flying behind her as she grabbed her backpack and the toasted bagel I'd left on the counter. As we approached the car, Lizzie yanked open the passenger door, tossed her bag inside, grabbed my arm and kissed it.

I kissed the top of her head and smelled her shampoo. I loved that Lizzie's blonde curls still tumbled in tangles around her shoulders and that she, of all the kids, cared little about the match of her clothing or the style of her hair. Lizzie, my free spirit.

"Got your homework?" I asked.

"Of course, Mom. Remember? I'm the responsible one."

I chuckled. All my kids claimed to be the model of responsibility. If only it were so. I held Lizzie's hand the two short miles to her friend's house where I dropped her off with a final hug and kiss. "See you, later, sweetie. Have a great day!"

"You, too, Mom. I love you!" Lizzie clambered out of the van and waved over her shoulder as she ran to the front door.

"Love you, too," I called after her.

I turned up the radio and let my mind wander to Jim McGrath as I drove the thirty-five minutes to my school, several districts away. I wondered if he'd changed, and remembered what I liked best about him. When he smiled, dimples grooved his cheeks, and his blue eyes sparkled against the striking contrast of his coffee-colored hair. His uniform consisted of a tweed sports coat, no matter what the weather, and jeans. Just picturing him made me feel alive again. I pulled out my cell phone and dialed Ed.

"Morning, Sam."

"Hey, Dad. How are you?"

"Fine and dandy. Got weekend plans?"

I smiled, comforted by our easy relationship. Ed asked me that every Friday morning, part of our usual routine. "Why? Do you?"

"Not yet, you'd better beat me to it."

"As a matter of fact, I wondered if you'd be willing to hold down the fort for a few hours tonight or tomorrow night."

"Your pick, my dear."

I thought for a moment. Much as I'd like to see McGrath sooner rather than later, I opted for later. That way I'd have time to primp. After all, it had been a good long while since I'd spent time with a man. "How about tomorrow evening? I'm not sure what the kids have planned," I said, "but I can guarantee, it involves chauffeuring."

"I know how to drive," Ed joked.

"Come early for dinner?"

"How about this… I'll worry about dinner and you take some time for yourself."

I smiled. "Sounds like heaven."

"See you then," Ed said.

I disconnected and phoned McGrath. When he didn't pick up, I left him a message. "Hi, it's me. How about tomorrow evening? I'll meet you at the Frozen Margarita at seven. Call me back if that's inconvenient."

Quite by chance, the Frozen Margarita had marked our first face to face meeting. It was almost a year ago, and I admit it. I'd been a bit devilish that night, realizing that McGrath was the detective who'd called to question me about my husband. After Rosie Stitsill had suggested to him that I might be married to her dead husband, he asked me a few questions verifying that I knew the man I'd married. Back then, the entire situation had seemed preposterous. And very confusing.

In any case, I'd kept my little secret, never letting on that I was Samantha Stitsill, or that we had spoken on the phone about this odd situation. Instead, I'd flirted with him. Out of character for me, a married mother of five. But what can I say? Margaritas have a dangerous effect on a woman who seldom leaves the house.

Seeing him there would be sentimental. And I suspected even more seductive than our first chance meeting.

CHAPTER THREE

DI MET ME at me at my classroom door. "Walk today?"
"Sure," I said.

She eyed me. "You look different. Do you have something you'd like to share?"

Di and her damned intuition. "Meet you at 4 p.m." I hedged with a sly smile.

"Can't wait." Di smiled back.

The day flew by. I rushed to my car after school. Today, I didn't mind not joining the rest of the staff as they headed across the street to the local bar for the ritual Friday post-work gathering. I couldn't wait to get home, settle the kids, and head out to meet Di.

After I arrived home, I paused to kiss each of the kids, check in with them, and load the counter with snacks. Then, I raced to Di's house.

She met me on the sidewalk in front of her home, and we began speed walking our usual route.

"Spill," Di said. "I haven't seen you this happy in a very long time."

"Coincidentally," I began, "Detective McGrath phoned last night."

"And?" Di narrowed her eyes but stayed focused on the sidewalk.

"I'm meeting him at the Frozen Margarita tomorrow night."

"Fantastic!" Di said. "Are you okay?"

"Excited, but nervous."

"What are you nervous about?"

"The possibilities."

Di nodded. "It's going to be great. I'm so proud of you."

"Me, too." My nerves chewed at my gut. I changed the subject. "Now, fill me in on Chris. Did you try cuddling again?"

"Funny. He's trying, but the poor guy can't bring himself to let me near him when he's about to fall sleep."

"The man has issues," I joked.

"Plenty," Di admitted. "It's what happens when a guy's single until the age of forty-four. Bachelor's in his blood."

"You'd think he'd be delighted to cozy up next to a hot mama like you."

"Yeah." Di tossed her chocolate brown pony tail. "But he likes his space. He won't even let me bring the baby to bed."

"Keep working on him." I grabbed Di for the second time in as many days as she dashed into the street without a glance. "Good God, girl, if you get yourself killed, he won't have anyone to sleep with and Ava won't have a mother."

"I know," Di agreed. "When we walk, the rest of the world fades away."

"Drivers don't stop for pedestrians in Dubois. Only in Worthington."

Di giggled. "I'm just excited about your date."

"Well, concentrate. I need you alive so I can run all the details by you. Now, back to Chris."

"Last night, I reasoned with him. I asked him to cuddle for five minutes more each evening. When we work our way up to twenty minutes, and cuddle that long for twenty-one days in a row, I think it will become a habit. I read it in a book somewhere."

Di had prescriptions for everything. She'd put the baby on a schedule when she turned three weeks old. Let her cry herself to sleep each night, fed her on a four hour schedule which she then lengthened to six hours during the night, then eight, until she'd put a solid night's sleep in place.

"It worked with Ava, so maybe it'll work with Chris. You could always guarantee him some kind of reward every few nights. That might work."

"You know Chris," Di said. "He still expects to have sex like we did when we dated, even though we now have a baby and a dog."

"Wait. The dog interrupts sex?" I shook my head. "Surely, he's trained by now."

"In that case, I'm the one who's trained," Di confessed. "I'm a sucker for that damn dog."

Thoughts of Di's golden retriever made me miss Rex, my own golden whom I'd lost when my life went haywire because of Jon's impostor. I was fairly certain the fraud had killed his wife, Rosie, my dog, Rex, and possibly my husband. But Di didn't know the entire story, and I'd decided she never would. Some matters demanded discretion. This was one of them.

As we curved around the last mile stretch, I went quiet, and felt an uncomfortable knot in my stomach. Evidently, McGrath's call revived more than just good feelings. Painful memories of loss flooded to the surface. I squeezed my eyes shut for a long moment, determined to block them out.

Di's voice distracted me. "What are you going to wear?"

"I haven't thought much about clothes this past year. When Jon was alive, he loved to shop with me. He'd watch me try on clothes then load them up and buy them for me. It pleased him I was thin and attractive. His friends called me 'Jon's hot wife.' I can't say I've thought much in a long while about the hot factor. The kids have kept me busy." I smiled. "It holds a certain appeal though. Tonight, I'm going to spend some time in my closet. See if I can resurrect a date outfit." I shook my head.

"What is it?" Di asked.

"I feel more than a little guilty."

"Understandable, but seriously, Sam, do you ever wonder why Jon had to be away so much. Were things really all that good between you?"

"Ouch!" I winced.

"Just saying," Di said.

"You're not wrong. Jon's absences were tough. It was his job though. He felt he had to take care of us. Do what he had to do to keep the family afloat. I can't blame him for that." My thoughts then wandered to my suspicions. A short time before his death, I'd phoned Jon in Japan. A drowsy-sounding woman had answered his hotel room phone, and she'd told me Jon had an afternoon meeting at the manufacturing plant. The woman seemed territorial when she'd spoken his name. Call it woman's intuition. Call it whatever. I'd felt betrayed. In truth, it stung whenever I allowed myself to remember that phone call.

Suddenly, I felt as nauseous as I had that morning. Jon died before I could confront him about my suspicions. Common sense dictated that he'd probably been unfaithful, but I didn't want to believe it… and even if he was, his infidelity didn't justify my pursuit of another man. I'd been confused enough when I'd found myself attracted to Jim McGrath before Jon's death. Now, guilt seemed to rear its ugly head again. It didn't make sense, but I recognized with increasing clarity that guilt ruled a fair portion of my life.

"Shit, this is complicated," I said.

"Life is problematic." Di glanced my way and giggled. "Want me to make an excuse and tell Chris I need to stop by your house after dinner? I could help you pick out an outfit."

"No, that's alright. It'll be late by the time I have the chance to search for clothing." I paused and glanced at Di. "Maybe I shouldn't go."

"That's plain stupid. Of course, you should go. You're single, Sam. You need to have a life."

"Easier said than done." I slowed my pace. I felt like I'd

been turned inside out. What the hell was wrong with me?

"One day at a time," Di advised. "And try not to be so hard on yourself."

I nodded. "You're right. I've gotten myself all wound up. It's just a drink, not a lifetime commitment to love, honor, and cherish."

"Exactly." Di placed a reassuring hand on my back.

We ended our walk in front of her house, both of us sweat-soaked and breathing hard.

I scanned the landscape. Leaves opened on the trees, tulips bloomed in flower beds. Life was good. I needed to focus on that now.

I gathered a breath. "Okay," I said to her and to myself, "I'm gonna get a life."

CHAPTER FOUR

I TUCKED LIZZIE into her bed at 9 p.m. The older kids lay sprawled across the family room floor with a tub of popcorn and a movie. I ducked upstairs with a glass of wine and entered my closet. I had plenty of clothes. After trying on several outfits, I picked one — a pencil skirt, a frilly blouse, and a cardigan. Not slutty. Not motherly. Pretty. Middle ground that wouldn't leave me feeling self-conscious.

I checked my cell before turning in. McGrath had texted back one word. "Perfect." My doubt and apprehension disappeared in an instant.

Saturday morning, I played board games with Lizzie while I sipped my coffee. Next, I tossed a load of laundry into the washer, then woke the rest of the household with the smell of pancakes and bacon. The kids tumbled into the kitchen and chatter filled the room. As I looked at them, my heart filled with happiness. They were good kids. And we had each other.

I played chauffeur all morning. Each child had a different activity until lunch. After sandwiches, I assigned chores and escaped to the bathroom for a leisurely bath. I finished preparations with time to spare. I puttered around the second floor, checked my makeup twice, changed, and then changed back. By the time I descended the stairs, Ed had arrived. He indicated his approval with a nod and a raise of his eyebrows. He was too polite to ask for details. I'd do the same for him. When the time came for either one of us to talk about someone new in our lives, we'd let each other know. In the meantime, mutual respect served as our MO.

Nick raised his eyebrows, too. Nick's my intuitive boy, always noticing nuances the others miss. "Where are you going, Mom?" he asked, alert to my heightened attention to make-up and wardrobe.

"Just out for a drink with a friend." I circled the room and planted kisses on foreheads.

"Hey, Nick," Ed interrupted. "Run out to the garage and grab a few Cokes. Stick them in the freezer so they get cold before the pizza arrives." He glanced at me and winked.

I thanked my father-in-law with a peck on the cheek. He bounced Lizzie on his knee as she chattered on about feeding ducks at the park and the huge play structure where she'd spent an hour hanging upside down. I smiled at the lot of them before I headed out to my van.

The drive to the Frozen Margarita took thirty minutes. I turned up the radio and let the lyrics set the mood for time with a man. Each song seemed to have a heightened meaning. By the time I pulled into the restaurant parking lot, I felt flirty and fun. I also recalled I'd always felt like a much younger girl around McGrath, when I wasn't leaning on him for emotional support, that is.

I walked directly into the bar and located two empty bar stools. I planted my purse on one and myself on the other. After I ordered a cold beer, I sat and waited, peaceful, content, and just a tad nervous. When McGrath placed a warm hand on my shoulder a few minutes later, my skin almost melted under his touch.

I turned to look at him and my breath caught.

I couldn't resist this man. That's what had scared me away from him eleven months ago. Those feelings still remained. Not gone. Not buried in the least. Right on the surface.

I wrapped my arms around him and held on tight, my

eyes welling with tears. "It's so good to see you." It had been a long time since anything felt this good.

"Likewise," McGrath said as he squeezed me tight. "And, by the way, nice choice of restaurants."

McGrath let go, settled onto the stool next to mine, and ordered a drink. He looked at me and smiled. It seemed like our gazes stayed fixed on each other for a very long time. Finally, I linked my arm in his and nestled my head on his shoulder. "Thanks," I said.

"For what?" McGrath looked puzzled.

"For calling." I gave in then, and allowed myself to feel how amazing it felt to be with him again.

"It's been an excruciating wait. You don't know how many times I've wanted to call. When you told me you needed time to grieve for Jon, I understood. I figured you'd call me when you were ready. I have to admit, there were days when I worried you'd changed your feelings, or you didn't feel as strongly as I did. As luck would have it, self-preservation and ego took over, and I told myself there was no way you didn't feel the same way I do." He chuckled. "Finally, I gave up waiting and called. I'm glad it's alright with you."

"Better than alright," I admitted. In that instant, I questioned why I'd denied myself this man for so long — risked losing him, in fact.

"I'm glad you're still single. I thought you might have given up on me by now. As a matter of fact, there were times when I'd hoped you'd moved on, just so I wouldn't have to decide," I confessed.

"Decide?" McGrath looked at his mug and played with its handle.

"That I wanted to be with you." I squeezed his forearm.

He leaned nearer and kissed my cheek. "So, you've decided?" He looked hopeful.

"You're funny." I laughed. "I'm just glad to be here... To see your face again."

"You look great, by the way."

"You have no idea how good you look," I said.

We drank another beer and decided to order dinner at the bar. As the crowd thickened, we moved closer to each other in order to hear. At least, we used that as our excuse. We caught up on our jobs and my kids, and then we compared notes on the impostor's death.

"I figured you'd let me know if you heard anything I should be concerned about," I said.

"No, it's like we said at the time," McGrath said, "nobody wants to hear another word about it. Once you got rid of Stitsill for the Feds, they were happy campers."

"Every now and then," I admitted, "I feel a twinge of guilt about destroying Jon's passport."

"We agreed, Sam, you had to protect your family. The less attention given to that thug and his past, the better."

"It still seems unreal. The entire series of events. Jon's missing passport. The unlikely appearance of Rosita. I mean, really, who would believe that this woman thought I was married to her dead husband?"

McGrath raised his eyebrows. "I remember calling you that first time, on official business, trying to figure out who was the fruitcake. Her or you."

"Thanks." I shot him the evil eye. "But you were just doing your job."

"It was pretty weird. She said her husband had died, but she suspected you were married to him. I don't investigate many polygamy cases." He laughed. "And then you recognized me when we first met in person, but you didn't let on."

"I'd decided to conduct my own investigation. You would have just gotten in the way," I teased.

"We can tell our grandchildren one of these days, although they'll think we made it all up."

"Grandchildren?" I appeared, I felt sure, as nervous as I suddenly felt. "You might be jumping the gun."

"Sorry. I'll slow down." McGrath wadded his napkin and set it atop his plate. "What next?"

I glanced at my watch. "I shouldn't stay out too late."

"You have a curfew?" he teased.

I came to my senses. "No," I said. "Not at all. What did you have in mind, Detective?"

"A nightcap at my place?"

I nodded. McGrath tossed a few bills on the counter to cover our tab and gripped my elbow as I eased down from my bar stool. I leaned over and kissed his cheek. He smiled and kissed me back. Full out. On the lips.

I followed McGrath home. Once we arrived, I kicked off my shoes and curled up on his oversized sofa. He served me a Bailey's on the rocks, and curled up beside me. I couldn't take my eyes off him. His wide shoulders, his square jaw, and the tender look on his face made my heart sing. He seemed to hang on my every word, just as I did on his. Surely, just tonight, I could leave my real life behind and enjoy this man.

I placed my glass on the coffee table and edged nearer to him. He encircled my shoulders with his arm, and I settled against him. Tipping up my chin, he kissed me. I held on tight as he ever so softly peeled away the resistance I'd worn like armor since Jon's death.

"I don't know if I can do this," I whispered, my throat clogged with emotion and my body shaking.

"Do what?" McGrath asked.

"Be with another man."

"What other man?" He held me at arm's length. "You got another guy waiting in the wings?"

I gazed into his gentle, smiling eyes. "Thanks for making me laugh." I tried not to descend into a total emotional meltdown before I admitted, "It's been a really long time, and I'm out of practice."

McGrath's eyes twinkled with good humor. "It'll all come back to you."

I bit my lip. "It's much more than that."

"Tell me."

"I feel as if I'm betraying my husband." Tears spilled down my cheeks. "I sound like an idiot. Jon's been dead for almost a year. Shit, I hate this." I stood, rifled my purse for a tissue, and blew my nose.

McGrath patted the cushion next to him. I sat back down, but a foot away, still trembling and teary. He placed a warm hand on my thigh. "We have all the time in the world," he said. "I might not be the most patient man in the world, but I've hung in there for almost a year. I figured out a long time ago that you're worth the wait."

I couldn't meet his gaze. I wanted to be with him. I might fall in love with this man someday. Who was I kidding? I was already halfway there. He'd been on the periphery of my thoughts for a year now, and I knew I would never forget his kindness through Rex's death, the loss of Rosie, and Jon's passing. McGrath. Steady and strong. The man I'd needed then, and the man I wanted now.

I shivered again. I'd become an expert at denial, convincing myself that my mother and teacher roles would fulfill me for a lifetime. One touch from McGrath, and my certainty melted away.

"I'm fat," I muttered, insanity gripping me.

"By whose standards?" McGrath's dimples deepened. "I'm a seasoned detective, remember? I'd say you're 120 lbs. soaking wet. Am I right?"

"123." I locked eyes with him.

"Well, then," he teased, "you've missed the cut." He patted my knee, shot another dimpled grin my way, and sat back. "Listen up, Sam. I want you. Pure and simple. But this has to be right for you in order for it to be right for me. For us. I'm in this for the long haul."

"I appreciate that." I nodded. "Can we sit for a while?"

"We can do whatever you'd like. Here's an idea. Let's play follow the leader." He tapped the tip of my nose with his index finger. "You're it!"

I liked the idea of being in charge. And the touch of his finger on my skin caused sensation to sizzle through my bloodstream. Not much had been up to me over the past year.

I bracketed McGrath's face with my hands and drew in a deep breath. His scent filled my senses. Calmed me. Seduced me. I took him in—his kind eyes, smooth skin, capable touch. He squeezed my thigh and inched me closer. His fingers trailed up and down my spine, causing long forgotten urges to surface.

I stood, reached out to him, and then led him down the hall to his bedroom. He paused to draw the blinds and turn down the bed. He stood before me, his eyes sparkling in a slice of moonlight. His tender smile melted my heart. I moved into his arms, and we eased down onto the bed as one. He reached past me, touching a button on his alarm clock. Strains of soft jazz filled the air.

"Do this often?" I asked.

"I was a boy scout. Being prepared is important." McGrath chuckled into my neck. Sensation sparked across my skin. "I've been rehearsing this moment in my mind for a very long time."

I claimed his lips, silencing him even as he slipped his hand beneath my sweater, pressed his palm to the small of my back, and drew me close. A few minutes later, we abandoned the bed and helped each other to disrobe. I lingered over him, savoring the act of unbuttoning his shirt and allowing my fingertips to sink into the pelt of fine silk hairs that covered his muscled chest. His skin felt soft. Warm. Inviting.

He sprawled back across the bed, drawing me down atop him. I sighed over the warmth of his skin pressed against mine. I stared into his eyes for a long moment, committing the tenderness and love in his gaze to my memory. Then I allowed myself to be transported by the fulfillment I found in being with this man.

When we shuddered to a stop a long while later, we

remained curled into each other. I lay within the safety of his arms, and I listened to the contented sound of our breathing. Our mutual serenity resulted from more than just the satisfaction we'd experienced in the final joining of our bodies. McGrath had captured my heart long ago. I knew this with utmost certainty now, and I silently vowed to never let go of him. Enveloped by Jim McGrath's embrace, I drifted into a sound sleep.

McGrath gently shook me awake at 2 a.m.

I fell headlong into panic mode when I spotted the time on the LCD. "Shit. Shit, shit, SHIT!"

McGrath propped himself on his pillow and eyed me as I shuffled through the sheets in an attempt to retrieve pieces of my clothing. He sat up and turned on the bedside lamp. Laughed at me.

"This isn't funny," I said. "I'm in so much trouble."

This really got McGrath going. "You? In trouble?"

"I didn't tell Ed I'd be out late. Or all night!" I yanked on my skirt, pushed my arms through the sleeves of my blouse before I determined it was inside out, and then started over.

"Deep breath, Sam. Five or ten minutes isn't going to make much difference at this stage of the game. If you're that worried, you could call your father–in–law."

"Hell, I feel like I'm in high school. I'll have to sneak into the house and hope he's fallen sound asleep on the couch, or given in and gone to bed in the guest room. If he realizes I've been out this late, I'll have to answer questions. Shit, I'm nearly forty years old. I don't want to explain myself."

"You really think he'd pump you for information?"

I sucked in a deep breath. "Thank you. You make a valid point. How do you do that? You're so damn good. Stop it."

"Me? Never." McGrath sat there, looking smug.

I found him even more irresistible. I ripped off my clothing and jumped back into bed. "Fine," I said. "You win. Ten minutes. I need to get home before dawn."

"Fifteen…" he whispered.

CHAPTER FIVE

THE LAST TIME I'd snuck into a house I'd been about eighteen years old. I struggled not to giggle as I locked the door behind me. It was 3:30 a.m. I stepped out of my shoes, then tiptoed through the back hall and tried to remember which of the stairs squeaked. With any luck, I could squeeze in a few hours of sleep before the house came to life again.

Not that I felt sleepy. I had to admit it. I was totally wired. Giddy. I tripped over the pile of shoes in front of the stairs, then caught myself, muttering, "Shit." At this rate, I'd have the whole house awake and questioning me. Face it, Sam, I thought, you're dangerous.

Sure enough the bedroom door at the head of the stairs creaked open and Lizzie peeked out. "Mommy?" she called. "I can't sleep."

I slipped up the stairs, taking them two by two, scooped her up in my arms, and toted her into my bedroom. "C'mon, sweetie," I told her. "You can sleep with Mommy." I set her down on the bed, pulled back the covers on my side, and rolled her inside. Then, I shed my clothes and slipped a nightgown over my head. I cuddled up with Lizzie and fell asleep in an instant.

When Lizzie flung her fist into my face hours later, I felt disoriented. It took a moment for reality to set in. Last night with McGrath hadn't been a dream. My cheeks flushed. In a moment of shocking clarity, guilt gripped me. I'd been unfaithful to Jon. Closing my eyes again, I drifted. I could almost feel Jon's arm draped across my body, feel his breath wash over my skin. But Jon wasn't here. He was dead, and he wasn't ever coming home.

Tears stung my eyes. I reached onto the nightstand for a tissue and wiped my nose. Damn you, Jon. How could you leave me without saying goodbye? Leave me with five kids to raise? Leave me feeling guilty for not wanting to go through the rest of my life alone?

I glanced at the bedside clock. 5 a.m. Too late for a sleeping pill. On Sundays the kids slept in, and Lizzie would probably sleep for another three or four hours. I wouldn't be so lucky. I threw my legs over the side of the bed, slipped into my closet to don my heaviest sweats, tip-toed downstairs, heated a mug of water in the microwave, and carried a cup of tea onto the front porch.

From the wicker rocking chair, draped in a stadium blanket, I gazed at the moon. With Jon's frequent trips to Japan, we'd always agreed we could still see the same moon. So whenever I felt lonely, I'd look at the moon and smile. It made me feel connected to him even when he lived a world away. Weird how I felt connected to him now.

"I miss you, Jon," I said aloud. "I'm sick that you left me. If you'd show up on the doorstep right now, I'd forgive you. For all of it." I imagined I'd be busy washing the floor or cooking or doing laundry, and there'd be a knock. I'd open it and Jon would be standing there, telling me it had all been a horrible mistake. He hadn't been killed in that fiery car crash.

I'd wrap my arms around him and drag him inside, up the stairs and into our bed. We'd make love and laugh, and then call the kids, who'd bustle into our room, climb onto the bed, and shower Jon with hugs and kisses. We'd share a group hug, just like we always had when he returned home.

Except it wouldn't happen. Not now. Not ever. I sipped

my lukewarm tea and cried. Anger replaced my melancholy. My children didn't deserve this. And neither did I.

After several long moments I shook it off. I didn't have time to wallow in self-pity. My life dictated I pull myself together.

The front door squeaked open. Ed, clad in jeans and a parka, delivered a hot mug of coffee. He sat down in the rocker beside me.

"I heard you come downstairs," he said. He did what he always did then, gave me that sideways glance that said he suspected I'd been crying. "Trouble sleeping?"

"I'd love to say no, but it's 5:30 in the morning and I'm sitting on the porch."

"Did you have fun last night?" he asked.

My mouth fell open. I didn't know how to answer.

"You need to have fun, honey. You're young. Life goes on." Ed sipped his coffee, then gripped his mug in both hands.

"It's so…" I paused, choking up, "…hard. I don't feel like life should go on without Jon. What about you? Don't you miss Betty?"

"Of course I do, but I have you and the kids," Ed said.

I laughed. "Aren't we something? You have me and the kids and I have you and the kids. We both want more, but we choose to deny it."

"I knew love, Sam. Betty was my soul mate. We raised Jon, lived to enjoy retirement together. It doesn't get any better than that."

"But you're young, too. Do you want to go through the rest of your life alone?"

"Hell, honey, I'm sixty-eight years old."

"But you're a young sixty-eight. You play in a tennis league, for God's sake. Singles. You're going to live forever. I think you could at least enjoy the companionship of a woman. Dinner. A movie."

Ed laughed. "There's plenty of time for that to sort itself

out. I'm not worried about it. I have plenty to keep me busy. If it happens, it happens. But you...you need to think about love again. You have your whole life ahead of you."

I turned away. I didn't want Ed to see that tears streaked my cheeks. He grabbed my hand and held it with a firm grip. "It's okay, Sam. Give yourself permission to have a life."

"I don't know if I can. I feel so responsible for the kids. They've been through too much."

"You'll be amazed. Kids are resilient. You know that. Remember the day we found out about Jon's death? They showed such courage and compassion. Toward you, toward Betty and me, toward each other. You've laid a solid foundation for them, Sam. They'll be fine."

"I don't know how to let go of Jon," I wept.

"You're doing it right now," Ed said softly.

CHAPTER SIX

I DRIED MY eyes, gave Ed a thankful pat on the back and headed inside the house to grab my tennies. My reflective running vest sat on the bench in the back hall. I tossed it on, along with a stocking cap, and headed out for a run. Running had been my mainstay for years. The power walking with Di had replaced it lately but now it felt good to set my own pace, warm through, and finally let loose in a full-out stride.

The crisp morning air had nothing on me today. Ed was right. I wasn't letting go of Jon, because somehow, I knew that I'd never let go of him. Instead, I'd carry him with me wherever I went. Good or bad. Clean or messy. He'd be right there beside me.

Three miles flew by and I wound up out back in the wooded area a mile or so from home. I slowed to a walk and thought about my day. Sunday breakfast. Pancakes, I imagined. Board games. Laundry. Maybe a game of HORSE around the basketball hoop. If it warmed up enough, we could all ride our bikes to Dairy Queen.

When I strode into the driveway a few minutes later, the sun peeked up over the horizon. I said goodbye to the last of the moon and entered the house. Ed had packed up his overnight bag and sat at the kitchen table, drinking coffee and reading the newspaper.

"Hi, hon," he said as I unlaced my shoes. "Good run?"

"Perfect." I grabbed a glass of ice water and sat down beside him. "What's on your agenda today?"

"Gonna head home. Got a few house jobs to do. Thought I might ride over to the hardware later and buy some replacement screen for that door of yours. Looks like one of the kids caught something sharp on it. I'll see to it later."

"No rush, Dad," I said.

He folded the newspaper, carried his coffee mug to the sink, and made the return trip to kiss me on the forehead.

"Thanks for staying last night," I said.

"My pleasure," Ed answered. "And remember what I said. Don't beat yourself up for having a good time now and then."

Ed jolted me back to reality. McGrath. How quickly I'd put him out of my mind.

"I'll work on it." I nodded.

Ed grabbed his bag and headed out. "Tell the kids I love 'em."

"Will do," I said. As soon as Ed left, I went to find my purse and my cell phone. Sure enough, I spotted a text from McGrath. It read, "Reentry go okay?" He made me smile. Sexy and thoughtful.

"Working on it," I texted back.

It was still early. The kids wouldn't be up for hours. I put on another pot of coffee and filled the counter with baking essentials. Flour, sugar, eggs, baking soda, baking powder, salt, walnuts. Plenty of time to whip up two coffee cakes. Ed deserved a treat for helping out, and I could drop it off at his house later. I could take whatever the kids didn't finish to work tomorrow. By the time they awoke, I had cakes cooling on the counter, eggs ready to scramble, and bacon warming in the oven for them.

Annie was almost fifteen. Marie had six months on her. Will and Nick were eight weeks apart, closing in on thirteen. Jon and I used to say we had two sets of twins. Step–twins, I guess, although we never referred to them as yours or mine, just ours. The four older kids got along amazingly well, and always watched out for each other. And when Lizzie came along, they welcomed her into the pack. It seemed like we'd been together forever.

The sleepy-eyed kids took turns with jobs. This morning Annie set the table while Marie served juice and helped me place the serving dishes onto the table. Chatter and teasing abounded at the table, a typical Sunday morning.

When the phone rang, I was too preoccupied to check the caller ID. I just grabbed it and said, "Hello." I immediately regretted my decision.

"I'd like to speak to Jon Stitsill, please." I went cold. It had been almost two years since I'd received a call like this. The caller spoke with an accent. Over-enunciated English. I recognized Mr. Bredel's voice and stepped out of the kitchen and into the study where I closed the doors. I didn't want the kids to overhear my conversation.

"Mr. Bredel," I said, feeling suddenly faint. "I'm surprised you're calling."

"I must speak with Jon," he demanded.

"No, Mr. Bredel, you will not speak with Jon. Not today. Not ever."

"You do not understand," he said. "It is of the greatest urgency."

Several years ago, Mr. Bredel and I had begun our relationship through a series of phone conversations. The long and short of it was this. He thought my husband had taught under his direction at a primary school in Botswana when Jon was supposedly serving in the Peace Corps. My Jon had never served in the Peace Corps though. He also thought that my Jon had fathered his daughter's child. My husband had never been to Botswana either. The last time I'd heard from the Bredel's, I thought that Mrs. Bredel had understood that my Jon was not the Jon they were searching for. I thought they knew that Jon's impostor was the guy they wanted. Had they not put this together? Why would

Mr. Bredel call Jon now, after so much time had passed?

On second thought, Mr. Bredel didn't know about the fraud. I hadn't shared what I knew with him. In fact, I hadn't known about Jon's impostor the last time I'd spoken to the Bredels. With both Jons now dead, what could Mr. Bredel possibly want?

"What's the sudden rush to speak with Jon?" I swallowed.

"I cannot share that information with you," Mr. Bredel said. "I must speak with Jon directly."

Call me crazy, but my curiosity got the better of me... again. I asked, "Have you spoken with Jon since you and I last spoke, Mr. Bredel?"

"I have new information," he simply said. "I must speak with him."

My brain cranked a four minute mile. I could call McGrath, have him pose as Jon and get the goods from Mr. Bredel. I still had questions about the impostor. Hell, I still had questions about my husband — his work, his extracurricular activities, and his death.

"Please leave your number Mr. Bredel," I said. "I'll pass along the message." There, I hadn't lied. I hadn't said I'd have Jon call back. Now all I had to do was get McGrath to agree to call Bredel. What harm would there be? It's just a phone call, right?

Mr. Bredel recited his number.

"Thank you," I said. "He'll call you when he can."

I clicked the off button on the receiver and walked back into the kitchen. The kids had scarfed down every morsel of food, the dishes lay scattered about the counters and the five of them had rooted to the family room floor to watch a movie. I leaned against the counter's edge and took a series of steadying breaths. Act normal, I told myself. Pretend today's just another day. A normal day.

As a rule, I would have put my foot down and called the boys back into the kitchen to load the dishes into the dishwasher. Today, I needed to do it myself, to soothe my anxiety with a menial task. I rinsed the plates, wiped down the counters, washed out the sink and thought. I replayed the history again and again.

Jon's impostor had lived in Botswana. I knew that for a fact. The guy had done a lot of bad things, including killing people for money. But I'd shot him dead. Hadn't I? My mind rehashed that night. I was alone, which was unusual. A stranger broke into my home. When I snuck downstairs to investigate the noises, I took Jon's gun. A dark shape loomed on the stairs and when it rose up at me, I fired the gun. But I never really saw the guy. I identified him from a photo that some government agent showed me afterwards. I narrowed my eyes, recalling the photo. It was more like a shot taken from a passport, rather than a snapshot of a dead guy. Plus, McGrath had checked the body to confirm that it was Stitsill, hadn't he? Wait. Holy freaking shit.

CHAPTER SEVEN

I WAITED TO be sure the kids were all sound asleep before I called McGrath at 11 p.m. I couldn't risk them overhearing my conversation about dead people. Or have them detect the fear in my voice. My knees buckled as I sank onto the side of the bed.

He picked up on the second ring. "Hey," he said. "How are you?"

"Not great," I said.

"Why? What's the matter?" he asked. "Are you having second thoughts?"

"No," I whispered. "It's not about you and me. Something's happened."

His voice changed, became more urgent. "What's wrong?"

"Before I tell you, I need to ask, did you actually see Stitsill's body that night?"

"I was shown a photograph. The body had already been bagged. Why?"

"I'm afraid he could still be alive." My heart lodged in my throat.

McGrath didn't answer for a long moment. "For what reason?"

"Do you remember the phone calls I told you about? The ones I started receiving some years ago from the guy in Botswana?"

"Yes," McGrath said, on immediate alert.

"The same guy, Mr. Bredel, called late this morning and asked to speak with Jon. First of all, it's weird. He's never called during the day. Plus, both my husband and the impostor are dead."

"When was the last time you heard from Bredel?"

I swallowed, trying to keep dinner from revisiting my throat. "Two or so years ago when he called looking for Jon. Remember? His daughter Suzanne called shortly after. She thought my Jon had fathered her child."

"It was a mistake, though," McGrath said.

"Yes. The guy Suzanne had been looking for was the impostor. The guy I killed."

"In self–defense. You're not a murderer."

"Well, if I were, I couldn't have offed anyone who deserved it more." I let that thought sit for a moment. "What if the impostor isn't dead?"

"Bredel is chasing shadows. Stitsill is dead," McGrath said.

He was trying to reassure me. It didn't work. "I don't know," I hesitated. "I suppose I could be overreacting, but he said he had new information."

"Did he give you any hints?"

"No," I told McGrath, biting at my bottom lip. "I asked him to leave his number. I told him I'd have Jon call him back."

"Sam, I don't mean to be cruel, but what were you thinking?"

I squirmed a little, unsure of his reaction. "I thought maybe you could call him? Ask him what's going on? Maybe he knows something."

McGrath cleared his throat, then went quiet. Did he think I was totally off my rocker? It seemed like several full minutes passed before he spoke again. "Tell me what's going through your mind."

"I want to know what happened to Jon. I mean, think

about it. All this weird stuff happened with his impostor. Then, Jon went to Japan on business as if it was just a normal trip. He never drove a car when he was in Japan, and he'd traveled there for ten years. Why would Jon have decided to drive on that particular trip? Something must have been different. And I trusted Jon. Why, then, after I'd reached him, was there a woman in his room?"

McGrath cleared his throat again.

"I know what you're thinking," I protested. "He'd been unfaithful. That it's not rare for someone who traveled as much as Jon did to hook up with another woman. Problem is, I knew my husband. He was true blue. He loved me. He was devoted." Once I stopped talking, I took a measured breath, and thought about what I'd just said. Maybe if I repeated this like a damned mantra, I'd convince myself as well as McGrath. "Do you think I'm wrong?"

The line remained quiet.

I heard a sigh. Then, after a long pause, McGrath spoke. "When you first contacted me, I made a mistake."

"What?"

"I didn't listen to you. During our very first phone conversation, when I interviewed you about Rosita Stitsill, you told me other strange events had occurred. The mysterious letter from Botswana, the phone calls from Mr. and Mrs. Bredel. I blew you off. It took me way too long to get on board. I've always felt guilty. If I would have taken you and Jon seriously when you first brought your concerns to me, I could have prevented Rosie's death, Rex's death, maybe even Jon's death. You might not have had to kill Jon's impostor…"

When McGrath paused, I waited.

"I'm not going to do it again," he said.

"Do what again?" I asked.

"Wait to take action. I'll call Bredel," McGrath said. "But I'll be myself. It's time Mr. Bredel understands that law enforcement is involved in the case. He doesn't, however, need to comprehend the extent of that involvement."

I swiped at the tears streaming down my face, took a deep breath, and felt relieved for the first time in a very long time. Maybe now we'd get some real answers. "Thank you," I whispered. "Thank you."

* * *

McGrath and I agreed on a plan. Since Botswana was six hours ahead of us, and five in the morning seemed too early to call anyone, we decided we'd each get a good night's sleep, go to work in the morning, and have as normal a day as we possibly could. We needed the perspective of time. It seemed essential to determine what we needed to know from Bredel, and McGrath wanted to be sure that the Jon who Bredel looked for was, in fact, the impostor. It made sense to me. We'd assumed all along that it was him, but we didn't know for sure. Finding out would at least answer that single question.

I slept fitfully that night. When I woke at 5:00 a.m., my head flooded with questions and concerns. What would McGrath discover? Would the news reframe my world? Was smoking really that bad for me?

The ground felt shaky. Running usually steadied me. Maybe I'd go for a run. But I felt nervous leaving the house this morning while the kids were still asleep. Get a grip, Sam. There is no reason to feel frightened over a phone call. Probably a simple mistake. I tried to convince myself.

I wrestled into my sports bra, a t-shirt and sweats. Then I tied my shoes, donned my neon vest, and headed out the door. A quick two mile run and I'd be home. It would clear my head and help me return to normal. As I warmed up, I thought about it. Two days ago, my life had seemed to be getting back on track. I had even considered dating McGrath. Now, all of that seemed like a distant fantasy.

I broke into a full stride. I knew it made little sense to

get in front of myself. If I slowed down my crazy thinking I'd be much further ahead. Take it one step at a time. My mind suddenly cleared, and I took in the hint of the rising sun. Next on my agenda were a shower, coffee, breakfast, and more normal. I cautioned myself. I'd ready the kids for school, head to work, and lose myself in teaching. No need to take on everything at once.

I also reminded myself of all I'd accomplished in the past year since Jon's death. I'd kept the kids afloat. Lizzie's nightmares were down to once a week, and she slept in her own bed more nights than not. Will was his typical self, oblivious to the world. Nick seemed a little overly concerned with being the man of the house, but even that seemed to be dissipating somewhat. Annie and Marie were devoted to being teenagers. They were all doing well in school, participating in all the regular kid things like sports and friends. I could handle whatever Bredel's madness brought and a relationship with McGrath. More than that, not only could I handle McGrath's re-entry into my life, I welcomed it.

CHAPTER EIGHT

WHEN I CALLED McGrath on my way to work, he explained the approach he intended to use with Bredel.

"I'll phone him, explain that I'm a detective and that the authorities have reason to believe that Stitsill has been involved in some questionable activity here in the States," he continued. "Tell him that you've shared some concerns with me that Stitsill is a bad guy who left more people than just Bredel in the lurch. See if I can get him on board."

He had my full attention now. "Mmm–hmm," I concurred.

"Then I can pump him for information."

"All of this makes perfect sense," I said. "Ready for my list of questions?"

"Sure," McGrath said.

I rattled off my list:

- "When was Stitsill in Botswana?
- When did he arrive?
- How long did he stay?
- Did he leave abruptly as Mr. Bredel's daughter, Suzanne, suggested in her previous call to my husband?
- Did he, in fact, father her child? Was there any real proof of that, like DNA testing?
- How well did Bredel know Jon Stitsill?

- What activities was Stitsill involved in while he resided in Botswana?
- How did Mr. Bredel make his acquaintance?
- While Bredel had suggested many years ago that Stitsill had come to him through his association with the Peace Corps, was that validated by their government? Our government?
- Who was looking for him then? Who's looking for him now?"

I paused for breath, then asked, "Are you getting all this?"

McGrath laughed. "Slow down. Who's the detective here?"

"It's my brain. It works overtime."

"You're something else," he said.

I ignored him and continued my train of thought. "When I first spoke with Rosita Stitsill at the parent–teacher conference three years ago, she said that her husband had served in Botswana in the Peace Corps. I always wondered how he pulled that off. He'd had to have assumed my Jon's identity at that point. Considering what I know so far, it would have been around 2005 or 2006, shortly after Jon's passport went missing. I've researched it. The Peace Corps pulled out of Botswana in 1997 due to Botswana's economic success, but they did keep a hundred or so volunteers around. So, that matches up."

"Got it." McGrath was all business now.

"Is that enough to start with?" I asked.

"Plenty. Basically, I want to open up a dialogue. Then, if we still need more information, I can take another run at him later."

Seemed like a solid start. We agreed that McGrath would phone Bredel the moment we hung up. It would be afternoon in Botswana, and we had no real way of knowing if he was calling Bredel's cell phone, a work number, or a home phone.

"McGrath?" I paused.

"What?"

"Thanks. You're helping me maintain my sanity," I said.

"I'm good for you that way."

I smiled. "You certainly are."

"Any chance you have time to let me convince you that I'm good for you in other ways as well?"

"Kids," I said. "I have these five kids."

"Hard to get around that, is it?" McGrath asked.

"Let's just let it evolve gradually. I can't even imagine."

"Which part?"

"Any of it. All of it. Will you call me once you've spoken with Bredel?"

"That's the plan," McGrath said. "I don't know if I'll reach him on my first try though, so if you're teaching, I'll leave you a message and you can call me back when you're free."

By the time I arrived home, it had started to rain. Lizzie's bus had just pulled onto our street as I neared my turn. The bus stopped, and she hopped down the steps. I honked, and she dashed through the quarter-sized raindrops to the van.

"There's my girl," I said.

She brushed the rain from her face and reached over to hug my arm. "And there's my mom."

We chatted on the short drive to the house, and then ducked inside for a snack and to begin homework. The rain intensified and pelted the windows. In another hour, we'd have to head back out and pick up the older kids from various sports practices. As long as lightning didn't strike, they'd still be running the track. Meanwhile, I whipped up a meatloaf and stuck it in the oven along with some potatoes, threw a load of laundry into the washer, swept the floor, and paid bills.

I couldn't take my eyes off the phone. I'm not sure what I expected. Patience is not my strong suit, what can I say?

My text alert must have sounded on my way home from

picking up the kids, but I'd missed it amidst the dissonance of my children's petty disagreements. I saw it after I sent them upstairs to shower and change for supper. McGrath had simply texted, "Call when you can."

I started to dial his number when Annie called down for help. Darn it all! I texted him to see if 11 p.m. would be okay.

During the ensuing evening, I tried to allow myself to become distracted by the kids. Once they were sound asleep, I finally phoned McGrath.

"What'd you find out?" I asked as soon as he picked up.

"What, no 'hello'? I'm going to start believing you're using me for my professional advantage if you're not careful."

"You're killing me here!" I hissed into the phone.

He laughed. "This all seems so covert when you whisper, even though it sounds like you're hissing at me. It's kind of sexy..."

"Detective McGrath, you're beginning to piss me off."

"Just having a little fun," he chuckled, then cleared his throat. "Bredel says that he's had other volunteers at his school over the years. Stitsill showed up on schedule, but as a last minute substitute for someone else. Bredel didn't think much about it at the time, because it had happened before. Stitsill told him the assigned volunteer had been stricken with illness. Bredel claims to have verified it with the authorities, and that everything seemed kosher. But, he also indicated that Stitsill rubbed him the wrong way right from the start. He said he couldn't put his finger on it, but Stitsill seemed to be playing a part. Plus, he was older. He guessed him to be about fifty."

"That matches what we know about him," I interrupted. "And the average age of a volunteer is twenty-eight, although there's no age limit."

"Yes," McGrath remarked, "but they appreciate the experience of older volunteers. Some volunteers are in their seventies."

I laughed. "We sound like a Peace Corps commercial. Did you ask him about Stitsill's background?"

"I'm a detective, Sam. Yes, I asked." McGrath sighed audibly. "He said Stitsill was a mechanical engineer who had graduated from Purdue."

"That totally matches what Rosie told me about him. So, he was posing as my Jon even then." I scribbled feverish notes.

"Evidently."

"Did you find out anything surprising or unexpected?" I fiddled with my pen, waiting for McGrath to supply more information.

"He told me that Stitsill said he was engaged to a woman in Mexico. He said Stitsill claimed to have met her the previous summer. Evidently, he'd exchanged letters with her during his time in Botswana."

"Rosie lied about that. She said that she'd met him on his way back from Botswana." I heard my voice rising as I grew more excited. "That's definitely news."

"We don't know for sure it was Rosie, but it's possible."

"Oh, I hadn't thought of that. I guess it could have been someone else."

"Hold on a minute," McGrath said. "There's more. Bredel discovered Stitsill brought an illegal firearm into Botswana. I'm not completely sure how Bredel found out about the gun, but once he did, he confronted Stitsill. He told Bredel he needed the gun for personal protection. His answer didn't ring true, and it alerted Bredel that Stitsill might not be who he claimed to be."

"So, what's Bredel's new information?" I drummed my fingers against my lips. "Is it...?"

"Let me finish." McGrath chuckled. "Bredel also said that he suspected Stitsill was hiding more than just a gun. Shortly after he discovered the weapon, Bredel began to keep a closer eye on Stitsill. While Bredel described him as a charismatic educator, he sensed that Stitsill had a colorful past. Not only did Bredel have questions about the guy, but so did the Botswana government."

"The government?"

"Apparently, a scandal rocked the community around the same time. A housewife who had lost her husband in a car accident a year or so previous was accused of killing her best friend. Authorities determined that she'd been sleeping with her friend's husband after her own husband's death."

"Wait a minute. That's confusing. How does Stitsill fit in?"

"Are you sitting down?"

"Yes, why?" I moved to the edge of my chair.

"I'm not sure if this is related or not, but there are some striking similarities. Far-fetched maybe, but remarkable."

"Go on." I braced myself.

"The husband traveled a good amount for business. Details of the fatal crash remain sketchy, but it sounds similar to your husband's accident. The guy was driving in Japan, like your Jon, as a rare occurrence. He normally used the rail system or had a driver. Supposedly another woman was with him at the time of the crash, which in his particular case, wasn't considered unusual."

"So the guy was a philanderer? And he just happened to be in Japan on business when his accident occurred?" Unbelievable.

"Seems so. Anyway," McGrath continued, "the woman survived the accident, but then disappeared shortly afterward."

I shook my head. None of this made sense. "I'm still confused."

"Hang in there. This guy, Darwin Coswell, had business in Japan, and he worked for the same company as your Jon."

I drew in a measured breath. "What?!?" I paused a moment, trying to take in this new information. "So, the real story is that Coswell worked for the same company as my Jon and the circumstances of his death, while seemingly accidental, cast suspicion. Maybe on the woman, maybe on Stitsill. Is that what you're saying?"

"Perhaps." McGrath paused. "I have to tell you, Sam. I can't ignore the parallels. What are the chances?"

I swallowed. I never expected this. "There's some probability Stitsill was involved? I don't get it. How?"

"According to Bredel, the authorities tied Stitsill to Coswell's widow."

I still couldn't wrap my head around any of this. I couldn't even speak. What did this mean? Was my Jon involved in something he shouldn't have been? From what McGrath had just said, it sounded like Jon's impostor had been involved in some kind of love triangle. He seemed like he had way more illicit stuff going on than being involved with married women. None of it made any sense.

"Sam, are you still there?"

"Sort of. My head is spinning."

"I know. It's complicated. I don't even get it, but it gives us a place to start. There has to be a connection between the two crashes. We can't ignore the similarities."

"Let me get this straight. Somehow, my Jon, his impostor, and this other guy, Darwin Coswell, are connected."

"That's where I wound up," McGrath admitted. "I'm sorry, Sam, but it seems like your Jon may have been involved in something more complex than you realized."

"I guess it's up to me to decide what I want to sort out, isn't it?"

"Of course, it is. You don't have to act on any of this," McGrath agreed. "In fact, I debated sharing these details with you. But I can't and won't lie to you. You deserve to know what I've discovered."

"I guess I need some time to assimilate this story. I have a hard enough time imagining my Jon with another woman. Right now, though, possible infidelity seems minor compared to the other implications of this mess."

"I know," McGrath said, "and I agree. There's probably

way more to this than meets the eye."

"How do we figure it out?"

"My chat with Bredel was interrupted. I made arrangements to speak with him again…"

"When?" I cut in.

"Next week," McGrath said.

"That seems like forever."

"I didn't want to seem too hungry."

I sighed. "I get it."

"And Sam?"

"Yes?"

"Bredel offered me another bit of information."

I braced myself. "Yes?"

"Bredel said he recently found a strong box. Inside, he found over \$500,000.00 in U.S. currency, and several passports."

My heart stuttered in my chest.

CHAPTER NINE

I T WAS IMPOSSIBLE to pretend my life was normal in the midst of all this craziness. How could Stitsill have been involved in Jon's company's business?

It's not like any of this was new for me. Before Jon's death, my life had been pure madness. Now, all that lunacy seemed to be starting up again. I could ignore it, as McGrath suggested. Get on with my life—teach school by day, wrangle kids by night, consider a new relationship after hours. But that's not in my nature. I like complicated. Maybe I should see a therapist. One of these days. When I have time.

I rose, ran downstairs to turn on the coffee pot, then dashed back upstairs to shower. Once I'd dressed, I lounged at the kitchen table with a cup of black coffee and a bowl of Cheerios. The house usually stayed blessedly quiet until 6 a.m. With any luck, I had another thirty minutes before the kids descended upon me.

My thoughts kept wandering back to McGrath's phone call. It raised so many questions my head throbbed. Perhaps I should instead concentrate on another date with McGrath. It was only Tuesday, but if Ed would babysit, I could sneak away for a few hours. Weeknights were a tough time for me to be gone. Homework, game time, sibling scuffles, dinner, laundry. The list was endless.

As I rinsed out my cereal bowl, I heard the shower turn

on upstairs. I smiled. Marie and Annie were great about getting themselves up and going in the morning.

Once I had everyone else awake and moving, I fed them, set out the lunches I'd made the night before, and then ushered them out the door to the bus. Lizzie and I left for her friend's house.

Although I was mentally drained, the work day flew by without a hitch. My life as a special education teacher often depended upon my student's moods. Thankfully, a lot of them had more academic deficits this year than behavioral. There is a God.

I ran into Di in the hall at the end of the school day. "The sun's shining," she said. "I missed walking yesterday. Are we on for today?"

I felt sluggish from lack of sleep, but I said, "4:30?"

Di smiled. "Yep. See you then." She turned to walk away and then stopped as if a bolt of lightning had struck her. "I can't believe I forgot. You saw McGrath Saturday night, right?"

"I did." I grinned.

"I'll want all the details." Her gaze bore into me.

"I'm not sure I can tell you all of them...," I teased.

"Can't wait," she said, angling toward her classroom door.

By 4:15 p.m. I'd settled the kids, changed into some exercise gear, and headed out the door. As I parked in front of Di's house, I spotted her on the sidewalk. She resembled a Cheshire cat, rubbing her hands together. I hadn't shut the van door before I heard her calling, "C'mon, give me the dirt."

I smiled, recalling my evening with McGrath. I told her about The Frozen Margarita, sitting at the bar, dinner, and then stopping off at his place.

"Did you sleep with him?"

"P–E–R–S–O–N–A–L."

"Did you?"

I grinned again. "Yes." I couldn't believe I'd told her, and I hoped I wouldn't live to regret it.

"And?"

"And what?" Di loved details.

"Is he… skilled?"

"Let's just say it proved to be one of the nicest evenings I've had in a very long time."

She clapped her hands together like I'd jumped off the high–dive board. "When do you see him again?"

"Um… I'm sure I will, but we didn't schedule anything. Quite honestly, I'm not sure how to manage it with the kids."

"You're a good mom. After my mom died," Di said, "my dad waited about three months before he started seeing Doris. THREE MONTHS. My life's been hell ever since."

"See what I mean? I don't want to scar my children."

"Yes, but Doris is a selfish witch. Your detective, he's not selfish, is he? Or wicked? Long, hooked nose?"

I laughed. McGrath could neither be described as egocentric or mean. Anything but. "No," I said. "I don't believe there's a selfish bone in his body. But we're still in the early stages. I suppose I should exercise caution. There's a lot I don't know."

"Don't be too careful, Sam."

"What? You think I'm going to pull back?"

"I'm just saying," Di said. "I know you. You always come up this long list of reasons. Kids, time constraints, work…"

"You're absolutely right." I shook my head. "I feel myself unrolling the register. Like the Dead Sea scrolls, it's never–ending. I'm convincing myself that I don't have the time for a relationship."

"Okay," Di said. "Let's be methodical about this. Recite the list, one item at a time, and we'll go through it and alleviate all of your excuses."

"Time," I said. "I already told you."

"Good one." Di nodded. "You have a horrendous schedule, true. But surely you could add a routine meeting to your week. Ed loves watching the kids. Build in a Wednesday engagement. Call it a "meet up" if you will. Tell Ed and the kids you're trying to hone your skills with adults."

"Like they care about that."

"Fine. Don't tell them where you're going. Make up some stupid excuse. You're creative."

"Got it. Wednesday meeting." I nodded. "My next problem? Exhaustion."

Di shook her head, not buying my excuse. "Did you feel tired Saturday night when you were with him?"

I snorted. Couldn't help myself.

"See, we're eliminating your cockamamie excuses, one by one." Di nodded with satisfaction. "Next."

"Nick," I said.

"Because he's the man of the house now that Jon's dead?"

"Precisely. But it's not just that."

"What is it then?" Di narrowed her eyes as she cast a glance my way.

"He gets stuff. Like when Jon died, he knew before I told him. And he has this sixth sense about me, too. I try like hell to hide my feelings from the kids, but if I'm having a particularly bad day, he knows. He'll wrap his arms around me, and I totally fall apart. The two of us butt heads, but when it comes right down to it, he's more aware of my moods, thoughts, and feelings than any of the other kids."

"So are you worried he'll be jealous?"

"No," I said. "It's way more than that. I'm worried he'll suspect I'm seeing someone long before I'd ever consider divulging that news to the lot of them. And that he'll, I don't know… know I'm sexually active. In some ways, he's like my conscience."

Di hooted. "Oh my God, you are in trouble."

"I'm screwed."

"Well, at least Saturday night you were." Di laughed again.

This time I joined her. "I need to enroll in an acting class."

"Perfect," Di said. "That's what you can tell the kids you're doing. Taking acting classes. Then, when you're at the detective's house, you can play cop and robber. He'll have to tackle you and then handcuff you…"

"Handcuffs. Hm. Why didn't I think of that?" We laughed harder. I sighed. "All of this talk of men and sex makes me nervous."

"You're scared shitless. I get it."

"You do?" I looked at her sideways.

"Not in your place, I know. But remember? I lost my mom. Hell, I think half of my angst over Doris came from the worry I'd let her replace my mom if I loved her. You know. Loyalty issues. And this other part may not make a whole lot of sense to you, but it was almost as if I felt that if I let Doris be my mom, I'd forget my own mother. Understand?"

"Completely. I feel like I have to be true to Jon's memory." I paused. "Or at least true to my memory of him."

"I get it," Di agreed.

I was glad she got it, because I sure as hell didn't.

Chapter Ten

I DROVE AWAY from Di's a short while later. As I rounded the corner toward home, I smelled smoke and immediately looked up. A huge dark cloud drifted overhead. I punched the accelerator, crested the street's only hill, and spotted flashing blue lights. Police cars and fire trucks lined both my driveway and the front of my house.

I slammed on the brakes, jumped out of the van and raced down the street, frantically scanning the landscape for my children, and Rex, our dog. Across from my house, in the neighbor's front yard stood several huddled figures. I counted, one, two, three, four, five. I burst into tears, my heart jack–hammering in my chest. I checked hair color and body sizes. They were there. All of them. They were alive.

I flew to their side while repeating my mental inventory. All kids accounted for. Thank you, God! Annie's arm shielded Lizzie, whose free hand clutched Marie's. Nick's hand rested on Will's shoulder.

"Where's Rex?" I asked.

Nick's soft sad eyes met mine. "Mom..." A simple reminder.

Reflex. Rex had died nearly a year ago. I extended my arms and my children rushed into them. We were so frightened; it was as if the earth shook beneath our feet. The sound of rushing water raged from somewhere behind us. The girls began to sob while the boys shouted in a cacophonous chorus, trying to make them stop.

"Shh," I calmed them. "One at a time. Tell me what happened." My gaze darted toward our house. I could scarcely see beyond the fire trucks to assess the progress of the fire or the status of our home.

"It was my fault, Mom," Nick said.

I knit my brow. Nick had spoken too quickly. He'd never hesitated to cover for someone.

"No, Nick. "Annie stepped forward. "It was me, Mom."

Marie angled in front of Annie. "No, Mom. It wasn't either of them. It was my fault."

I narrowed my eyes. This would be another of those times when they all claimed responsibility. "It doesn't matter who's to blame. As long as you're all safe, we'll get through this. But tell me please, what happened?"

Just then, a local firefighter, Marty Jaeger, approached me. Marty and I had attended high school together. He also coached basketball and knew both of my boys well. "Sam?" He passed me a sympathetic gaze.

"Yes," I said, resting my hand on Marie's forearm.

"Talk to you for a moment?" Marty turned and strode away from our group.

"Okay, guys," I said to the kids as I closed their circle by linking Marie and Will's hands. "Hang tight while I speak with Mr. Jaeger."

Marty led me to the rear of one of the units. "You okay?" He reached out and patted me on the back.

My knees turned boneless. I tried to breathe, but it seemed as if all the oxygen had been sucked from the air. I backed away from him and straightened my shoulders. His eyes went soft, and his lips tightened before he spoke. "We're very lucky, Sam."

I nodded as I glanced back at my children. Then I took a long moment to survey our home. Jon and I had purchased the old Victorian farmhouse about twelve years ago. We'd spent months fixing it up—redoing electrical, replacing cabinets and countertops, refinishing hardwood floors, installing carpeting, restoring staircases. You name it, we did it. From the front, our home looked intact, safe, and sound. I could have pretended that the smoke still canopying the house simply posed as an overcast Midwestern afternoon right before a thunderstorm broke loose. As I peered closer, around the side of the house, just behind the garage where the kitchen sat, the exterior of my home looked charred and dreadfully exposed. I'd only been gone a little over an hour. And hadn't they all been snacking and working on homework when I'd left the house?

I nodded as the shock took hold.

"You should be very proud of your kids," Marty said. "Annie called 911 and alerted us about the fire, but only after she had gotten everyone out of the house and across the street."

"Our meeting place. We practiced," I said through tears. "After Jon died, I tried to imagine every eventuality…"

"Good work, then." Marty rested his hand on my shoulder.

"Do you know what happened?" I continued to try to assess the damage but I felt frozen to my spot, unable to move.

"Sounds like a candle was left unattended. A curtain caught fire, and the flames spread quickly."

"I wasn't gone that long. Honest."

"Don't feel guilty, Sam. It was an accident. Your kids are good kids. Responsible. It could have happened even if you'd been at home."

"Thanks for saying so, but I'm not so sure. I shouldn't have left them." I closed my eyes and shook my head. "What's the damage? Is the fire out? Can I go inside?" I knew even as I spoke, I was kidding myself. The hoses still pushed water over the side of the house and the police officer, Dave Duggan, seemed to be cordoning off the perimeter of our damaged home. "Is that crime scene tape?" I asked Marty.

How often have I told them to be careful? Did they not understand how dangerous it could be to burn a candle? The thought of losing them ripped me apart. For now, it made sense to stay grateful they were unharmed, rather than to be pissed. I'd save that for later.

"No," Marty said. "It's barricade tape. We were able to contain the fire, but we want to secure the place. You may be able to go inside to pack up some belongings after we're sure the fire is extinguished." He paused. "It'll be awhile before we can assess the full extent of the damage. At the very least, you won't be able to stay here tonight. In fact, it will probably be some time before the house is habitable again."

"I'll have to get someone over to patch the exterior. I know this is a safe neighborhood, but I can't leave a gaping hole in my home."

"Let me take care of it for you, Sam." Marty's hand rested on my arm. Indeed, my life had become a soggy, destroyed mess once again. If anyone required soothing, it was me.

The pit in my stomach grew deeper. I heaved a sigh. The kids were safe, I reminded myself. In a fog, I muddled down the street to fetch my car while Marty made small talk with my children. When I reached the van, I opened the driver's door and climbed inside. I reached inside the console for my cell phone. Seven missed calls. All from home. I phoned my friend Julie Black. She also happened to be my insurance adjuster. Julie warned me not to enter the house until the fire marshal gave me the go ahead.

"Take the kids to a hotel in Worthington tonight, Sam. If need be, buy whatever's required to get through the week. Once we know if you'll be allowed to re-enter the home to recover any salvageable possessions, I'll give you a call. After I complete an initial assessment, I'll enlist a crew and have them secure your home. You sleep tonight. No worries."

Julie knew me well enough to know that sleep wouldn't

come easy tonight, but I thanked her and disconnected the call. I dialed Ed and filled him in. He took the news well—both of us were numb to catastrophes by now. He offered to drive right over, but I reassured him that I had everything under control. Then he offered us shelter for the night before I pressed the end button on the call.

I hesitated and held onto my phone after disconnecting. More than anything, I wanted to call McGrath. I eyed the kids from where I sat in the van. I knew I should hustle down there, but instead I dialed his number. When he picked up, I told him what had happened.

"You okay?" he asked. A tear trickled down my cheek at the sound of his soothing voice.

"Trying to be," I said.

"Want me to come over?"

"No," I said. "The kids need me right now. Plus, if you showed up, I might fall apart."

"In any case," McGrath said after a moment's pause, "I'm here for you."

"Thanks," I said. "Hearing your voice is just what I needed. I'll call when I can."

"It kills me not to be there for you," he said.

"Kills me not to have you here," I answered.

I drove the van the short distance to the neighbor's yard, then loaded the kids inside. "Listen up," I told them. "I'm incredibly proud of all of you. Well done." I smiled at them. "Hungry?"

Without pause, they began yammering about food choices. I pulled up the van to where Marty stood with the fire marshal and rolled down the window. "I'm going to feed these kids some pizza."

Marty nodded. "Great idea," he said. "That'll give us time to check the electrical. In any case, you'll want to stay somewhere else tonight."

"I'll stop by after we eat." I checked my watch. "Say in about ninety minutes. Does that work?"

"Perfect. And by the way, I'm so sorry." Marty locked his eyes with mine, resting his hand on my arm.

"Thanks," I said, feeling a warm buzz where his hand had been. I rolled up the window and wheeled down the street.

I had just pulled into the parking lot of the local pizzeria when my cell rang. It was Ed, reminding me that the kids each had pajamas and clean clothes at his house. They also had essentials like toothbrushes and toiletries available at grandpa's kid heaven. After Betty had died and Ed had moved nearby, he'd made sure to purchase a home large enough to accommodate my troops. A regular handyman, it took him only six weeks to turn the basement into a Man Cave boasting handcrafted loft beds, an oversized television equipped with video devices, and a ping-pong table. Ed had played ping-pong with Jon for years and the kids loved playing their dad's favorite game.

Upstairs, the girls' pink bedroom held a set of bunk beds and one twin. Regularly, Annie and Marie gave Lizzie permission to sleep on the top bunk. They acted as if they were doing her a huge favor, letting her have top spot, when in actuality they loved gossiping into the wee hours of the night. Lying across from each other meant their words were somehow protected from little ears.

In any event, after I hung up the phone, I told the kids that I'd be dropping them off at grandpa's house after dinner. Afterward, I'd run by the house, try to gain entrance inside, and collect backpacks and anything else I could set my hands on.

We filled up on pepperoni pizza, Cokes, and breadsticks before loading back into the minivan and heading to Ed's place. As I eased into his driveway, he stepped out onto the front porch and waved. I slid out of the van, herding the kids in his direction. Ed gathered them around in true Ed style, and asked them to tell him all about the excitement.

One by one, I kissed them, gave them my usual behave-for-your-grandfather instructions and headed back to our home. I truly hoped I could get inside and gather up essentials for myself. I had no idea where I'd sleep tonight, on Ed's couch, or squeezed in the bottom bunk with one of the girls, but beyond tired, it wouldn't matter.

I rolled onto our street and sighed. It looked as if the fire trucks were all but gone. One unit remained parked in front of the house. I pulled into the driveway, parked on the apron, and walked slowly up the drive and around to the back of the house. The kitchen was completely exposed to the outside. I swallowed hard. It almost felt like another death, as if pieces of me were being sucked dry, one after the other. Jon and I had toiled long and hard, but happily on this place. The house that Stitsill built, we'd called it. Our homemade place for our homemade family.

Marty must have spotted me, because he appeared from out of nowhere. "Hey," he said as he approached me. "Did you lose the kids?" He chuckled.

"Dropped them off at my father-in-law's house. They'll be busy there, and I'm guessing we'll need to spend several nights with him."

"I'm afraid so."

I surveyed the house. It was destroyed. I felt broken.

All 6'6" of Marty watched me closely and I avoided his sympathetic gaze.

"I warn you," he said, "the first floor is totaled. Water-logged and charred."

"Stairs?"

"Wet but sturdy."

"How about if I sneak in the front, go upstairs and grab a few things? Is the second floor stable?"

"Yes. The fire is completely extinguished and was contained to the first floor. Upstairs, you'll find only smoke and water damage. I'll come inside with you," Marty said. As we turned toward the house, he wrapped his arm around my shoulder. "Tough year, huh?"

"That's one way to put it." I leaned into him a little, appreciating the warmth of his comfort. Then, I reached into my purse and grabbed my keys.

"It's unlocked," Marty said.

I nodded. Of course it was. There was a gaping hole in the kitchen.

He opened the front door, then stepped aside so that I could enter first. The smell slammed me in the face. Pungent scents of melted paint and scorched wood. It seemed almost bitter as it hit my nostrils. My head began to throb, and I felt as if I might melt, too.

"You okay?" Marty asked. "You're pale and clammy. I'm worried about shock." He placed a steadying hand on my arm as I sank down onto the front hall steps.

"I think it's the smell." I rested my forehead on my knees.

Marty planted his hand on my shoulder and knelt down in front of me. "It's a normal reaction. Just give yourself a minute." Then, he returned to the front door and opened it to let in some fresh air. I inhaled a couple of deep breaths, but the air wouldn't seem to clear. I decided to stand up, gather what I needed, and get out fast.

"Be right back." I stood and hurried up the stairs.

"Need anything from down here?" he called out.

"I can't imagine that you'll find five dry backpacks that don't smell to high heaven. I'm sure the textbooks are soggy and homework papers are ruined," I said. Unbelievable. "Will the house be alright overnight?"

"Julie Black came by and phoned a clean-up crew to secure the place. They'll be here within the hour. Try not to worry. You have enough on your plate."

"Thanks for being here, Marty. You're a saint."

I ran upstairs, retrieved a couple days worth of clothing that didn't reek of smoke for myself, the back-up items I kept in my swim bag, and my sleep medication. Sadly, I was pleased when I found it, undisturbed, in my cabinet. Then, after pausing for a few moments, trying to catch my breath and not retch right there on the ruined floor, I entered the kids' bedrooms in a feeble attempt to gather some clothing for each of them. Since their rooms were at the rear of the house, I faced more devastation than I could have imagined in their water-logged rooms. I grabbed my fire-proof safe, then called Marty to help me lug the thing to my car. At least I had all my important papers and my jewelry. Everything else would have to wait.

By the time we loaded everything downstairs, evening had settled and moonlight streamed through a settling veil of fog, which created a yellow haze in a misty sheen of radiance on the wraparound portico.

Shit. I'd miss my front porch.

CHAPTER ELEVEN

BY THE TIME I made it back to Ed's at almost 8:30 p.m., Annie and Marie had phoned friends and borrowed textbooks. With Ed's computer, they finished their homework. Lizzie had emailed her teacher to explain our situation and she'd received a pass on the evening's assignments. True to form, Nick and Will had hidden in their Man Cave, playing ping–pong, oblivious to homework or the fact that tomorrow still meant a school day, crisis or not.

After I shed some light on the subject for them, they buckled down and emailed their teachers and filled them in. As I ascended the basement steps, I overheard Nick tell Will the fire seemed like a good way to obtain a free pass for a few days' assignments. I stopped in my tracks and called out, "I heard that!" then listened as Nick sighed audibly.

"Just kidding, Mom. You know, a little levity in a bad situation?" I'm sure he rolled his eyes as well.

I made my way to the second floor, stood on the bottom rung of the lower bunk, and leaned over the edge of the top bunk to find Lizzie softly snoring. Dressed in her favorite cotton nightgown and cuddled up with a stuffed dog she'd inherited from Marie, she looked like an angel. I kissed my fingertips before planting them on her flawless cheek.

The girls lay sprawled on the family room floor with Ed's laptop, watching something or other on YouTube. I found Ed in the kitchen. He'd put on the kettle and was just pouring me a cup of tea.

"You don't need to do that," I said, settling in an old ladder back chair.

"Yep, you sure are a lot of trouble." He smiled. "You okay?"

"I've learned a lot of lessons over the past year. Lesson number one? Don't let the little things get you down. The kids are safe, that's all that matters."

"You know me, Sam. I love to tinker. I'll help out however I'm able with the house, and you know my place is home for you and the kids for as long as you need it."

"What did I do to deserve you?" I walked over and wrapped my arms around him.

"You married my son."

I nodded, mumbling into his chest, "Well, thanks, anyway. You always seem to do way more than your fair share."

"Listen," he added as he handed me a mug of tea, "the pull-out in the study is made up for you. I'll get the kids off in the morning. You go ahead and attend to business, go to work, carry on with your life as usual. Go for a walk with your friend. I've got dinner and chauffeur duty. You'll have plenty to do in the next few days. Leave the kids to me."

I shook my head in amazement. "Really?"

"Really," he simply said.

I sat down at the kitchen table, took a deep breath, and then a sip of my tea.

Ed headed downstairs to harass the boys. I pulled out my cell and discovered a text from both the insurance adjuster and then the fire marshal. I messaged them back and we agreed to meet the following morning at 6:30 a.m. so that I could still get to work on time.

* * *

Meeting with the insurance gal and fire marshal took much longer than I'd anticipated. The adjuster predicted it might take three months or longer to get things back in tip-top shape. I'd had the foresight to keep good records. Receipts from all of our renovations were in the fireproof strong box I'd retrieved from my back closet. I'd decided on my drive over to meet Julie that I'd replace cabinets, floor, carpet, the works, just as Jon and I had originally done. It would lighten my load not to have to make those major decisions. God help me when I actually had to reenter my home and sort through what was left of our belongings.

The fire marshal seemed satisfied with our interview, especially after I explained that the kids had confessed to the circumstances surrounding the fire's origin, and it matched what they had told Marty. Marie had lit a candle in order to cover up the smell of burnt popcorn, then the boys had decided to toss a football in the family room, hit the candle and knocked it into the curtains. By the time they'd realized what they had done, it was too late. Two bad decisions equaled a house fire.

I craved a decent cup of coffee when I finished my meeting, so I stopped off at The Daily Grind.

On second thought, I needed something stronger than coffee. Later.

As I pulled into the school parking lot, I heard the final bell sound. I high-tailed it to my classroom, all the while questioning the wisdom in my attending school today. I focused on the task at hand instead. My students were milling about outside our tiny classroom, but, far as I could tell, hadn't caused any major incidents before my arrival. I unlocked the door and ushered them inside. "Into your seats, people," I ordered as I settled my cell phone onto my desk, and then locked my purse inside my bottom file drawer. I checked my calendar, which reminded me that I was scheduled to spend the morning co-teaching with my friend, Jack Kowalski. After twenty minutes of homeroom,

I hustled my students out the door and headed for Jack's classroom.

"Hey, Ms. Sit Down, Sit Still, Sit Tight. How's it going?"

"Small fire at the homestead last night," I said nonchalantly while cringing inside. Jack spent so much of his life shaking his head at me. He'd never let this one go.

"What?" He gaped at me in obvious shock. "Small fire? What does that mean?"

I shook my head. "It means that the kids and I will be staying with Ed for a while."

"What the hell happened?" Jack hurriedly wrote an assignment on the board, barked at the kids to begin working, under penalty of death, and returned his attention to me. "Sit down," he ordered.

I sat, explained what I knew about the fire, the reconstruction, and our plans to stay with Ed for the duration.

"Shit," he murmured under his breath. "More of 'As the Stitsill's Turns'."

"It's okay, Jack. Cool your ever–loving jets. We're all fine. That's all that matters."

I looked up at him. He towered over me. At 6'4" and with the build of a basketball player, Jack drove the 6th grade girls and his fellow teachers crazy. I swooned a little bit, too, every now and then when I just looked at him and forgot that he was more like my little brother than a good–looking guy. He was something, but Jack was ten years my junior, and I was way out of his league. Besides, he occupied my best male friend slot at work.

He shook his head so fast, I thought it might begin to spin. "Have you told Di? She's going to flip."

"I hate to tell her. She overreacts to everything. She'll make me jittery."

Jack laughed and slapped me on the back. "That's why she's your BFF, and not mine." Then, he returned to the class and began an entertaining lesson on what my special education students called alphabet math…beginning algebra.

At lunch time, I entered the lounge, sat down in a rickety office chair, and undid my brown bag. Ed had packed my lunch. A sandwich and an apple. I'd just taken my first bite when Di entered the room.

"Samantha Stitsill," she howled. "How could you not have phoned me?"

Di never howled. She normally had a voice like a fairy princess, soft and sweet. Damn Jack. He'd told her.

"It was late by the time I made it to Ed's. Besides, there was nothing for you to do."

"What can I do? Are you okay? What more can happen? Your life gets more complicated by the minute."

I narrowed my eyes and pleaded with her. "I need you to calm down. You overreact every time I have a crisis. Can you go to your happy place, so I can come with you?"

Di's lunchbox hit the table with a thud. "This place is filthy," she said.

Silly me. Di didn't know calm.

I watched as she leaned into the cupboard under the sink, came out with double-duty cleanser, and sprayed it over the table. I shielded my sandwich from her frenzied spritzing, and yelped, "Hey, trying to eat here."

"I hate it when I'm the last to know." Di sat down and glared at me with her beady Italian eyes.

"Sorry," I said before changing the subject. "Ed's signed up for kid duty after school." I glanced out the window. "Sun's shining. I'll fill you in on every last detail when we walk. Deal?"

Di shrugged, her eyes still narrowed. "Don't you have to do fire cleanup or something?"

"I'm not 'allowed' for another day or so. So I can sit in Ed's house and be crazy, or walk…"

"Let's go by your house. I want to see."

"Di," I barked. "I need a break from crises. Let's walk our

usual route. Once I'm allowed back in the house, you can come over and help me sort through the wreckage."

Jack walked in as Di opened her lunch and began to set it out like a dinner at a five star restaurant. He rolled his eyes as he paused behind her. I smiled into my PB&J on whole wheat. We spent the next ten minutes scarfing down our food.

* * *

By the time I met Di for our power walk, my fanny dragged and I hoped like hell that exercise would rejuvenate me. For the life of me, I couldn't figure out why I'd gone into work. Any normal person would have stayed home. Shit. I no longer had a home. My legs turned to mush, and my life flashed before my eyes. I shut them tight and said a long prayer, asking God for strength. I wanted to sound halfway decent when I phoned McGrath later. I hate it when people think I don't handle things well. And I wanted to impress McGrath. Although he'd already seen me at my absolute worst and still seemed interested, I couldn't risk it.

Being myself with him still scared the shit out of me.

Di shut her front door and met me on the sidewalk. "Ready?" she asked.

"Let's do it." I yawned behind my cupped hand.

"Tell me," she commanded.

I shared every detail I knew. It wasn't a heck of a lot, considering all aspects of rebuilding the kitchen were only in the initial stages. I still had a slew of phone calls to make, a contractor to decide on, and tons of other gory minutia I'd decided to postpone until tomorrow.

Di studied me. "Let me know if I can help."

I nodded.

Seemingly satisfied that my life was contained, she said, "Now, on to my problems."

"Is it serious?"

She shook her head. "It's Chris."

I laughed. "What now?"

"He's completing car checks."

I narrowed my eyes. "Not sure what that means."

"Last night we went on a date. Downtown. By the time we got out of the restaurant and back to the parking garage, it was chilly." Di mimicked shivering as she recalled the event. "Seriously, it was freezing."

"Go on," I said, poised for some serious laughter.

"He forced me to wait in the cold while he investigated the exterior for scratches, bird droppings, and God knows what else. I swear, I thought he was going to pull out an automobile diagram like they do at the car rental."

I pictured Chris with the full knowledge Di's report was completely accurate and true. Di's frustration increased as she relayed the scene to me. "And?" I asked.

"I'm not kidding. He made me wait for almost five minutes." She shook her head. "Then, I had to stay outside while he backed out the car. He was afraid I'd ram the door into the car parked next to ours."

By this time, I could hardly walk. I was too busy holding my sides. True, it's a new car. True, Chris deserved the title 'Mr. Particular'. But what really cracked me up? Di's the most OCD person on the planet, yet she's upset and confused about Chris' obsession with his vehicle.

"Do you expect anything less from him? He's a freak about his things," I said.

"Speaking of men, what are you going to do about McGrath?" she asked.

I sputtered, "McGrath?" Where did that come from?

"You finally have a chance at a relationship and you're moving in with your father-in-law? That's not going to make dating any easier."

This time, I shivered, despite the sweat forming on my brow. "Dating. I hate that word."

"It's dating, Sam."

"I know. I get it. I just don't like the idea." I lifted my head and took in the half-mile shade-less stretch ahead of us.

"Then don't think about it," Di advised. "Just find time to do it."

I seized Di's recommendation and phoned McGrath on my way back to Ed's. "I have to talk fast," I said. "Only five minutes to Ed's house."

"We have to find a better way. Either you're at work, or I'm at work, or you have kids."

"Complications." I realized, just as Di had said, I didn't feel tired any longer.

"Middle of the week meeting?" he suggested. "Meeting with the fire marshal? Something like that?"

"What if the kids need me?" I said.

"I thought Ed was on duty," McGrath reminded me.

"I won't have much time."

"I'm quick," he joked.

I laughed. "Now that, my dear…" I chuckled, "…just isn't true."

CHAPTER TWELVE

I WONDERED IF I'd always feel this giddy when I snuck off to see McGrath. I also wondered how long I'd call him McGrath. I noticed that every now and then I broke down and called him Jim. Would that ever take permanent hold? And if so, when?

I glanced at the speedometer. Speeding. I eased up on the accelerator. It felt good to feel this alive, to have a smile permanently carved on my face despite the fact that my house lay in ruins. Life kept trying to hang a steady black cloud over my head. Tonight, I intended to kick that cloud in the face.

I'd warned McGrath this would be a Bredel/Jon and fire free night. No discussions about death, assassins, or blazing homes. I needed a break. I pulled into his gravel drive a little past 6 p.m., climbed out of the car, and strolled up the winding brick path to his front door. He met me with a sweet, prolonged kiss, and I calmed with each passing minute. I followed him inside and accepted a glass of cabernet. He putzed around, sprinkled seasoning on two bacon wrapped filets. Way better than the macaroni and cheese Ed had served to the kids by now.

While McGrath walked outside to light the grill, I buttered two slices of ciabatta bread and dressed the salad. When he returned, he turned on some music. A cool spring breeze blew into the dining area as I set an intimate dinner table.

"So," he said. "How was your day?"

"I'm frazzled," I said. "But work was a breeze, and the kids have settled into Ed's like they've always lived there. Seriously, it's amazing how adaptable they are."

"You don't have to keep it together for my sake. It's okay. I'm here for you." He planted another affectionate kiss on my cheek.

"It's weird," I said. "I'm so comfortable with you. We didn't see or talk to each other for almost a year and here we are, like an old married couple, moving around the kitchen in total sync. This 'normal' time is exactly what I need." I glanced around his kitchen. Friendly Formica countertops, oversized pine table with rustic chairs. Comfortable. Homey.

McGrath smiled. "I'm glad."

"Thanks for waiting," I said, contemplating for a moment where I would be without his comfort.

"My pleasure." He patted my hip on his way outside to set the steaks on the grill.

I heard the faint ringing of my cell, and ran to the living room in search of my purse. I rifled through my bag, found it, and answered.

"Sam?"

"Here," I answered.

"Marty Jaeger."

"Oh, hi, Marty. Is something wrong?" My heart picked up speed. Knee-jerk reaction.

"Nope, just wondered if I could stop by the house later this week. I think I left a shirt there."

I frowned. A shirt? Really?

"You're welcome to go by and pick it up," I said. "The house is locked, but truthfully, at this point, I think anyone can enter without too much trouble."

"I'd feel better if you were there," he said.

"Sure," I agreed. "I'll be there tomorrow after work. It's time to begin sorting."

McGrath stepped into the living room, questioning me

with his eyes. I shrugged my shoulders.

"Tomorrow's great," Marty said. "How about I stop by after work? Say around 5:30?"

"No problem. I'll see you then." I disconnected the call.

McGrath waited.

"One of the firefighters, an old friend, left something behind at the house. He wants to pick it up tomorrow."

"He's hitting on you," he said matter of factly.

"I don't think so." I settled back on the sofa and smiled at McGrath. Jealous, huh?

"You don't think so, but I know so," McGrath continued. "Trust me, I'm a detective. I discern things others fail to notice."

I laughed. "You remind me of Jack. He told me you were hitting on me a year ago when you took me to the gun range."

"He was right. I was hitting on you." McGrath walked over to me, pilfered my wine glass, and placed it on the table. He pulled me up, gathered me into his arms and kissed me.

I smiled at him after the kiss. "And you're hitting on me now."

"You possess succinct deductive skills of your own, Samantha. Now, let's eat, so we can spend time on dessert before you have to rush home."

"I do like to linger over dessert. And it's a school night, after all," I said.

We enjoyed our supper, steaks and adult conversation laced with more serious flirting. I slid my toes up his pant leg before he pushed away from the table, took my hand, and guided me down the hall to his bedroom. I stood before him, silently watching while he unfastened each of the eight pearl buttons on my silk blouse and slid it off my shoulders. I returned the favor, undoing the buttons on his shirt before I helped him remove his khaki's. He looked great, standing in front of me in his BVD's and socks. I laughed.

"What?" he asked. "You don't find this look attractive?"

"Very," I said before pulling him down on top of me.

McGrath caressed my breasts as I rolled atop him. I offered myself to him in a way almost unfamiliar. And then, I devoured him. I could get used to this. Love-making proved a delectable dessert.

I showered before heading back to Ed's. Acclimating to my "real" life proved the hardest part of all. I had to pull myself together and regroup into Mom mode before I headed back to the kids. I laughed to myself. Could the clandestine love affair of a single mother of five cause schizophrenia?

McGrath peeked into the bathroom as I toweled off. "Need anything?"

I smiled. "Nothing more this evening, thank you. I'm a mom. I have to hurry home."

He laughed. "Mom. Right. Hard for me to think of you that way at the moment."

* * *

Living out of a suitcase reminded me of what my late husband's life must have felt like. Only difference, I had five kids and my father-in-law within the same 2,000 square foot space, and I didn't have the opportunity to dine out, enjoy room service, or have maids arrive to make up my bed and clean up my mess. In any case, I fell onto the lumpy sofa bed and closed my eyes after arriving back from McGrath's place. My body craved rest. Inside my head though, sparks flew. I couldn't turn off my brain long enough to settle into sleep.

I suddenly felt haunted by McGrath's upcoming Bredel call. What new wrench would get thrown into the mix? Would I learn something new about Jon's impostor? Would the information turn my world upside down? Would I uncover details about my Jon that would ruin the fond memories I'd worked so hard to preserve? That was the real question. The upsetting question.

I gave up on sleep since it was too late for a pill, and began pacing the tiny room before I finally sank onto the side of the mattress and held my head in my hands. There had to be a better way to manage late nights than flopping like a fish on dry land. I plucked my headphones from the suitcase pocket and reached for my phone. Music usually helped on sleepless nights when it was too late for a melatonin. I pushed the home button and the screen instantly lit. A text message signaled everything I'd been worried about. It read, "Call me. I've heard from Bredel."

I dialed and waited. When McGrath answered I whispered, "What? What did he say?"

McGrath cleared his throat. Not a good sign. It signaled his discomfort—a hesitance to deliver bad news.

"Okay," I said, posturing myself. "I can take it." I stared out the window at the murky streetlight for a long moment, then shut my eyes, bracing myself for the worst.

"He found some paperwork that indicated that Stitsill had ties to Jon's company. Not just a receipt with Darwin Coswell's name on it, but something more."

"What?" I asked. I couldn't imagine.

"He wouldn't say, but he's dangling a carrot, hoping I'll give him something if he hands over information. He knows I'm law enforcement. He knows I'm desperate for information. I've explained to him that Stitsill is missing."

I stopped and thought for a minute. What did Bredel want? He couldn't know about the $500,000 that Rosie had found in the strong box and had me deliver to a trust lawyer to care for her boys. No. Maybe he was a greedy bastard and felt that the $500,000 he'd found could somehow be multiplied by getting in touch with my Jon. Maybe he guessed that McGrath was an intermediary. "It's something else, isn't it?"

"It's a gut feeling, Sam. I'm worried Stitsill killed your Jon, too, and got paid for it."

A shiver snaked down my spine. Was that even possible?

My Jon died in the car accident a week before I'd killed his impostor on my basement steps. How could he have flown to Japan, killed my Jon, and then arrived back in the U.S. and shown up at my place twenty-four hours later? Goosebumps rose on my arms.

"He could have, couldn't he?"

Silence met my words.

I tried clearing the lump in my throat. "Did he kill my Jon because I was onto the fact that he was poisoning his wife, or was it something else?"

"I don't know yet."

I began to feel very guilty. And scared. Had Jon been killed because of me? "This new tie to Jon's company mixes things up, doesn't it?"

"At least."

The more I thought about this, the less I felt like it could be described as news. Either I was in denial, or McGrath had left something out.

"Detective McGrath," I tensed. "Is there something you're not telling me?"

"Remember what Bredel said the last time I spoke with him? He said that people had been looking for Stitsill after he'd left Botswana. Because his departure occurred so abruptly, it raised suspicion."

"Yes, I remember."

"Evidently the same organization has resurfaced in Botswana, looking for him again."

"What? Who are they? And why are they looking for him if he's already dead?" My breath caught in my chest. "He's dead, isn't he? I mean, I killed him. I saw a photo of him after I shot him. I identified him." I inhaled a measured breath.

"Sam," McGrath interrupted. "There are other possibilities."

"What? Like the whole thing was a set up?" I felt sick to my stomach.

"That's one," McGrath said.

"I realize that, but denial is easier than facing that fact." I didn't know what more to say... This was all so much bigger and scarier than I ever imagined.

"Sam?"

"So... So who were these guys?"

"Not sure. Maybe Interpol."

"Interpol?" I asked.

"You know who they are, right?"

"I'm afraid so."

CHAPTER THIRTEEN

I ENDED THE call with McGrath, pulled my laptop off the nightstand and Googled Interpol. International Criminal Police Organization. Although my heart raced and thudded like a bass drum in my chest, I felt more energized than fearful. It made no sense. I should have learned something from my last escapade. Walk away. No. Run away. But no. A slice of excitement zipped through my veins.

I read the home page first, discovering that Interpol had been around since 1923, with members from almost two hundred countries. The organization facilitated cross-border police cooperation, as Pakistan supposedly did in helping the U.S. to uncover Bin Laden's whereabouts. Its mission statement: to prevent or combat international crime, like the events of 9/11.

I discovered flow charts that illustrated the command hierarchy, and photographs of the past General Secretariats. I quickly scrolled to the member nations. Botswana was, indeed an affiliate, along with Canada (where Stitsill had been born) and Japan.

For some weird reason, I felt extremely satisfied to discover this, because I felt it would aid me in securing their cooperation to solve the mystery that now surrounded my husband's death. Never mind that I held a full-time position as a schoolteacher. Never mind that I was the widowed mother of five. Never mind that I no longer lived in my own home. In the naive place my mind seemed to visit with ever increasing frequency, I assured myself that I'd be in charge of the investigation, and Interpol would supply me with a team of inspectors. Yeah. Right.

I clicked back to the home page, reading the list of crimes that Interpol investigated. Drugs, corruption, pharmaceutical crime. Pharmaceutical crime. Interesting. Stitsill had acquired tritiated water and used it to kill his wife, leaving their two boys without a mother or a father. Nice guy.

I read about crimes related to pharmaceuticals. There were organizations that sold counterfeit and illegal medicines. Some were located in Southern Africa. Bells and whistles. Botswana. Southern Africa.

I felt as if I'd been living in a bubble, like that boy without an immune system. How simple a life I'd led until a year ago.

I turned my eyes back to the computer screen. Interpol projects were listed, some of which targeted serial murders and rapists, maritime piracy, corruption, genocide, and war crimes. Sheesh. I briefly scanned the fugitives file and inspected the WANTED list. Stitsill's name wasn't there. Not like he would have been identified by that name. When I'd turned over the strong box to McGrath, which contained a slew of false passports and payment receipts for Stitsill's successful assassinations, I'd also relinquished access to any clues to his past. At the time, it made complete sense. And as far as I knew McGrath had handed the documents over to the proper governmental agency. McGrath had said it was the right thing to do. I'd agreed because I'd thought the nightmare had ended. Damned hindsight.

I clicked on each of the remaining links, but nothing seemed appropriate.

Completely baffled, I made a list.

- My husband's passport, stolen in Toronto, led to his identity ultimately being stolen by a hired gun. The impostor had lifted Jon's name and life history and used it when necessary.

- The imposter then killed someone to fake his own death (the body never positively identified), and left the country…ultimately arriving in Botswana under the guise of being a Peace Corps volunteer. When?
- While the impostor served in the Peace Corps in Botswana, he kept over $500,000 dollars, fake passports, and at least one firearm in his possession.
- Either before going to Botswana, or while he lived there, he did something, or was thought to have done something which had given grounds for various groups (governmental, law enforcement, others???) to search for him in a "threatening" way. He'd fled Botswana.
- He'd left money and several passports behind when he departed Botswana.
- When he'd moved back to the States, he'd left his wife and sons behind, along with large sums of money and fake passports.
- The impostor poisoned his wife, causing her cancer and subsequent death. Why??? And what about his wife? Did I know everything about Rosie's involvement???
- The impostor was suspected of killing a man who also worked for the same company as my Jon, two years prior to his arrival in the States. He was involved with the man's wife.
- My husband died in a car crash in the mountains of Japan, just like this other gentleman.
- I'd killed someone (according to "authorities", the imposter), who was looking for the passports and/ or the money. I didn't actually see the guy I'd killed because it was dark. The authorities showed me a photograph of the impostor and asked me if he was the man I shot. I'd said "yes", plus I thought

McGrath had seen the guy after I'd shot him. Had I imagined that? Who were the "authorities"??? Who did I shoot?? Why are people…"authorities", or "others"…still looking for the imposter?

With that final notation, my eyelids fluttered. I tucked the list inside the pocket of my purse, lay down, closed my eyes, and instantly fell asleep.

I awoke in a fog. It took me a minute to get my bearings. Ed's house. School day. Tired. I managed to start coffee brewing in the kitchen, then trudged to the bathroom on the second floor and turned on the shower. After dressing, I woke the girls, then headed downstairs to get the boys going.

Once I finished my first cup of coffee, I felt tons better. I couldn't help a quick sneak into the study to click on the Interpol site again. I tried searching for criminals in the Red Notice category. I guessed Stitsill would be wanted for way more than just questioning or verification of his identity. But the site didn't make it easy. Since I didn't have a name to search for, I played with various searches. I tried the sites listed tips, but they didn't help either. I wished they'd post photos of the bad guys like they did on the Post Office bulletin board. Why couldn't this be easy?

Just then, I heard Lizzie screeching at Nick about breakfast cereal, and Ed's familiar footsteps descending the stairs. I felt sorry for him. The poor guy had finally retired. An eligible widower as well. I imagined he had about five hundred million things he'd rather be doing.

I met him in the hallway.

"This weekend, I'll go out and look for a furnished apartment. The construction on the house won't be completed until the end of summer. That's way too long for us to impose on you."

"Tell you the truth, I like having you guys around. It's been way too quiet for me since Betty's passing."

I chuckled. "She did like to talk."

Ed smiled at the memories. "Yes, my girl had a lot to say. I miss her." Ed turned away. A familiar gesture I recognized in myself whenever I teared up about Jon.

"These kids will sure enough distract you," I said.

"Exactly what I'm saying. Honestly, your being here is just the right medicine. In fact…"

I followed Ed into the busy kitchen, swiped the bowl Nick held over his head and out of Lizzie's reach, placed it back on the table, and gestured to him to sit down and eat before I subjected him to my wrath. His sheepish grin, an expression that I knew far too well, made me smile. I ruffled his curly mop once he sat down at the table and handed Lizzie the milk.

Ed poured two fingers of cream into a mug, just like his son had done, then doused coffee over the top and winked at Nick and Will.

"What's going on?" I asked. "Looks like you guys have something up your sleeves."

Ed grinned. "We were going to wait until I could discuss this with you alone, but what the heck, huh, boys?"

"Yeah, Grandpa," the boys chorused, "ask her now."

Will jumped out of his seat and rushed to my side, resting his head on my shoulder.

"Is someone in trouble?" I sighed. What had happened during my absence last night?

"No," Ed began, "but we do have a proposition for you."

I ushered Will back to his seat so that he could finish his breakfast and be ready for school on time.

"Be quick about it, then. Fifteen minutes and we're outta here."

The girls winked at each other, and my suspicions increased by the second.

"School's out in four weeks, right?" Ed asked.

I nodded, then furrowed my brow.

"The cottage is ready and waiting," Ed raised his

eyebrows at the kids.

They shrieked with excitement.

"What? For a week or two after school gets out?" Ed and Betty had taken the kids to their rustic lake cabin for several of the previous summers, a few weeks at a time.

"We were thinking we'd head up to the lake the day after school gets out. Then, we could dive right into summer. Fishing, canoeing, jet–skiing, campfires, picnics." Ed smiled at the kids.

I breathed in their hopeful expressions. It was only 6:30 a.m. and they looked ecstatic. "What about summer sports' camps? I have you all signed up."

Lizzie surprised me with an audible sigh. "Mom, boring."

I stopped and recalled how Jon and I had vowed not to over–schedule our kids. We'd believed they needed free time like we'd had as kids. Hours to play outside, build tree houses, fish in the creek, ride old–fashioned bicycles, and slurp on homemade popsicles.

I stepped over to the kitchen counter and poured myself another cup of coffee. As I sipped it, I leaned against the oak cabinet and reminded myself this would be the last summer before my boys entered high school, the last summer before my girls were licensed drivers, the last summer they'd really spend together before each branched off with their own interests. We weren't far away from boyfriends and girlfriends, either.

"I can't do the entire summer," I said. "There's too much to manage."

"We've done it without you before," Ed said.

"But you're by yourself this year."

"All the more reason to keep myself busy," he argued.

I tossed the idea around. It was the last summer I'd have with them as kids. I felt bad about letting them go, yet my brain raced through a thousand scenarios of what I could do in their absence. While the kids were at the cottage with Ed, I could travel. Japan? Botswana? I'd be sure to be back by August. That would give us a month together before school started again.

"I'll think about it," I said, knowing I'd already given in to the idea.

I could hardly wait to phone McGrath and convince him that we could work together to solve this mystery once and for all. I'd tempt him with benefits, plus, it would afford us the chance to know each other, really know each other. Travel together. Solve a crime. There's that.

There are times, now and then, when I wish I would/ could curb my impulsivity. I'm a sensible woman. I teach full-time and special education students at that. I raise five kids, pretty much single-handedly. I pay my bills on time and attend church on all major holidays. I drive the speed limit. Okay, maybe that's an overstatement, but seriously, I'm pretty together. So why did I already have one foot headed down the jet way?

Lost in thought, I blinked back to the present as Marie waved her hand in front of my face. "Mom, are you okay?" she asked while the rest of them laughed. Even Ed joined in.

"You're ganging up on me," I teased.

"It's just for June and July," Annie piped up. "And you always say the best place for kids to grow up is outdoors."

I nodded. She had me there.

"And we'll be out of your hair," Nick said as he smirked.

"Because I act so anxious to get rid of you," I said. "And Annie, I realize that a good part of August is wrapped up in summer, too. Who do you think you're kidding?"

I grinned at her. They got up from the table like spectators rising at a winning baseball game, and carried their dishes over to the sink.

"C'mon, mom," Lizzie said. "We're gonna be late."

Nick wound up beside her and elbowed her. She shot him a look, then understanding settled on her face. Nick then knotted his arm into mine and looked directly into my eyes with his clear blue ones. "We love you, Mom. And think about it. You'll have the entire summer to pull the house together, spend some time with your friends, even go on a date."

Heat rose up my neck. I swear to God, Nick is like a bloodhound. He knows what I'm up to almost before I do. What the heck?

"Fine," I agreed. "You can go." I couldn't believe it. I'd done it again.

CHAPTER FOURTEEN

AFTER BLOWING MY desire for calculated decisions well before 7 a.m., I determined I would not phone McGrath on my drive to work. I needed to practice self-control, a necessary skill if I ever hoped to become a decent amateur sleuth. It would be difficult enough to stay off the Interpol website once I arrived at school. The least I could do was resist my urge to call McGrath and suggest international travel.

Despite my best efforts, another impulse gripped me. I phoned the absence line at school, requested a sub for my morning classes, made a sharp U-turn, and sped towards home. I can't say why, but I needed to go there. I cautioned myself to slow down. The house would be there no matter when I arrived.

It's not like this hadn't happened to me before. I often craved control when my life took a sharp left turn towards hell. When my house had been invaded and tossed upside down a year ago, I prided myself in my level-headed handling of the situation. I put the house back together, better than ever, in record time. Today? Well, this was just me being me.

As I'd hoped, a dumpster had already been positioned in the driveway. Perfect. I could dispose of ruined items, yet salvage what was left of our belongings, precious or not.

A sudden surge of energy swept through me. I knew I'd

made the right decision. As I exited the car and rounded the rear of my home, I checked the exterior. The crew had done a nice job boarding up the outside of the kitchen and family room. Yes, I was searching for a hair tie in the junk drawer, but the need for positives outweighed my desire to face reality.

I stepped back to the car and grabbed the list that the insurance adjuster had given me. My first mission was to secure valuables that I'd overlooked the first night, then I'd begin listing what had been destroyed. I shook my head, surveying the damage. If I smoked, this would have been a good time for a cigarette.

Determined not to allow the current state of affairs to defeat me, I unlocked the front door and headed inside. I methodically traveled from window to window, fully opening each one on the first floor. Next, I climbed the stairs and cracked open those on the second floor. As the stale smoky air cleared, the place cooled down. I threw on a heavy sweatshirt.

The electricity had been turned off, so my first order of business was to clear out the fridge. Five garbage bags later, I'd completed my task. I decided, in spite of the still soggy floors and smoke and heat–damaged walls that I would remain in the kitchen area and focus on the area of my home where most of the damage occurred. This would encompass the most difficult process of the clean–up. The rest of the house would involve only inventorying needed replacements. Get the crap job out of the way first, I told myself, the rest will be a cake–walk.

It didn't seem like much in those two rooms was salvageable, and I knew the insurance adjuster had said that a restoration crew could complete this task for me, but I felt better knowing I'd scoured the place first. I left the canned goods in the pantry, tossed a dozen cereal boxes and snacks in the trash, then pulled my stool over to the liquor cabinet. Tempted as I was to pour myself a couple of fingers of Jon's favorite whiskey, a glance at my phone reminded me it was merely 8 a.m.

Surprised to find the inside of the cabinet dry, I considered saving the unopened bottles. I made a mental note to Google this later, and determine the safety and wisdom of doing this. If Jon were here, I knew he'd say "It's alcohol. It'll kill the bad stuff. It's fine."

I felt a pang of longing. For him. For the years of crazy that had been my normal, but I shook it off, and returned to my mission. I had a helluva lot of liquor in my home. I said a silent prayer that the wine in my basement cellar had survived, and made another mental note to move the job of checking that to the top of the list.

I pulled out bottle after bottle, setting them on the water-logged countertop. Enough bottles of sake to fill a tub. Each with a card taped to its back. All gifts from Jon's travels. I tossed them all. The last bottle, a fancy bottle of Glenfiddich, stood like a lone soldier on the shelf. It, too, had a card attached.

My curiosity piqued, and I peeled the scotch tape from the envelope and slid my nail under the seal of the envelope. Even weirder. A newspaper clipping from the *Asahi Shimbun* had been placed inside. I recognized it as the English publication Jon had read while in Japan. He'd often brought it home to show the kids. I peered at the clipping, skimming once, and then reading it again a second time. Then, a third time.

It referred to the accident which Bredel had spoken with McGrath about. Darwin Coswell, the guy who worked for Jon's company. The guy whose wife was tied to Stitsill.

I turned the article over. On the back, at the edge of the paper, in bold block letters, I read the handwritten message. "You're next."

I leaned over the trash bag and vomited. My limbs began to shake uncontrollably. I couldn't stop them. I placed my head between my knees, still gripping the article.

I told myself to STOP. Think.

This was a warning Jon had never received, right? Who'd given him this bottle? Was it Stitsill himself?

Panic filled every cell of my being. After I'd shot the impostor on the basement steps, the police had taken the gun I'd used. Jon's gun. I'd retrieved it from the police station shortly after, and replaced the weapon on Jon's closet shelf, safe and sound back inside its case.

I ran upstairs and positioned a stool in front of the shelf, located the case and pulled it down. Relieved to find the gun, I held the cold metal, fingering its weight within my hands. It provided me with a measure of security. I replaced the gun in its case and placed it in the hidden boot of the van. My intention was to hand it over to McGrath for safe-keeping. It would be much more secure with him, rather than sitting in my shell of a home.

I phoned McGrath, and he picked up on the first ring. "I've found something."

He waited for me to continue.

"It's an article about Coswell's car crash. From a Japanese newspaper. With a threatening note on the back. I think it was meant for Jon, but I'm sure he never saw it." I couldn't stop shaking. I explained where I'd found the article and waited for McGrath to respond.

"Tuck it in your bag. Bring it to me. We'll figure it out. Try not to worry."

"Easier said than done. I need this to be over."

"You and me, kid. We'll get to the bottom of this."

"Thanks," I said. "I can't tell you how much it means not to face this alone."

* * *

I determined that I'd accomplished enough for one day. My recent discovery left me exhausted and mentally spent. I changed into my running duds and headed for the sunshine.

A run would clear my head. Three miles in, my body and mind relaxed. It was still early, and I had the entire day ahead of me.

I did what any crazed woman would do after finishing my five miles, headed for normal, stopped off at the gym for a quick shower, dressed and headed back to school.

I arrived at lunchtime amidst the puzzled looks of my co-workers.

"Sam," Jack said. "What the hell? I thought you called off. Why are you here?"

"Strange as it sounds, I just called off for the morning. I have classes to teach, lesson plans to write, plus, I need normal. As much of a pain in the ass this place is, it's where I need to be."

"You've lost your mind." Jack placed a reassuring hand on my shoulder. "Let me know if you need anything."

I nodded and headed toward my classroom.

I met Di halfway down the hall.

"I have an emergency," she said.

Had she not noticed my morning absence? Her steady gaze indicated she had not.

"Serious?" I asked.

"Chris. He wants to go away for the weekend. He feels like it's his turn now that Ava is a little older. He claims we need some alone time."

"Honestly, Di," I patted her wrist, "this is very common. Guys are jealous of babies. Think about it, you married so soon after you started dating, and then simultaneously got pregnant. It's not like you spent a lot of alone time before Ava came along."

"My biological clock was ticking double-time. I had to have a baby. I hate it that he's so high maintenance. Isn't it the woman in the relationship who's supposed to be moody and needy?" She waved her arms as we hurried down the hall.

"So, what's your angle? I know it's hard to think about

leaving Ava for the weekend, especially now that you're back at work, but she's so tiny, it would almost be easier to leave her now than when she's older and experiences separation anxiety."

Di groaned. "My life will never be normal again."

"No, it won't." I grinned.

"Would you watch her?"

I stopped dead in my tracks. "What did you just say?" I had to be hearing things.

"Would you watch her? It would just be from Saturday evening till late Sunday afternoon. You're so good with babies. I can't think of anyone I'd trust more."

Okay, I thought. I'm Mother Earth. Di could go away and relax if she knew Ava was in my charge. But seriously, I don't babysit. I DON'T BABYSIT. Now, could this be the time where Di pulled out all the stops and reminded me that I owed her one? She did, after all, tutor Joey when I needed someone in the Stitsill home to gather information for me. I opened my mouth, but nothing came out.

"Chris wants sex every other night," Di continued. "I just got the go ahead from the doctor two weeks ago, and it's all Chris wants from me. I'm exhausted. I'm fat. I'm a mess." Tears began to roll down Di's cheeks.

I hate tears. I'm a sucker for tears. And I hate hormones, too. "Honey, I'd love to help you out, but I've got a heaping full plate right now. The reconstruction is supposed to start on the house next week. The kids have track meets, volleyball tournaments, and Lord knows what else. Let's see if we can find some single teacher from our building. Maybe Tracey Wilson can do it. Heck, you could give her a couple hundred bucks and call it good."

Di eyes beseeched me, but I held firm. The silence grew. When I glanced at her again, she looked downright wounded. Don't relent, I told myself. I felt like saying, "How about them Tigers?" But what would that accomplish?

Students filled the halls. As they greeted us, I seized the

opportunity for a quick getaway. I touched Di's arm and urged, "Don't worry, we'll figure out your drama king hubby. It'd be great if we could clone ourselves after giving birth. That way, our husbands could have sex, and we wouldn't need to participate."

Di laughed and we both headed for our classrooms. I spotted Jack again on my way down the hall. I locked eyes with him. He slapped me on the back, reading my plea for help. "Stitsill, can we talk?"

I felt so tempted to spill everything new about Bredel, Jon's impostor, my recent discovery of the newspaper article and the tie-ins which McGrath and I had just learned, but today, I reminded myself, I was determined to focus on restraint. I simply shook my head.

"I'd love to, but I've got to get to class. I'll talk to you guys later."

I broke away from Jack and Di and bee-lined to my classroom. All I wanted to do was get inside and hide. But kids stood there, waiting for me to unlock the door. I did. They bustled through the entry, chatting and bumping into me. This was going to be an interminable day.

By the time my planning period rolled around, I was starving. I grabbed a box of crackers and headed to the lounge, looking forward to kicking up my feet, if only for twenty minutes. As I rounded the corner, Di bumped into me. "I was just coming to look for you."

I sighed, bracing myself for a guilt trip. "Why?"

"I wanted to talk about Chris, but there's something else, too."

I couldn't imagine. "What's up?"

"Can we go into your classroom and talk? This matter requires privacy."

Di can be a drama queen—perfect match for her husband, the drama king—and I could never tell ahead of time a real from a faux emergency. "Sure," I answered, shaking my head.

We entered my classroom, and Di walked over to my bucket of cleaning supplies. She sprayed and wiped off a student's table and sat down. I opened my crackers, poised myself against the edge of a desk and began to eat.

"You'll never believe it."

"Just tell me," I said, glancing at the clock and slightly bored at the thought of another problem. Whatever her issue, we had only fifteen minutes to discuss it. I was determined to finish writing my lesson plans.

"I haven't even talked to Chris about this yet, his continual obsessing has put me over the top." Di paused.

Tell me about it!

"Mrs. Erickson contacted me yesterday," she continued.

"The High School principal? Why? You didn't request a transfer, did you?"

Di shook her head. "Nothing like that." She laughed nervously. "She remembered right after Rosie died, when I'd visited the school in early fall for a meeting, I'd mentioned that I'd adopt the Stitsill boys in a heartbeat."

"Uh-oh." My churning stomach surprised me. Those boys were special, and, like all of us, they'd been through unimaginable loss.

Rosie's dying wish had been for her boys to be raised here. After her death, her mother had stayed on for a while, took them for a short visit to her home in Mexico, found a family from Rosie's church to raise them, and then returned there.

"So, what's happened?"

"The couple who took the boys were elderly. The woman died last week and the husband is a known alcoholic. Neither he nor Mrs. Erickson think it's the best place for the boys, and she's asking for legal aid to help her find a more appropriate placement."

"Wait a minute," I said, "custody can't just be switched in the blink of an eye. It takes forever. I understood the couple had been appointed as legal guardians so the boys would be allowed to remain in the States. Right? What are you thinking, Di?"

"I want the boys," she said, casting her eyes to the floor.

My stomach flipped, and I tossed my cracker box to the side. "Really? That's great! But you just had a baby. Are you sure you want to take on two teenage boys? I know they're great kids, but seriously, I'm raising teenagers, and even with good kids, it can be a challenge. Plus, those boys have been through so much. You have to talk to Chris about this." As I spoke, my mind whirred. What if Jon's impostor, the boy's father, was still alive? What if he came after Di? Or me? With the latest news from McGrath, I questioned his death. Then again, he hadn't come after me since my own Jon's death. Still.

"I wanted to bounce it off you first. I don't want this to come between you and me," Di admitted. "I know you were close to Rosie and the whole mystery thing around the boys' father. It's never been resolved. We've never been certain what became of their dad. You might feel funny."

As far as Di knew, it never was resolved. "You've got bigger issues to worry about than me. Chris is going to have a full-blown tantrum when you tell him."

"It's got to be a mutual decision, I know, but I did tell him I wanted to adopt the boys when Rosie died. He supported me then."

"Makes sense. You were dating. He was enamored. At that point, he would have climbed Everest for you. Having an idea and bringing it to fruition are two very different things, especially in the case of adopting two teenage boys."

I glanced at the clock. Two minutes.

"Di, you need to think about this. It's a monumental decision. You do need to talk to Chris. At length. Maybe your weekend away will provide you the opportunity. After you've filled his needs, of course." I chuckled and placed my hand on her wrist. "I know that losing your mom early has made you sensitive to kids like this, but you have to keep it all in perspective. You can't adopt every child who loses his mom."

"Look who's talking? After Jon died, you pursued custody of Will and Marie."

I locked eyes with Di. She was a good friend, but she'd just crossed the line. "Totally different," I reminded her. "Those kids had been mine for ten years before Jon died. They visited with their mom, but lived with us. I've raised them since they were preschoolers."

"Still, you took on an enormous responsibility, and now you're all by yourself. You don't even have a husband."

The words stung. Surely, Di didn't mean what she'd just said. I sat there, frozen and silent. The bell rang.

CHAPTER FIFTEEN

I NEEDED A fight with Di like I needed another pencil stub. Plus, she'd distracted me from doing more research on Interpol, writing lesson plans, living a normal life. Adopt Joey and Emilio? Was she fucking crazy? I avoided setting up a walking date with her, unwilling to complicate my life further. By the time I'd left work, chauffeured kids, made dinner, and busied them with homework, seven bells had struck on the grandfather clock in the hall. I'd persuaded Ed to spend the evening with his golfing buddies, so we had his house all to ourselves. That part I welcomed tonight. Preoccupied and irritable, I poured a glass of wine, wandered out onto Ed's deck, settled into a lawn chair, and savored the solitary silence.

I hadn't spoken with McGrath since the previous night. Seemed like a week ago, so much had transpired in the meantime. I switched gears. The thoughts I didn't want to face crept in as I kicked my feet up on the railing. My Jon. What had he been involved in? What had his company really been about? Did they have secrets? International secrets that Jon knew? Had those secrets put him in jeopardy? Had he put us in jeopardy as a result? Accidentally or knowingly? Had Jon's secrets provided the impetus for Stitsill to pose as my Jon? Was that why Jon had been killed? Had someone made his death look like an accident?

My mind spun. I sipped my wine and winced. Too

painful to imagine even half of the answers. Anger bubbled up. More than anything, I wanted to know the truth. If Jon had gotten himself involved in something ugly, I needed to understand the why, what, and how of it in order to understand myself and determine my future. I'd start gathering information soon, fitting the pieces together as I'd done when Jon's identity had been stolen.

But for tonight, I wanted to pretend, just for a few moments, that peace shrouded my life. I watched as a cardinal and his mate drifted from tree to tree, splendor in their flight and dance. I allowed my mind to float, thinking about McGrath and hoping that we could simply fall in love more deeply every day. Our life would be simple. Ordinary.

The door wall slid open behind me. Annie. She opened a chair and positioned it next to mine. I reached for her hand and held it tight. "See the cardinals?" I asked. "Aren't they beautiful?"

"Mom, the birds are great, but I need to talk to you."

I took a closer look, and saw the worry wrinkles on her brow. "What is it, sweetie?"

"I'm forgetting Dad. I used to be able to see his face and hear his voice by just closing my eyes. Now, even when I try to do it, I can't seem to. I hate it." Tears filled her eyes.

"Oh, Sweetheart, I know. It happens to me, sometimes, too. But then, other times, I see him clearly. Think of a memory. That will help you to visualize. Or walk into Dad's closet when we get home. It still smells like him. When I go over to the house next time, I'll grab some photo albums."

"I don't understand why he had to die. It's not fair." Tears spilled off her lashes.

"Totally unfair," I agreed. "All that you're feeling, honey, it's a part of the grieving process."

"But what if I do... forget him?" The tears were streaming now. I wrapped her in a tight hug.

"You won't, I promise. Close your eyes, right now," I said. "Can you see him? His brown hair, his green eyes?

Remember all of his funny sayings? 'Haven't had this much fun since the rats ate my little brother. Be careful out there, it's a jungle.' Can you hear him cheering for you at track meets? In his suit and tie, holding a golf umbrella?"

Annie giggled. "His umbrella turned inside out, but he kept holding it over his head."

"You can see him, can't you?"

"I can." Annie opened her eyes and smiled. "Thanks, mom. You're the best."

She stood, eased her long body into my lap, and tucked her face into the hollow of my shoulder. I held her close, smelled her hair, wished her back to infancy. But my life hadn't been simple then either. I, like many other young women, had married an alcoholic, thinking I'd be the woman to change him. When Annie turned two and just after I'd given birth to Nick, I realized the only thing I could change about my first husband was his marital status. We'd parted ways before Nick turned eight weeks old. Long before Jon's death, my kids had already dealt with too much loss in their lives. Marie and Will had lost both their mother and their father.

I'd learned a long time ago that it didn't help to dwell on the past. Figure it out, sure. But spend time on regrets? No way. Move on. So why did I still feel the need to figure out Jon's death? Would I ever learn to heed my own advice?

I squeezed Annie tight, and she hugged me. "I'd better finish my geometry."

"That's my girl," I said. We walked inside together, and I refilled my glass. Lizzie lay parked in front of the singing show, as Jon used to call it. I grabbed my laptop before heading back out to the deck, where I searched for mid-June flights to Japan. I remembered Jon's flights had left mid-afternoon. Thirteen hours in coach at $2200 dollars a seat. Ouch. And I'd have to pay for McGrath, too. I couldn't expect him to cover his ticket. And then there would be the hotel, the food, and the transportation costs. How could I justify all of this? I knew myself well enough to know I'd figure out a way.

The door wall slid open again. Close to 8:00 p.m. Nick handed me my cell phone. "You missed a call. It might be important."

"You didn't check to see who called, did you?" I asked out of curiosity, hoping it hadn't been McGrath. I'd never asked him not to call when I was with the kids, but it seemed like it might be a good topic for a later discussion. I looked at the readout on the screen. Di had called.

"It was just Mrs. Harris."

I waved him back inside and pressed the call back button. She picked up on the third ring.

"Hi," she said. "Thanks for returning my call. I wasn't sure if you'd ever talk to me again."

"It's not like that, Di, but you hurt me today. I understand why you want to adopt the boys. I really do. I just want you to go in with eyes wide open. Adoptions like this are complicated. The boys have a Mexican heritage and living relatives. It's a lot to juggle on top of the emotional traumas they've both had to endure. You're tough, I know, but it's a hell of an undertaking, especially when you're still establishing your own life with Chris and Ava."

"You're totally right to warn me about what I'm getting myself into. Mostly, though, I want to apologize. I can't even believe myself, saying those hurtful things to you. I hope you can forgive me."

Forgiveness is my middle name. I liked Di. If not for her, I probably wouldn't get out of the house much. Or at all. Running hadn't appealed of late. Exercise time with Di provided therapy. I needed someone with whom to bounce my issues around, and I wanted and needed her encouragement when I felt tempted to back away from McGrath.

"I forgive you," I said. Sometimes, when I weighed the options, it was just easier to let go of the bad stuff. "How are the plans for the weekend coming along?"

"I feel duplicitous," she said. "I found a sitter, started pumping extra breast milk, and all the while, I'm chomping at the bit to get Chris to agree to adopt the boys."

"I understand the internal struggle, but don't set yourself up for a fall. I know you're bent on raising Joey and Emilio, but it's going to be a process. First, you have to let Chris mull it over. It'll be a major issue for him. Keep in mind, Ava's still an infant, and he's already feeling abandoned. My guess is, it's going to take some pretty steady convincing for him to agree. And if you do adopt the boys there will be quite an adjustment period for all of you."

"I just have a feeling about this. It's the right thing to do. Chris and I are older. He's always wanted more than one child. And this way, he'll have boys to play ball with and teach all the man things he believes are so important. We may never have another child of our own."

A few sprinkles of rain dotted the deck. My laptop lay open on the patio table. I shouldered the phone and gathered up my things. All I really wanted to do was finish my wine, curl up on the couch with Lizzie, and read a good mystery.

Good-old Di. Naive, headstrong, Di. She reminded me of someone else I knew. I laughed. "If you said anything different, I'd be worried. You've got a big heart. Those boys would be very lucky to have you." If only it were that simple.

CHAPTER SIXTEEN

R AIN DAPPLED THE windshield, those silver dollar–sized drops that indicate a drenching rain will soon begin. I slowed my speed as the rain increased in intensity and I approached the orange cones marking the narrowing of the highway from two lanes to one. I had planned on an extra long drive to work this spring morning, aware that it would give me some extra time to think.

I'd awakened out of sorts. I needed to understand why. I'd been on edge with Ed and the kids, anger simmering just beneath the surface. Before long it would bubble over and create a huge mess, something I didn't want to take out on my students or colleagues.

Damn Jon. How could he have left me with all of this? In his position with the company, he'd known and kept company secrets. I remembered his last call home before his death. He'd told me he'd discovered money missing and the top dogs were plenty miffed. Had it been Jon's job to sort it out? Probably. That had been his reason for extending his Japan trip. Of course, he'd neglected to mention the woman who would be staying with him during that time.

Mad at a dead guy. How would I resolve that one? I'd been episodically angry with Jon over the past eleven months. Now that the first anniversary of his death approached, I felt guilty about that anger. He hadn't intended to die and leave us husband and fatherless. My recent relationship with McGrath had probably made it even easier for me to be mad at him. If I was mad, it almost felt like permission to continue my life with another man. And far easier to push aside my guilt.

Had Jon felt guilty? I knew, way down deep, that a housekeeper hadn't answered his hotel room phone. She'd spoken plain English. No one at the hotel had spoken plain English. Not in the eleven years I'd phoned him there. I'd always had a horrid time trying to reach my husband. No one had ever answered his hotel room phone but him. Who was she? Would I ever know? If I knew, would I feel better or worse?

My anger escalated. I'd pushed through a year of my own grief, my children's grief, my mother–in–law's death, two funerals, life insurance red tape, recovering from shooting someone (and now I didn't even know who I'd shot) and much, much more. Those items were just the tip of the emotional iceberg.

I recalled my studies on Kubler–Ross' stages of grief years ago in college. They had helped me make sense of the loss of my parents, and arrive at some conclusions of my own about the grieving process.

The grieving stages were fluid, not linear. Denial overlapped anger, and bargaining, and depression. Through my work with parents of disabled students, I learned that the initial denial parents experienced upon the birth of their impaired child reared its ugly head over and over again as developmental milestones served as an assault on the parents, a fierce reminder of what was never to be — normal. I'd also postulated that acceptance was a crock of shit. How did one ever accept that their child would never walk, read, drive, date, or marry? The best parents could hope for was a new normal, one that they created. An adjustment. It didn't necessarily fix the problem, but it did make them feel better for a little while.

Maybe I required an adjustment. Living at Ed's didn't

help. One more thing to add to my list of NOT NORMAL. I simply needed to ground myself with my own NEW NORMAL. Adjustment, not acceptance. Just like I did after the death of my parents. Just like I did after I lost Jon.

I blew out a puff of air as traffic began to clear. I sped up. The clogged traffic had been a costumed blessing. By the time I arrived at work, I felt much better.

Jack pulled into the parking lot as I eased my car into a spot. I waited for him to lumber towards the building, and I joined him under the overhang. Rain continued to pound the pavement, so we slipped inside the back door.

"Mornin', Jack," I said.

He slapped me on the back. "Hey, Stitsill. What's up?"

"Searching for normal."

"You're such a freak," he said. "I've been through so much with you over the past few years, woman. There is no normal for you. Face it, would you?"

"Shut the hell up. You're depressing me. I need to hope, okay?"

"Normal. Stitsill normal. Let me think. What would that consist of? Tailing bad guys. Befriending their families. Shooting bad guys. Call me crazy, but that's just not normal."

"You're getting on my nerves." I nudged him with an elbow.

He laughed. "How about dating? You got pretty female on me when I brought that up yesterday. Are you seeing the detective?"

"Am I that transparent?" I shook my head. There were things about myself I just didn't like: my naïveté, my optimistic nature, my ease of forgiveness when someone hurt me. I hated that Jack could see right through me. I hated Nick picking up on my moods at home and now Jack at work. I couldn't escape the scrutiny. Secretly though, I felt glad someone on the planet got me.

"You have that glow." Jack shrugged and looked embarrassed.

"Shit, you spotted my glow?" I sighed. Was nothing sacred? "When did you first notice it?"

"Yesterday," he said.

Now that's just plain scary. "Are you psychic, or is it something I'm really giving off?"

"It's your smile," Jack admitted somewhat sheepishly. "It's open, relaxed. And oh, yeah, your cheeks are flushed."

"Crap," I said. "I'm going to have to work on that."

We stood inside the double doors now, our eyes momentarily locked. I knew it made Jack uncomfortable when he admitted what he considered to be deeply personal information.

"Can I touch base with you after I tuck my bag inside my room?" I asked.

"Sure," he said. "Something's up, isn't it?"

"Yep, your Stitsill detector is right on this morning. Any guesses?"

"I have no idea. I've already been way more perceptive than I can handle, and it's not even 8 a.m."

After I unlocked my classroom door, tossed my book bag on my chair and delivered my lunch to the lounge refrigerator, I headed to Jack's room. I wavered a bit. Divulging information was something I indulged in with Jack. A year ago, I had shared the deepest parts of me on a regular basis, but I hadn't done that in a long while. I'd retreated like a wounded pup after Jon's death. Opening up to Jack again after so long felt odd and unfamiliar, scary, in fact, but I knew I needed him. Maybe I was opening up to the world again since McGrath had pierced my armor. That had to be a good thing, didn't it?

I strolled inside Jack's classroom and pulled up a student's chair beside his desk. Jack, organizing his day, opened and closed drawers, pulled out grade books and lesson plans, worksheets and pencils for those who'd left theirs in their lockers. Jack cracked me up. Since he taught Math, he refused to enlist the available computerized grading program. He felt it posed an insult to his intelligence, and he delighted in his ability to figure out average scores and final grades with only the smarts–between–the–ears, as he called it. Jack didn't wear a watch either, yet he knew, often to the minute, the exact time.

Now, he peered at me. I recognized the probing look. Jack always used it on me when he tried to sort out my inner thoughts, even though he'd told me a million times he'd tired of trying to figure me out. He reminded me of Pavlov's dog. Once, he'd gotten it right, he felt confident he'd succeed again. Men and their false sense of competence.

"What?" I asked. "Have you got it?"

Jack shook his head. "No, darn it. I don't. Just tell me," he said. "We've only got six and a half minutes before the kids invade our surroundings."

"Right." I glanced at the wall clock and confirmed his statistics. I had to hurry, so I came right out with it. "Di wants to adopt the Stitsill boys."

"She's loony!" Jack decreed.

I nodded. "I know, but you know how she is."

"Loony," Jack repeated. "Chris will never agree."

"But he's devout. Devout Catholics are good people. They help other people in need." It was the only reason I could imagine Chris raising the boys.

"Heck, Stitsill, I consider you more of a bleeding heart than either Di or Chris. Actually, I'm proud of you. I thought for sure you'd adopt those boys after Rosie died. I guessed that after you shot their dad, you'd feel sorry for them, and guilty, too. I'm glad you didn't succumb to remorse or obligation. It would have been misplaced."

"Their dad was an assassin. And I'll never feel guilty about protecting my family. So, you can just hang that idea in your back closet, mister. Clear?"

"Chill, woman," Jack said. "I was surprised is all. Don't take it personally."

I inhaled a measured breath. Much as I loved him, Jack

had a knack for getting under my skin. The bell rang. Jack washed his hand over his sandy mustache and goatee. A sort of 'let's wrap this up' warning.

"I couldn't adopt them. I have five kids. I'm single," I reminded him.

Jack nodded. "Not criticizing, just sayin'." He stood and loped to the classroom door, opening it to the throng of sixth graders who promptly poured through it.

"I've got to head to class. I'll talk to you later, okay? And Jack…" I paused and looked him right in the eye.

"I know. Not a word to Di." He locked his lips with an imaginary key.

"You're a weirdo," I teased.

Jack slapped me on the back, and I went my way. I thought about Rosie's boys. All alone. Without a mother or a father. It tugged at me. I understood why Di wanted to adopt them, and I understood why it made me fearful. I turned abruptly and headed back to Jack's classroom.

"What now?" he asked as I entered his room.

I motioned him into the hall. He looked worried. I guessed I did, too. He shut the door behind him as he joined me.

"I don't know for sure if Jon's impostor is dead."

"He's dead. I was there, remember?"

"I know you were, but consider this. You didn't see the dead guy. I didn't see the dead guy. It was pitch black. The dead of night. I pointed at the looming figure on the stairs and fired the gun. Heck, I didn't even aim. We thought the guys that showed up afterwards were Feds. FBI or CIA or something. We believed them when they verified Stitsill's death by showing me his photo, but who's to say it was really him? Maybe they wanted me out of the way, and they knew they could keep me from pursuing anything more by declaring him dead."

Jack shook his head, deep grooves forming on his forehead. "I thought Detective McGrath checked." I could see Jack searching his memory.

"We may have been duped." My lips narrowed as I turned to walk away. "I have to get to class."

"Sam." Jack's hand circled my wrist.

I turned to look up at him, fighting tears.

"Watch your back, woman."

I nodded and walked away.

CHAPTER SEVENTEEN

I HARDLY HAD time for anger. The school year was wrapping up for both me and my kids. Plus, the upcoming anniversary of Jon's passing felt like a noose around my neck, constricting my oxygen intake and paralyzing me as I relived the horrendous days surrounding his loss. Add the possibility of the Stitsill boys becoming part of Di's family; it left me feeling powerless and anxious to tie up all the loose ends surrounding both Jons' deaths.

I knew it would take time for Di to work out the details of an adoption. Still, the noose tightened. Whenever I feel out of control, I scramble to organize what I can. Being that I wasn't even living in my own home, I headed there directly after work to assess the progress of the reconstruction. I couldn't help but hope by the time I moved back in, I'd have this entire mess figured out.

As I rolled into the driveway, I noticed Marty's truck parked on the street out front. Wouldn't you know it? I must have shelved the memory of Marty suggesting we meet so that he could pick up his shirt. Suddenly, I felt an overwhelming desire to circle the wagons. I hadn't planned to let him in. To my house or to my life.

I climbed out of the van and smoothed my skirt. Marty hopped out of his truck and sprinted up the driveway.

"Sam," he called, his smile wide. I noticed his eyes light up when I turned to greet him.

My conviction softened. Marty, one of the good guys. Did I really need to be such a hard ass?

"Hey, Marty," I answered as my eyes traveled to the slim brown paper bag he held tucked under his arm.

"Whatcha got there?" I asked.

He handed over the bag and I peeked inside. Word seemed to have spread about my current love for wine. Trefethen. My other new boyfriend.

"Thank you," I said, smiling back at him. "This is one of my favorites."

"I guess you could say we're on similar wavelengths. Got a corkscrew inside?"

A glass of wine sounded great after the day I'd had. Come to think of it, Ed had offered to coordinate kid schedules tonight. What could one glass hurt?

I nodded and led the way inside through the garage. The new cupboards were stacked in my parking space. Sheets of drywall were positioned against an inside wall as well. Signs of progress. As we entered, I noticed that the smell had changed from stale smoke to a mixture of raw materials and cleaning supplies. The cupboards were still attached but the furniture had been removed, the window coverings discarded, and the family room carpeting ripped from the floor. I tiptoed through the maze and opened a cupboard drawer. Sure enough, the corkscrew sat there, waiting like a port in a treacherous storm.

I scrubbed, then handed the tool to Marty and searched for a couple of stemmed glasses. As I rinsed them out in the sink, I remembered McGrath's warning. But I knew men. I could handle whatever Marty threw my way.

Marty poured two glasses and we headed to the front porch. Once I sat down in one of the wicker rockers there, I relaxed and took a long sniff from my goblet. The smell of oak and vanilla tickled my senses, and I allowed myself a moment to enjoy the soothing scent before I sipped. Jon and I had traveled to Napa, but I refused to let the memories of the trip replay. I just savored the seconds as they passed. I knew, without a doubt, I required a break to recharge and clear my thinking.

I forgot about Marty until he cleared his throat as a way of getting my attention.

"Sorry," I said.

"It looked as if you'd gone somewhere pleasant. I hesitated to disrupt you. I know you've got the world on your shoulders right now. Anything I can do to help?"

I looked in my glass, brought it to my lips and let the liquid coat my tongue. Solid red fruit, balanced by a slight hint of spice, coated my taste buds. My pulse slowed to that of a bradycardia patient. Then, I tipped my glass toward his and clinked.

"You've already helped. Thanks for the wine. I needed it."

"I'm a coach, remember? I know what the end of the school year looks like." He paused, sending a warm smile my way. "Chaos."

I thought about the boxes littering my classroom floor, the stacks of papers I still had to correct within the next week, the untaught lessons I still felt rushed to finish, the emotional strings with students that needed binding before next Friday.

"There's a lot left to accomplish. And, truth be told, you're right. I guess I hadn't realized till just this moment. I'm beat."

I grimaced. I hated to admit my weaknesses. Why the heck was I letting Marty in?

"You're entitled. I know you, Sam. You see yourself as invincible. I get that. You've had to be. But, seriously, I'm worried. How much can one person take?"

I laughed uncomfortably. "Don't worry." I tried to reassure Marty, at the same time angry with myself for being so damned transparent. "I'm Wonder Woman's identical twin. Honest."

Marty raised his glass toward mine and then took a drink. "I've always admired you, Sam. Even back in high school. Seemed like you had it all over the other girls in class. What with your swimming, being at the head of the class, your leadership. Seems like life could have been a little kinder to you, doesn't it?"

I chuckled and drank more than a small sip of wine. "None of us can control the hand we're dealt. Doesn't make sense to wrestle with stuff like that. Just leads to ill thinking and hostility."

"You're so damned level-headed. Don't you ever want to scream? Or swear? Or throw caution to the wind and do something totally out of character?"

Tempting, I thought. I narrowed my eyes at him. "Like what?"

Marty leaned back in the rocker, his gaze drifting to the blue sky. "Cliff diving?"

"Actually, I toyed with the idea a long time ago. But by then I had kids and it seemed too risky. I don't always have good luck with adventure." I thought back to my investigation into Stitsill's life, my relationship with Rosie, my heart softening to their son, Joey. None of that had worked out. I'd brought misery and heartache into my life, whether I chose to admit it or not.

"It's good for kids to see their parents take risks. They need to learn to push themselves. Think of it this way, you'd be modeling for them."

"Listen, Marty, four of my kids are adolescents. They can come up with enough risk-taking behavior on their own. Just because their frontal lobes aren't well-developed yet, doesn't mean I have to demonstrate my brain never fully formed." I smiled at him and sipped my wine. It felt good to talk to an adult who knew me, knew from whence I came.

"What did you do in high school?" I asked. "Tell me the truth. Were you one of the closet drinkers? You never got caught that I can remember. Yet, I can't imagine a good-looking strapping guy like you not partying every now and then."

Marty laughed a long and hearty laugh. "Caught." His eyes crinkled at a memory.

"C'mon. Tell me," I coaxed.

"You remember Brian and Fynn?"

"Of course," I answered as I smiled. They were spunky kids, I recalled. The Irish cousins. Freckle faced trouble-makers. Exactly the types of kids I most loved to teach.

"One August night, hot, humid. Hotter than a coal furnace, as I remember. The three of us climbed the access ladder behind the school and hoisted ourselves onto the roof. We'd picked up some pink spray paint from the hardware store, lying to the clerk and telling her Fynn's mom had sent us for it because she'd decided to repaint an old dresser for his sister, Mary Sue. We slipped the cans into our shirt pockets and, once we got situated on the roof with the paint and the six packs we had strung onto our belts, we drank until we were more than a little sloshed, peed over the side of the school, then painted huge penises on the roof. Still there, far as I know."

I peered at Marty. I'd never have guessed, and my heart filled with a new admiration. I nodded my approval. "Ever been back to check?" I laughed.

"Not lately." Quiet laughter filled the air between us as Marty refilled my glass. It felt healing not to be worried, or overwhelmed, or hurried. This might be the flip side of my current life. Interesting. Easy. Comfortable. Friendly.

"How long have you been divorced, Marty?"

He looked surprised by my question. "A long time."

"Why didn't you remarry? You're still young. Still got the looks going for you."

He smiled. "Why, thank you, ma'am," he said. "Gun shy, I guess."

"That surprises me. An athlete. A firefighter. A coach. Somehow, that doesn't seem to fit."

"What's that saying? Twice burned, once shy?"

"Twice?" I scrunched up my face. I couldn't recall Marty having been married more than once.

"High school. I dated Sarah Becker, remember?"

I didn't remember. Where had I been? Sarah had been a couple years younger than we were, but I couldn't recall her and Marty being an item. "Did she break your heart?"

Marty's easy manner shifted. "Seems like I'm best at getting my heart broken," he admitted. He refilled his glass and slugged down a good-sized gulp.

"Sorry," I said, chastising myself for changing the tone of our conversation. "I didn't mean to bring up unpleasant memories."

Marty laughed. "That's one way to put it. It's not manly for us big guys to admit our frailties."

I looked at Marty, sure he was right. He proved to be the model of a broad-shouldered firefighter. Tall, like Jack, but with the clean chiseled lines of a true German. Long nose, high-cheekbones, clear blue eyes. Nice guy. Simple life. No kids. No spouse.

"Hungry?" I didn't know about Marty, but suddenly I felt famished.

He looked startled. "Why? Are you?"

"A little. Plus, I'm beginning to feel this wine. Showing up at Ed's tipsy probably isn't a great example."

"You could sneak in after the kids are asleep," he joked.

"Been there. Done that," I confessed.

Marty's turn to nod in approval. "Good for you."

I rose from my chair, tripping over my own feet and tumbling into Marty's lap. We shared a not so uncomfortable moment. Then, I thought better of it and forced my composure back to the forefront. "I'm such a klutz." Get it together, Samantha.

"No problem," he said.

"I'll just go to my car and see if there are any crackers or something for us to munch on."

I walked past Marty and found an unopened bag of pretzels in the van, then stepped inside to take a deep breath and allow myself to relish in the comfort of being home, even if only for a few hours. Home. Relaxed. Unencumbered.

I moseyed back to the porch. The blue sky above me held a few patches of puffy clouds and a soft breeze blew a few curls across my face. I swept the strands back into place.

My footsteps clattered on the wooden slats of the porch. I set the food on the wicker table in front of Marty's and my chair, noticing that Marty had refilled our glasses in my absence. He made quick work of opening the snack bag and offered me a handful of pretzels.

I settled back into the company of an old friend.

CHAPTER EIGHTEEN

I HAD ONE week to make plans. Japan, here I come. I phoned McGrath and shared my idea with him. He had vacation time coming. Although he didn't appear completely onboard with my idea, he knew better than to let me loose in Asia on my own, so he agreed to accompany me.

"Sounds exotic," he said. "Hey, maybe we'll even find time for a little romance."

Romance sounded good to me, although I wasn't sure how romantic it would be in the midst of a full blown investigation into my dead husband's dealings on his last trip abroad. As I hurried through the house to pack appropriate clothing for the trip, I unearthed an old negligee from my single days and tossed it in my bag. To my surprise, I'd located reasonable flights through an Internet site, and reserved two seats on a nonstop flight to Nagoya the Monday after school finished. I gathered all of my notes on the Stitsill mystery, tucked them inside a manila envelope, then proceeded to place them, along with my passport, securely in the sleeve of my carry-on bag.

Some time ago Ed had suggested I take a month off to heal, and he helped me smooth over the arrangements with the kids. Truth be told, they were adolescents, and their main concern was themselves. As long as Grandpa tipped the scales in their favor with his plan to take them to the cottage for the entire summer holiday, they were happy.

Lizzie experienced a moment or two of clinginess until Ed reminded her that her friend Eva would be right down the beach with her folks. Then, she couldn't pack her duffle fast enough. Add that to the fact the contractor I'd hired to do the reconstruction assured me the house would be in livable condition by August 1st, and we were all good to go.

I had also agreed to join them at the cottage for a brief memorial to Jon's memory, so we would have a few strong family days before I headed out for my "vacation".

I double-checked my list and couldn't think of one thing I'd forgotten. I sailed through the week feeling a strange and unexpected peace I hadn't experienced since Jon's death.

That Friday, with the van packed, the kids loaded, the cooler teeming with peanut butter and jelly sandwiches and sports drinks, we headed out at precisely 4:05 p.m. I drove as fast as safety allowed, listening to my kids banter amidst loud the rock 'n roll music Nick insisted on blaring from the dashboard CD player. We laughed and joked the entire drive north on I-75, arriving on the cottage doorstep at 8:37 p.m.

Lizzie's eyes were heavy, so Will carried her up to bed and I tucked her in after we unpacked the car. By then, she'd already fallen soundly asleep. I pushed back her thin sunny curls and kissed her forehead, a twinge of regret touching my heart. Letting go had never proved easy for me.

The next morning, Ed and I built a bonfire on the beach. He left me unattended for a moment as I rounded the pit with rocks and tossed a few sticks into the center. He returned a short while later with two mugs of steaming coffee.

"Thought this might help," he said.

I sipped, savoring coffee spiked with a touch of Bailey's. "A man after my own heart." I wrapped an arm around his waist and squeezed. "Thank you."

"My pleasure, my dear. You're doing an impressive job raising all of these kids on your own. It's the least I can do."

We fed the kids, then ushered them down to the fire pit. Each one carried something special they'd made for the occasion. Annie, a picture she'd sketched, Marie, a scrapbook she'd compiled, Will, a boomerang that he and Jon had made together when he was younger, and Lizzie, a stuffed bear that Jon had gifted her with after one of his trips. She had dressed him in Daddy–like attire: overalls, old T–shirt, a ball cap, plastic boots, and a makeshift fishing pole. Nick followed the entourage with his guitar. He had written a song for Jon, which we would hear for the first time at the conclusion of this memorial service. All in all, a fine tribute to Jon.

I'd been saying goodbye to Jon in stages. I couldn't help but wonder how much longer it would be before I found some final peace with the grieving process.

We gathered around the fire, each sharing a special saying that Jon used. A couple of years previous, we compiled a list of what we entitled 'Daddyisms'. The fact that he'd come from Kentucky provided us with a wealth of material, we often teased Jon as his Southern drawl thickened whenever we headed south.

Lizzie started with, "This is the most fun I've had since the rats ate my little brother."

The kids always laughed at this. Since Jon had been an only child, it made perfect sense.

Marie followed suit with, "Be careful. It's a jungle out there." Jon used this phrase whenever the kids left the house without us.

Annie then piped up with, "Tomorrow's another day." The kids laughed, still convinced that their father had been a master of the obvious.

Once Will and Nick added their quotes, Annie showed us a picture she had drawn of Jon. My amazingly gifted children. Marie shared her album. Will clutched the boomerang to his chest.

Then, under the bluest of skies, Nick lifted his acoustic

guitar and his soft music filled the air. I immediately felt stunned by the breadth of my son's talent. He had entitled his piece, Dad's Lullaby, and sang in his newly acquired and sometimes creaky bass voice.

> *You left our home but not our hearts*
> *Our father strong and tall*
> *And it won't be long till we meet again*
> *At heaven's pearly wall*
> *In the meantime I will take your spot*
> *Let no one come to harm*
> *For I'll shelter my family as you would have done*
> *And hold them close in my arms.*
> *You left us much too soon, Dear Dad*
> *But you watch us even now*
> *Smiling down as you've always done*
> *From a shining dark blue moon*
> *You are in the sun*
> *You are in the rain*
> *You are in our very souls*
> *We miss you Dad but we always know*
> *That you're never far from home*

We held hands and cried as my heart filled with overwhelming joy and pride. My son had grown into an amazing young man. Talented, insightful, and with a heart bigger than the entire Western Hemisphere.

Ed and I coordinated the rest of the day as a party, doing all of the things with the kids Jon would have done had he still been alive. We shot the boomerang, built ornate castles in the sand, formed a solid line, holding hands, and ran full–speed ahead, plunging into the frigid Lake Michigan waters. Ed stocked a plastic container with worms and took the kids fishing, first the boys and then the girls. When the expeditions were complete, we cleaned the walleye, perch, and bass at Ed's workbench, scraping the scales as Jon had expertly taught all the kids to do, and then gutting them and filleting them. Then we searched the shore for sticks to string them on before we roasted them over our seasoned fire.

We spent a long day celebrating the legacy that Jon and I had created over the ten plus years we'd been together. We'd created a family. A bond much stronger than blood. A joining of hearts.

CHAPTER NINETEEN

MCGRATH PICKED ME up at the house. I wanted to check on things before I took off, and it made sense for a control freak like me to leave a list of last minute items I expected the contractor to be sure to complete in my absence. It killed me, the not being there to supervise, but after weighing all of my options, it made much more sense to make this trip to Japan while I could. I sensed that my future would depend on it.

We boarded the coach section of the Boeing 747. I wore comfortable sweats and tennies, while McGrath stuck with his standard issue Khaki's and sports coat. I questioned his wisdom. We would be flying for 13 hours and 5 minutes, if everything went according to plan. An interminably long time for someone like me who could barely light in any one spot for ten minutes. I placed my Kindle in the seat pocket in front of me, along with my water bottle and magazines. McGrath opened the standard Delta issue red blanket and placed it over my legs with a reassuring pat.

He knew things about me without me having to tell him. Nirvana.

I rested my head on his shoulder and slept like an infant for five hours. I awakened famished, and McGrath pulled out the sandwiches I'd packed. Peanut butter and jelly on whole wheat, another standard issue, but of my cupboards, not Delta's. We finished off our sandwiches with a shared banana, and I rifled my notes out of my backpack.

A single fact gnawed at me above all others. I may never know for sure who I'd shot that night on my basement stairs. I had a nagging suspicion it wasn't my husband's impostor, but someone he had sent in his stead. Made perfect sense now that I had some distance from it all. Why would a hired gun like Stitsill pursue me on his own? Why not send one of his minions? Unless the hit had been personal.

I pointed to the bullet point on my list and shoved it under McGrath's nose.

"Relax, Sweetie," he said. "We'll make plans once we hit the hotel. Maybe after we cuddle up and take care of a few more important items first." His smile was sly, his hand warm on my thigh.

Despite my brooding, I felt myself relax. An unbidden smile graced my lips. "God, you're good for me." I snuggled into him, resting my head back against his muscular shoulder, and promptly fell back to sleep.

Seemed like no time at all before the flight attendants were serving us yet another glass of water and announcing our arrival in thirty short minutes. I slipped on my shoes, squeezed past McGrath with my toothbrush and paste, and waited in line at the restroom door as the window shades rose automatically. My stomach buzzed with excitement. Answers. I'd soon be getting answers and putting this piece of my life to rest.

I knew I'd indulged in naïveté yet again, and I hated that about myself, but I couldn't help but long for a clean slate. Find out what Jon had really been up to, reassure myself he was who I'd believed him to be, and then tie things up in a neat, tidy package. Didn't seem like too much to hope for, did it?

McGrath must have been reading my thoughts, because when I returned to my seat, he recited a prepared speech.

"Now," he began. "I want to warn you that we may not find what we came here for. Let's not get too serious and remember to take things as they come. No serious agenda, just a light-hearted exploration of Jon's life. I can't imagine a straight-shooter like him could have been involved in too much intrigue."

"Here's the thing," I answered a bit sourly. "I'm not so sure about that, after all we've learned. But whatever we find, I need to understand it with a fair amount of certainty in order to get on with my life."

He squeezed my shoulder. "Either way, Sweetheart, you'll get on with your life."

I suppressed a scowl. Jim McGrath possessed wisdom. I appreciated it. Mostly. As we strolled down the jet way to Immigration, I thought about his comments. As usual, he was right. My sentry. My voice of reason.

I texted Ed of my safe arrival. He returned my message with one of equal reassurance. The kids were well, busy and happy. After we'd made it through Custom's and collected our luggage with that good news, we caught an electric train to the Meitetsu Station. I'd mapped out all the details, going as far as figuring out what our stop would look like. My research proved accurate right up until I hit the restroom, where I was greeted by a pit in the concrete floor, which I was evidently supposed to squat over to do my business. I decided to wait until we reached our hotel, just across the street. Outside, I took in the skyscrapers amid odd sculptures of steel girders, throngs of Japanese signs, and taxis darting in and out of traffic amidst blaring horns.

Early evening had descended, and the neon lights flashed at us from every direction. All city, all the time. Throngs of Asian faces crowded around us. I noticed a wide assortment of women, some dressed in traditional bright kimonos, others in cotton slacks and light jackets. A bit intimidated, I allowed McGrath to lead the way as we crossed a driveway and stepped into the hotel. My head spun. I craned my neck like an Amish child. I'd never seen anything like this city. Twin towers loomed overhead. The buildings went on as far as the eye could see. Just as Jon had described to me for years. Something out of a movie. Unbelievable and surreal.

We unpacked and, needing to stretch a bit more, we headed down to the 12th floor to a restaurant Jon had routinely mentioned. I recognized it from photographs he'd shared after one of his trips. It was called Torafuku, and was a Japanese Izakaya, or share restaurant. I didn't feel like sharing food or a table with anyone other than McGrath, but the truth of the matter remained, neither one of us could speak or understand the language. Essentially, we were alone no matter where we sat. We entered, removed our shoes and sat Indian–style on the floor's tatami mat at an intimate table for twenty, way in the back. The menu, written entirely in Japanese, caused me to thank the good Lord for the plated food in the window. At least the display provided an idea of which sushi we would eat. Once our server arrived, McGrath and I followed him to the front of the restaurant. We pointed to the dishes we desired. McGrath even figured out how to order Asahi beer. Good man.

I listened to the piped string music as it played in the background. And as I ate, I recited my agenda to McGrath. "After a good night's sleep, we should eat a big breakfast and head out for the day. I have a list, but I can't figure out where to start. Part of me thinks heading to the police station makes the most sense. I can't wait see the accident report from Jon's crash. Surely, the name of the woman with him will be listed in the documents."

"You going to hunt her down and take her out?" McGrath asked, deadpan, and popped an entire marinated chicken wing into his mouth.

I frowned. "We have a lot to cover while we're here."

"Haste makes waste, Sam. Throttle back."

"We're only here for a month."

"An entire month." McGrath winked at me.

I nodded and raised my beer. "Point well taken."

McGrath laughed, then placed his hand over mine. He clinked his bottle against my own. "To us," he said, grinning sheepishly. "To a productive trip, and to us."

I took a long pull on my beer and relaxed.

The next moment, I felt his fingers on my cheeks and he turned me toward him, interrupting any thoughts of my life of innocence. His lips gently joined mine as he wrapped his arms around me and drew me close.

"Let's go upstairs," he murmured. I moaned into his neck.

We rode the elevator to the 30th floor.

I didn't need the negligee after all.

CHAPTER TWENTY

JET LAG LEFT me jittery. I lay awake, trying not to breathe or move for fear of waking McGrath. One of us needed to be rested for the day ahead. Finally, I couldn't take lying still for another minute. I slipped out of bed, shuffled into a pair of shorts and a t-shirt, scribbled a quick note to McGrath, grabbed my room key and my shoes, and tiptoed out of the room. Outside at 3 a.m. Nagoya time, I'd hoped to find a quiet spot for reflection, but the streets were alight and crowded with people, all Asian. They bustled like ants searching for their own special hill. Frantic and focused.

I took in the panorama. The lights of the city obscured any chance of a starry sky, but the view proved stunning. Fountains, skyscrapers that resembled space shuttles, street lights that looked like robots. A far cry from the small town in which I resided. I'd grown up in a cave. The world was much larger than I'd ever understood.

I felt like I'd been abducted by aliens.

How had Jon done this?

I scowled. He'd done it for approximately three of our eleven years marriage, a week or two at a time, of course. I guessed, unlike me, this had become second nature to him. Me? I didn't weather change very well.

One thing about Jon, he'd been exacting in his descriptions. He had told me about a McDonald's located in the adjacent Meitetsu train station. I glanced down the street to my right and found it exactly where he'd described it. I'd had the foresight to zipper some yen into the pocket of my exercise shorts, so I headed in the direction of the Golden Arches. If everyone else was awake and traveling the city in the middle of the night, why shouldn't I join them?

A quaint cashier stood at attention, a miniscule, older Japanese woman, probably 4'10" and retired, I imagined, as I walked through the entrance. Next in line, I ordered a large coffee, in English. No problem. With no idea of the exchange rate or of which currency equaled what denomination, I simply handed over a bill and received change. I had to trust I wasn't getting screwed, but in reality, in that moment, I would have paid an outrageous sum of money for a decent cup of coffee.

Jon had reassured me many times little crime occurred in Japan. Still, I felt a little intimidated at the prospect of finding a contemplative spot outdoors in the middle of the night. Once I located a booth in the back of the fast food establishment, I seated myself away from view, and curled up my legs in front of me while I sipped my coffee.

It made sense that I felt out of place. Some 6,500 miles from home, away from my kids for the first time in a year, and with a strange man who wasn't my husband. Get a grip, Sam. Stop the histrionics. He's not a strange man. He's a good man. A cop. A trustworthy man who makes your blood simmer and your heart swell. Not only that, he's traveled all these miles with you so that you can put your dead husband to rest. Only the best kind of man would put himself through that!

I shook off my doubts. Japan. This could be an adventure. Hopefully, what I discovered about Jon wouldn't be so horribly shocking that it would rock the image of him that I still held dear. Everything happens for a reason, I reminded myself. The path you have chosen has value.

What, I'm already reciting Japanese proverbs? I chuckled and allowed my thoughts to wander back to the previous night with McGrath.

It felt good to laugh again. To surrender to his embrace. I had begun to realize, in inches, I'd been so busy trying to keep myself together for the sake of my kids, that it was as if I'd been holding my breath for the past year. A long time to go without oxygen. With McGrath, I felt pieces of myself creeping back to life, if slowly, and it felt exhilarating. Albeit a little scary. Alright, a whole lot scary. Sometimes the inclination to pull back felt so strong, it carried the strength of a magnetic force. Yet, when I spent time with McGrath, I knew love once again tugged at my heartstrings…in a very nice way. I knew better than to ignore those feelings or to fight them off.

I thought about his skin and the way he let me brush the soft blond hair on his arms. And the fire from his lips whenever they rested atop mine. Sometimes, my lips stayed hot long after he kissed me. Like a radiant heat had taken residence there. All of this seductive thinking made my body temperature rise. Suddenly famished, I abandoned my coffee on the table, returned to the register, and ordered a sausage muffin with egg and an orange juice.

After I devoured my food, I sat back, closed my eyes for a moment, and took a measured breath. When I opened my eyes, McGrath stood in front of me.

"Oh, you startled me." I smiled at him and offered him my pursed lips.

He stared at me with fire in his eyes. "Don't ever do that again."

"What?" I said, knowing full well that I'd overstepped my bounds.

He cocked his head. I'd done the same with my kids when they scared the shit out of me.

"I'm sorry. Forgive me. Please?"

He rested a heavy hand on my shoulder. "I'm just glad you're alright. God, woman. Wake me next time. I'll come with you."

"Deal," I said.

He looked as if he didn't believe me, so I added, "Cross my heart."

He leaned over and kissed me. At first a quick peck, then he returned again and lingered with a forgiving kiss. "Couldn't sleep, huh?"

"Jet lag," I admitted. "How'd you know I was here?"

"I'm a detective, remember?" Then, he paused. "You told me that Jon came here after his morning runs."

I nodded. "Hungry?" I asked.

"Starved," he said. "Want something?" He looked at the crinkled wrappers on my tray and arched his brows.

"All that exercise last night." I grinned at him.

"You deserve more food." McGrath stood, squeezed my shoulder and looked down at me.

I shook my head. "I'm full," I said. "Satiated, as a matter of fact."

"How disappointing." McGrath tossed the words over his shoulder as he strode toward the cashier.

When he returned to the booth with his food, I asked, "So, what do you think, Detective? Police station?"

McGrath nodded. "I wonder if we shouldn't make a trip to the American Consulate first. Have them pave the way for us. When a foreigner dies in the U.S., procedures are different than for native citizens. We don't just hand over accident reports. It's essential we follow protocol."

I felt an immediate let down. Red tape. McGrath seemed to sense my disappointment. He rested his hand on mine. "I'm with you every step of the way, Darlin'. Trust me, doing this right from the get go will save us mountains of aggravation. I know you well enough to realize that bureaucratic procedure makes your skin crawl. I want my girl happy on this trip, and I'm going to do my absolute best to make sure that happens."

Tempted to argue, I bit my lip. What McGrath said made absolute sense. God must have sent him to me. I took a long moment and then smiled. "Thanks."

"Good girl," he said. McGrath ate a bite of his breakfast.

"We need to find it first," I said. "Have you looked it up? Do you know where it is?"

McGrath shook his head and closed his eyes, a familiar gesture overcoming him. He fought his frustration with me well. "I'm sure we can figure it out. We'll Google the Consulate when we get back to the room. It can't be more than a taxi drive away."

I felt reassured, but also anxious to hurry back to the room and set things in motion. McGrath narrowed his eyes. "You need to relax. It's four o'clock in the morning. We have plenty of time."

"Yes, but the sooner we get answers, the sooner we can have fun."

"Good point, but let's think of it this way. We'll get the answers in the way we were designed to receive them. One at a time. Then, we'll still have a puzzle to put together. It won't help to rush. Let's try to stay balanced."

"Geez," I joked. "You'd think I was a fruitcake."

"Teamwork. That's all it is. Teamwork."

"And what's my contribution? What do I bring to the team?"

"You bring instinct, motivation, ambition, and an undeniable ability to keep my blood flowing in the right direction each and every moment that I'm with you."

I smiled, quite satisfied with his answer.

CHAPTER TWENTY-ONE

THIRTY MINUTES LATER we were back in our hotel room, in bed, cuddling up and making sure, after our long plane ride, that our blood was circulating properly. Afterwards, we slept like exhausted puppies. I finally felt relaxed, knowing with McGrath by my side, we'd figure out this mystery.

At 8 a.m., we went for a morning run before we even fired up the laptop. McGrath was right. I needed to slow down, take my time, do this right.

"Sweetie," he called to me from the bathroom. I peeked in and admired his naked form as he towel-dried his buzz cut. His shoulders couldn't have been broader or more well-defined. His abs bragged more of an eight pack than a six. And he had shapely legs. As attractive on a man as a woman. I couldn't help but notice his other equipment as I took inventory. None of it disappointed.

"Sweetie?" he repeated.

"Oh, sorry." I smiled at him. "Got distracted."

McGrath grinned. "Glad to hear it," he said. "Just wanted to mention. As we go through this, you may be surprised at what pops to the surface. Not just in terms of information, but emotionally."

I swallowed. McGrath was wise to warn me. I'd tried to stave off the most difficult facts surrounding Jon's death for a year. Facing the music now might prove less than harmonious.

"I know you don't like being told what to do or how to feel."

I nodded.

"Just a suggestion, but you may want to try letting in as much emotion as you can allow at the time. My gut feeling is it'll help you move more quickly through the process."

I nodded. Unexpected tears rolled down my cheeks. "I have no living parents, a dead husband, and five very lively kids and you're giving me advice on moving through the process?" I had no idea where my ire had come from, and I felt ashamed and embarrassed.

McGrath fastened his towel at his waist, wrapped his arm around my shoulders, and led me back to the bed. He sat me down, then sank down beside me. "I'm just saying this. You don't have to put on a brave front for me. I've been through things. Things we haven't shared yet. But will... someday. I'm not trying to tell you what to feel or how to feel it, just letting you know I'm here. If you need to talk, to cry, to have a couple more glasses of wine than typically necessary, I'm your guy. Whatever you need. No judgment, no expectation."

I caught my breath. "Okay." I rested my head against his shoulder. "Got it."

My turn for a shower. Hot water pelted my skin. I felt better, ready to face the day thanks to McGrath's well-spoken words. Today could be tough. Really tough.

According to the website, the U.S. Consulate opened at 8:30 a.m. At 8:30 sharp, I phoned the Consulate office.

"Mushi, mushi," a female voice answered. Next, I heard a rush of Japanese.

"Hello," I said. I flashed back on the call to the Marriot—the last time I'd tried to reach Jon. I'd heard a woman's voice on the line and my stomach dove. Acid filled my throat. I'd swallowed, paralyzed, unable to speak. The scene repeated itself now.

I must have turned green because McGrath, now clad

in his routine khaki's and sports coat, stopped filling his pockets and came to rest a steadying hand on my shoulder.

"Mushi, mushi," she said again.

"Sorry," I apologized. "Do you speak English?" My panic shifted to calm intent.

"Certainly, ma'am," she said in English. "This is the U.S. Consulate. How may I help you?"

I cleared my throat before saying again, "My husband died. A year ago. In an automobile accident in the mountains outside Nagoya. I have a death certificate that was issued here, but I'd like to secure a copy of the accident report, as well."

"Of course. We can help you to arrange that."

Relief flooded me. McGrath had been right. I appreciated him even more.

"What do I need to do?" I asked with increasing anticipation.

"We will need to meet with you. Appointments are available on Wednesdays. We can see you next Wednesday, June 23, at eleven. Your name, please?"

Next Wednesday? My heart sank. "This is Samantha Stitsill. I don't have much time in Nagoya," I lied. "Isn't there a chance you could see me tomorrow? I have five children waiting for me at home. I can't afford to spend another week waiting." The panic in my voice may have helped or hurt me. I held my breath as I waited for the woman's reply.

"Hold on a moment, please," she said.

McGrath stood before me at a distance that left me feeling independent yet supported.

He nodded.

I tapped my foot. I breathed. In and out. In and out.

"Ma'am?" she said, coming back on the line.

"Yes?" I said, breathless.

"Mr. Drummond has an unexpected opening tomorrow morning at 10 a.m. Be on time, and bring any pertinent information with you."

"Specifically?" I asked.

"Your husband's death certificate and his passport. Your passport. Your marriage license."

I remembered one of Jon's favorite phrases. "A pint of blood, too?" he would ask sarcastically. Tempting as it was, I zipped my lips and replied with a simple 'thank you.'

With a second thought, I asked, "Mr. Drummond. Is he an agent?"

"Agent?" she asked. A short moment of silence ensued. "No, ma'am," she said. "Mr. Drummond is the Principal Officer here."

I severed the connection, told McGrath of our meeting tomorrow, and what documents I was supposed to bring, while I reached for my computer, and Googled the Consulate once again. I read Drummond's job description while McGrath sat in a chair, trying hard not to look worried as he sipped a glass of ice water and pretended to be busy on his cell phone.

Sometimes, my stupidity amazes me. Nathan Drummond was an American. Duh. Of course, he was. A veteran Foreign Service officer, he'd received honors for helping to break up a smuggling ring, had attended college at Kansas State, and had served as Director of the American Center in Nagoya prior to his assignment at the U. S. Consulate. I now felt at ease as I anticipated my meeting with him.

McGrath glanced at me when I snapped shut the laptop.

I reiterated what I'd learned. McGrath nodded his approval. "Well done, kiddo. Mind if I come along?"

"Of course, you're coming! I need you there!"

"Just checking."

"You said it yourself," I told him. "We're a team."

"Here's a thought. Let's play it by ear, but we can choose whether or not to tell them I'm a cop. As an American, Drummond might welcome a law enforcement officer from the U.S. into his circle. Then again, he may not. Depends on what kind of character he is and his past experience with U.S. cops."

I shared more with McGrath about what I'd learned about Drummond. The fact that he'd helped to break up a smuggling operation in Los Angeles seemed to indicate to me that he might be exactly the right person to help us. Someone with whom we could be honest. Someone who'd be on our side.

McGrath cautioned me to play it close to the vest at first. We didn't know this guy. He encouraged me to curb my gut instinct, even if I felt safe. Wait. Nothing would be harmed by waiting until we had a solid handle on the guy.

His way of warning me to be patient. Sheesh.

CHAPTER TWENTY-TWO

W E HAD THE entire day ahead of us. I'd dressed professionally in anticipation of a meeting at the Consulate, so after McGrath and I decided to do some sight-seeing in the absence of any fruitful detective work, I changed into more comfortable shoes and we stepped out the door. At the Concierge's desk, McGrath quickly arranged a temple tour. Forty-five minutes later, we were whisked away in the back seat of a Corolla driven by a tall, thirty-something, well-mannered Japanese man named Toshi, who appeared to speak better English than I did.

Our first stop was the Ohsu Kannon Temple shrine. As Toshi parked our car, we observed a priest and a small entourage standing in front of a couple and their vehicle. Toshi explained that newlyweds came to this temple to pray for fertility and that the priest would bless their car before sending them on their way. Toshi then asked us if we minded if he excused himself for a cigarette. We agreed, and then McGrath leaned over to whisper in my ear. "Blessing their car? Seems a tiny space to expect fertility to occur. I think they're driving a stick, too."

I elbowed him as we climbed the wide, steep staircase to the entrance doors. Once inside, I bit back my laughter. This was a temple. A shrine. People came here to pray. I needed to control myself, but the place was filled with giant phalluses. They stood like soldiers in a solid line. Rows and rows of them. I tried not to look at McGrath. My real impulse was to run. I needed fertility like I needed a hole in my chest.

I located the nearest exit and stepped out into the excruciating heat of the noonday sun. A few steps further yielded a spot of shade. McGrath followed and grabbed my arm, laughing. Guffawing, really.

Not two seconds later, a dozen or so Japanese men dressed in white robes and tall, black, brimless, stovepipe hats struggled as they made their way through the center of the main path, balancing thirty-foot two-by-fours on their shoulders. On top, and inside its own black temple, a giant crimson sculpture of a superbly erect phallus, perhaps twenty feet in length, lay secured to its base and enshrouded inside. From the way the men slaved, the humongous dick must have weighed a ton. Every man's dream.

McGrath's eyes widened. I knew we needed to get out of there quickly. Within moments we were bound to make total jack-asses of ourselves, alienating our tour guide when he showed up, and winding up without a ride back to the hotel.

"Looks like the Japanese take procreation seriously," McGrath said as he snickered.

"I think this is the place where every man comes to pray for long and lasting erections. Will you look at the size of that thing? Makes me want to cross my legs for…FOREVER."

McGrath grinned. "Let's get you out of here before you decide you never want to see another penis again."

"No," I said. "This is just what the doctor ordered. I'm sure this investigation will get tough at times. We may need to return later for more comic relief. Let's try not to get thrown out. Now, put your head down and say a prayer. A fervent one. That your equipment continues to stay in working order for many years to come." I clamped my hand over my mouth to contain a case of the giggles that refused to stop.

We quickly made our way to a park-like courtyard.

McGrath guided me to a bench. He nodded at Toshi, who followed at a respectable distance.

"I think that's the funniest thing I've ever seen," I said. "Once, when Nick attended kindergarten, he took a postcard of a water tower, shaped just like that..." I pointed to the phallus ala carte, "for show and tell. His teacher called me, horrified, but here, people come to pray and worship family jewels."

"Personally," McGrath said, "I think the Japanese have the right idea. The male appendage should be honored and revered." He leaned over to kiss my cheek.

"You're losing credibility," I joked.

Toshi approached us, asking if we were ready to move on. I passed him my camera so he could snap a few photos of McGrath and me in front of the temple. This needed to be recorded for posterity. After clicking the photos, Toshi informed us that it was a short distance to the next temple and he wanted to be sure to treat us to lunch in between stops. He dropped us off in front of what I assumed to be a small storefront in the middle of nowhere. After saying a few short things to the owner, she hurried us inside and sat us at a tiny corner table in what appeared to be the living room of a family home. Certainly not where we expected to lunch, but the cooking smells beckoned. Ginger, soy, and garlic.

While we waited to be served, we noticed Toshi in the kitchen, kissing the top of the head of an elderly woman. Evidently, Toshi had brought us home for lunch.

For some reason, it didn't feel strange. I relaxed, and savored the Asahi that Toshi's relative served. Shortly into the meal, I ventured into untraveled waters. "So," I said, "tell me more about yourself."

McGrath shrugged. "Nothing to tell."

"Liar."

"How about at dinner?" he suggested.

"Chicken." I narrowed my eyes. I didn't want to pry, but

I did want to know this man. Every inch of him.

Toshi walked in, rescuing McGrath from further torturous questions, to inform us that our next tour would begin in thirty minutes. He showed us down a narrow hallway to the restroom where we each took a turn, and then loaded us back into the Corolla for a harrowing drive down winding roads and through impossible traffic. A New York cab trip was a balloon ride compared to this. I held tightly to McGrath, gritting my teeth.

The next several stops were mild in contrast to our first stop of the day. The temples were serene—beautiful architecture, gold-walled exteriors atop long steep climbs through deeply wooded paths, one in particular in the midst of a quiet pond, reverentially poised. A deep peace filled my soul.

When we arrived back at the hotel, McGrath spent several minutes speaking privately with Toshi. I busied myself checking for emails on my phone. One message from Di, inquiring as to my trip, which I answered in the quiet seclusion of the air-conditioned back seat. Another from Jack, questioning my abrupt departure without explanation. I put that message to rest with a quick reply as well, assuring him that all was well.

Safe and sound in Japan with a police officer. No worries necessary.

I made a swift call home at the same time, speaking with each of my five kids and Ed, catching up on the latest news on the home front. All bases covered. McGrath tapped on the window. I crawled out of the car.

McGrath was spent, in need of a power nap. While he rested, I power-shopped and bought myself a soft flowy dress to wear to a nightclub that evening. I rode the elevator to our floor, dressed in my new frock, and slipped into a pair of spiky heels. McGrath changed into a fresh pair of trousers and a pressed white shirt.

Toshi had offered advice on a restaurant near the hotel,

and a night club to visit afterwards. After an evening spent dining and dancing, one in which McGrath escaped filling me in on his deep, dark secrets, we fell into bed at 1 a.m. We had a big day ahead, and we needed our rest.

CHAPTER TWENTY-THREE

MY EYES POPPED open before dawn on Wednesday as well. Anticipation of the day ahead and jet lag held equal responsibility for my wakefulness. To keep from waking McGrath, I padded into the bathroom and plugged in the coffee maker. I didn't have the energy for another trip to the Golden Arches, so I sat on the toilet and sipped my coffee, then snuck back into the room, collected my laptop and backpack and returned to my new office. I set the computer on the bathroom countertop and opened my files.

I pulled up the clipping about Coswell's accident, which I'd scanned. I kicked myself once again for having turned over Stitsill's many passports to McGrath, who'd turned them over to the F.B.I. the day after I'd killed him. Or may have killed him. I sighed as I picked up my note pad, rereading the facts, and occasionally jotting down an additional thought. For the life of me, I couldn't remember a single name on any of those false documents. I considered searching the *Asahi Shimbun* for an article about my Jon's accident, but the thought of finding one headed me toward a full–out meltdown. I stood, steadied myself against the counter and inhaled a slow, measured breath.

I fought the temptation to take the laptop with me, and I wrestled with my hope to confide in Mr. Drummond. I had no real reason to think he'd be an ally, just a ton of desire. I wanted help in this foreign country, wanted desperately to find someone who could wrap up my jumbled life with a neat and tidy bow, hand me quick and satisfying answers, and send me on my merry way. Unlikely.

McGrath knocked lightly on the bathroom door. I gathered my papers and stuffed them back inside the manila envelope.

"Sam, you okay?"

I flushed the toilet and stashed my computer inside my backpack while I ran the water in the sink. Next, I slipped my backpack beneath the counter and stepped back into the room.

"I'm fine." Somehow, I thought McGrath might find me overanxious, or notice the fact that I was snowballing downhill. I also worried he might suspect me of being the impatient, impetuous woman that I am.

McGrath climbed back into bed and patted the mattress. I crawled in, nuzzled my head into his shoulder, and fell fast asleep, waking next some four hours later to the sound of the screeching alarm clock.

My stomach bubbled with nerves, but I tried to remain calm. McGrath plugged his iPhone into the bedside table accessory and American music, welcome and familiar, played. The man had a way of meeting my every need. I could only hope that when he fell from his white horse, and I knew and sort of hoped he would, that the fall would be gentle and forgivable.

I headed to the shower while McGrath ran downstairs to fetch us some real coffee. I spent the next hour blow-drying my hair, brushing on make-up and dressing. McGrath decided we needed a nutritious breakfast, so we made our way to the hotel restaurant and enjoyed an all-American breakfast: eggs, toast, bacon, hash browns and orange juice.

I glanced at my watch. Almost time to catch a taxi, so I returned to our room, gathered all my documents, and rejoined McGrath in the lobby.

"Ready?" he asked, a gentle expression on his face.

"I'm fine, really," I lied.

The Consular office was fifteen minutes away.

* * *

Feeling as if I'd been turned inside out, I attempted to distract myself by taking in my surroundings, wondering if every U.S. Consular office in every foreign country looked the same. While respectful of the Japanese heritage, this place boasted American strength. Flags flying high in the bright Nagoya heat greeted us.

We walked inside. An eagle graced the circular emblem which adorned the wall above the reception desk. I kept my gaze focused on the eagle's eye, feeling as if he were spying on all of us. The receptionist smiled, and I told her of our appointment. She asked for our passports, made copies, and directed us to a collection of chairs and couches at the far end of the lobby.

My mouth felt stuffed with cotton, and I clenched McGrath's hand so hard, he gave me a pained look, then loosened my grip. "It will look more professional if we don't appear to be a couple," he said.

"Of course," I answered. "I don't know what's wrong with me."

"Nerves. Breathe while I'll get you a glass of water."

McGrath returned moments later with a cone of water. I drank it in one gulp before the woman behind the desk led us down a long hallway to an expansive office at the rear of the building. We settled into two easy chairs positioned in front of a massive oak desk. McGrath murmured, "You know what you're here for, so stay focused."

I nodded, drinking in his encouraging words like a much needed blood transfusion. I steadied my breathing. As footsteps sounded behind me, I turned. The man stood with his back to me as a Japanese woman extended a manila file to him. Staring at the back of his salt and pepper head,

I noticed he was tall, 6'4" perhaps, lean, and possessed the bearing of a statuesque man. His movements were concise. Nothing wasted. His hand barely moved as he accepted the file. He turned then, and it was as if his turning radius had been structurally developed to assure minimal movement.

I finally saw his face. I reflexively reached out to McGrath, remembered his advice, and froze, stifling a gasp.

"Mrs. Stitsill, I presume." He strode forward silently, forcing a faux smile my way.

I peered up at him, searching for a look of recognition from him. There was none.

As he extended his hand, I inhaled a measured breath, stood, and stared into the eyes of my husband's impostor. Jon Stitsill II.

CHAPTER TWENTY-FOUR

IT TOOK MUCH longer than a millisecond for my brain to restart my heart, but it finally did. The man who had stolen my husband's identity, most likely killed my dog AND my husband, the man I had supposedly shot to death breaking and entering my home, the Jon Stitsill impostor, stood before me as Consul General Drummond.

I fought off all those natural urges — gasping, vomiting, screaming, fleeing — and summoned a calm exterior from the deepest recesses of my being. McGrath seemed to sense my need for a moment and stepped forward, shook the demon's hand, and offered polite conversation.

This guy had ruined my life. That pissed me off. Royally. I wasn't about to let this lying, cheating assassin get the better of me. Then, for some unknown reason, I experienced this flash of bureaucracy at its finest, and a list of scoundrels in public office appeared in front of my eyes like the rolling credits at the closing of a film.

I took a cleansing breath and did what any woman with an agenda would do; I smiled brightly, and shook the son of a bitch's hand. I figured Drummond, or whoever the hell he really was, already knew McGrath was a cop. Let Mr. Fucking Drummond figure a few things out on his own, like what I knew about him. I'd done my own spying. I had my own information. The fact that I couldn't remember one damn thing in that instant seemed inconsequential; it would come back to me.

Mr. Drummond turned on the charm, asking us if we'd like coffee. I hoped that meant he'd leave the room for a moment so I could ask McGrath if he recognized the guy. In reality, McGrath had only ever seen two photos of Jon's impostor, the one that had been delivered to me at school two years ago, and the one of his head after I'd supposedly shot him dead. McGrath had never interacted with the man. It was entirely possible he had no clue who this guy really was. I, on the other hand, possessed several advantages.

One, I'd seen this guy arrive at his wife's home and sneak inside. I'd witnessed his determined stride as he eased down her street after dark. I could still summon the fear his mannerisms had created in me that night. His movements remained precise.

Two, those heart-to-heart talks I'd had with Rosie gave me first-hand knowledge of what a manipulative sociopath this guy had been. He'd wooed her, bribed her away from her shallow existence in Mexico to a richer life in the States. I still didn't understand why he'd done that. The only thing I'd come up with so far? He'd needed a cover. The fact that he'd actually fathered a child with Rosie — well, that reality still buffaloed me. This guy was evil. The devil incarnate.

"Coffee?" I heard the words again, as if being shaken awake from a deep dream.

"Yes, please." I summoned every ounce of inner strength, locked eyes with my husband's impostor, and smiled widely. "Black."

Drummond picked up his phone and made a quick call. He wouldn't be going anywhere. I couldn't risk alerting McGrath to the fraud's true identity, so I made pleasant conversation with my husband's killer while we waited for our drinks.

"How long have you been at the Consulate?" I asked. I knew what it said on the website but I couldn't wait to hear the line he'd invented.

He stood, walked to a nearby credenza, and picked up a file folder. "I've been here since last May, a little over a year." He returned to the desk with the dossier, smiled again, and sank into his chair.

"How do you like Japan?" I fought the urge to scratch out his eyes and through some kind of miracle, kept my screaming heart silent.

"I've been here for quite some time," he said. "I served as director of the Nagoya American Center for three years before my appointment here."

I turned my thoughts to practical details. That would have given him plenty of excuse for travel to the U.S. Plenty of opportunity to acquire false passports, kill people, and impregnate women. Sufficient time to establish a long trail of duplicity. I suspected his over-inflated ego allowed him to do whatever he wanted, whenever he wanted.

My mind and body disengaged, and I watched as an offhand observer as the Japanese woman reentered the room, this time carrying a shellacked tray which held a pot of coffee, cream, sugar, and three china tea cups painted in traditional Japanese colors with ornate flowers. The young woman poured us each a cup and I sat back, steadying myself against the back of my seat, trying desperately not to faint. I could never have held a cup and saucer without it clattering into my lap. I willed my knees to calm and focused on deciding how to broach the topic of acquiring the report of my husband's accident. God interceded, and I regained my bearings.

I didn't want to alienate this guy. I didn't want him to feel that I was on to him. I needed time to think. In the meantime, I'd act dumb and focus only on what I'd come for — a guiding hand to the Nagoya police's cooperation in handing over the documentation.

Only problem I could anticipate in that moment was Drummond wondering why I wanted the report. A year had passed. I wasn't sure it would make sense to him that

I'd waited so long to obtain the paperwork and worried it would make him question why I'd decided to travel all the way to Japan to get it. Good question.

Pleasantries over, earth under my feet again, my brain whirled like a spinning top. After a long moment, I let my instincts take over and dove in, headfirst.

"Thank you for seeing my friend and me today. As I explained to whomever I spoke with on the phone yesterday…" Crap. It hit me right then. The woman who'd taken my call the previous day had said there were no available appointments until the following Wednesday. After I begged, pleaded, and told her my name, she'd put me on hold, then returned to tell me I had an appointment the following day with the Principal Officer, Consul General Mr. Drummond. My late husband's impostor. He knew, didn't he? He'd been waiting for me. I'd been set up.

"…I'm seeking a copy of an accident report involving my husband. Jon died in an automobile crash in the mountains. One year ago."

"I'm happy to pave the way for you."

A knot clogged my throat. This was a lot to handle. Even for a tough cookie like me. I caught McGrath's gaze. He looked like a cheerleader, rooting me on with his kind eyes. He smiled at me encouragingly, too. I swallowed, convincing myself I could handle the next thirty minutes. Then, we'd be outside and safe. I couldn't wait to spill my guts to McGrath. Was he clueless? Or was he just that good a cop?

Stitsill checked through the file with my paperwork. He narrowed his eyes, checking the documents thoroughly. This guy didn't carry out stupid red tape inconsequential tasks like this. This should have been handled by an underling. I started to feel pissed off again. Framed and scared.

He pressed the intercom button on his desk. Less than ten seconds later, the high-heeled Japanese woman reentered. They spoke Japanese, then he handed the papers to her and she left the office.

"We'll get everything straightened away for you. You'll have no problem obtaining the accident report, but you were right to come here first. The protocol is a bit different in Japan and the Consular office is here to assist you in matters of this nature, so that you don't have to negotiate the bureaucracy. It should only take a moment for my assistant to phone the police precinct for you. If you'd like, I'd be happy to have her call a cab, and ask the driver to take you there once we're finished."

McGrath spoke up, the first time since we'd gotten the small talk out of the way. "Thanks, but we have a driver."

I frowned at him, a sure mistake.

He covered for me. "Mr. Yamoto," he said as he looked my way. "I phoned him while we were waiting in the lobby. He's available to take us wherever we need to go today."

I smiled. Brilliant. Getting into a car arranged by Stitsill couldn't possibly be a good idea. We needed to get the hell out of there in a hurry. And I wasn't all that sure I wanted to visit the police precinct just yet. McGrath and I required time alone.

CHAPTER TWENTY-FIVE

THE HEAT WAS stifling. I couldn't catch my breath. But being outside the Consulate met my immediate need to be away from Stitsill.

"You okay?" McGrath touched my arm, his hand cool, and I instantly exhaled. "I know we need to talk," he continued, "but right now, I think I should call Toshi and have him pick us up. Stitsill might be watching, and we want him to think we're here on a simple errand. I'd love to check the car for bugs, but now isn't the time. Just watch what you say when we're in the car."

"Alright," I agreed, gripping his arm for strength.

McGrath pulled out his cell and made the call. Toshi explained to him that he'd arrive shortly and take us wherever we needed to go. We stood together, waiting for what felt like an absolute eternity. In reality, only twenty minutes passed before his Corolla pulled up and whisked us away.

McGrath handed over a wad of bills. Toshi smiled. Now at our service, he delivered us back to the hotel in fifteen minutes. Fifteen minutes of excruciating small talk. McGrath excused Toshi, asked him to give us an hour or two, then ushered me inside.

"Let's find a quiet place," he said. He placed a reassuring arm around my waist and guided me into the restaurant. The hostess led us to a corner table that overlooked the city, and McGrath ordered two black coffees and a fruit plate.

"Talk to me," he said.

"You know who he is, right?" I dabbed my brow with a napkin, and practiced deep breathing exercises.

McGrath nodded. "Yes. By the way, you were great. You couldn't have done a better job if you were Clarice Starling chatting up Hannibal Lecter."

I managed a slight smile. "Thanks for that."

"Look at the bright side," McGrath said. "At least we know he's alive, and where he's stationed." He popped a pale green grape into his mouth.

In a shocking moment of clarity, I returned from the deep abyss and was immaculately able to focus on the present. "Who does he work for? Do you remember what we thought when we opened the strong box and found the receipts and the fake passports? We thought he was an assassin for the U.S. government."

"I don't know that we have any reason to think otherwise, given the fact that he's still alive and still working for them."

"I've lost faith. Faith in the world. Faith in my country." My head dropped to my chest, and I sighed, weighted down by the enormity of my new reality.

"It's a serious blow. But, face it, kiddo, the world's always been like this. It goes back to the Bible."

"The Bible?" I knit my brow.

"Pillaging, corruption, all of the worst of humankind. It's been around forever."

"But it's reaching out to grab me right now." I struggled to blink back tears.

"And that sucks." McGrath sipped his coffee. "Most of the population is allowed the luxury of never having to be involved in this kind of deceit. For whatever reason, you're in the mix now. We have to decide what we're going to do about it."

I nodded and took a deep breath. "You're right. We know he's alive. We know he's involved. Jon was somehow tied to him. The question is, why? And how?" A sudden wave of nausea revisited. Was this really happening?

"My suggestion…let's get some rest."

"We have to keep up the charade. We need to visit the police department and retrieve the accident report. Stitsill will be waiting to hear we've been there. If we don't show up at the precinct, he'll figure out we've got another agenda." I fought to display a calm exterior. And failed miserably at squelching the heebie geebies.

"We don't have to have another agenda. Let's simply claim the report, then do whatever we please for the rest of the afternoon. Tomorrow's another day. One step at a time."

"What if we aren't safe? What if my kids aren't safe? And how do we find the answers we need with Stitsill hot on our trail?" I stopped and locked eyes with McGrath. I read a familiar look in his gaze. The look that said SLOW DOWN. Take a breath. He was right. Clear-headed thinking would serve me better than leaping off another cliff. One cliff per day.

"Sam?" He waited while I collected my thoughts.

"You're right, as usual. Call Toshi and ask him to drive us over to the precinct, alright?"

McGrath nodded, patted my hand, signaled our server, and pulled some cash from his billfold. He called Toshi, made the arrangements, and then stood. "C'mon, let's go."

Thankfully, McGrath took the lead with Toshi, and at the precinct. I felt too shell-shocked to do anything other than place one foot in front of the other, but I did manage to take a few mental notes. A bright gold star appeared above the entrance door of the police station. That, as well as Japanese script and a red light, which I guessed might flash in the case of a city emergency. On one of the shuttered double-paned glass doors, the word POLICE appeared in English. A uniformed officer, clad in typical blues, sat behind the counter. Behind him, posters of cartoon characters were plastered to the walls. A wall clock, nailed high and to the right, read 12:00 p.m.

In my heightened state, I worried everyone would be at lunch, even though an officer sat at the reception desk right there under my nose.

"Konichi wa," he said.

"Hello," McGrath said. "Do you speak English?" He retrieved the backpack from my grasp, searched the file folder tucked into the inside pocket, and withdrew the necessary documents. "I believe that Mr. Drummond from the U.S. Consulate phoned you on our behalf." He gestured at me. "This is Mrs. Jon Stitsill, and we would like a copy of her late husband's accident report."

"Yes," the officer replied in perfect English. "I have it right here."

He quickly perused our paperwork before he handed the report to McGrath. I might as well have been invisible. McGrath thanked him, grasped my elbow, and guided me outside.

"Let's head back to the hotel. We're going to get you a stiff drink, put you to bed, and deal with the details later."

As always, Toshi drove expertly through the dense lunch-hour traffic. I'm embarrassed to say I don't remember much of the trip back to the hotel. I don't think I took in a breath of air, blinked, or swallowed once.

The next thing I knew, I found myself dressed in my pajamas and gripping a tumbler of amber liquid that tinkled in my shaking hands. McGrath helped me to bring the glass to my lips and instructed me to swallow. I did as told, once, twice, and then again. McGrath eased my head back onto the pillow, kissed my forehead, and tucked the covers under my chin. Then, he sat at my side and waited for me to fall asleep.

* * *

When I awakened two hours later, I felt like I'd been hit over the head with a club and dragged by my hair into a cave. It was pitch black. I wasn't at all sure where I was, or if I were dead or alive. I must have shifted though, because McGrath quickly sat up. He rested his hand on my shoulder.

"You awake?" he said.

"I think so." I rubbed my eyes and inhaled a measured breath. Then I sat up, rose to my feet and shuffled into the bathroom. Turning on the cold water, I splashed some on my face, then squinted at the mirror, horrified by my reflection. Deep circles haloed my once bright blue eyes. My strawberry blonde hair, which had once cascaded in soft ringlets around my neck, was now matted to my sweaty skull. I looked like crap.

I felt an overwhelming urge to pack my bags. I longed to set eyes on my kids. Hold them. Couldn't I just go home? I brushed my teeth, turned on the shower, stepped out of my pajamas and into the streaming jets of hot water. I stood there for a long while, then soaped my head and body and waited again beneath the hammering pellets of the spray, praying that I'd feel alive again before too long.

Once I climbed out of the tub, I toweled dry and wrapped a second towel around my head. By then, McGrath stood at the sink, naked and brushing his teeth. He kept his distance, stepping out of my way as I walked out of the bathroom and sat on the edge of the bed. For a moment, he kept watch, making sure I could still function, I guess. Once he saw me plug in the blow dryer, he must have assumed I was alright, because he disappeared into the shower.

I turned off the hair dryer and picked up my phone. I started to dial Ed's cell phone, and then remembered it was 4 a.m. back in the Midwest. Later. By the time McGrath returned to the bedroom, I'd finished putting myself together. He eased himself up against my still naked back. Drawing him into me, I tumbled across the bed. A desperate longing overcame me. Now, more than ever before, I needed McGrath.

CHAPTER TWENTY-SIX

I GUESSED WE had slept a good fourteen hours. We didn't talk much as we pulled on our running duds, laced up our shoes, and jogged east out of the Marriot the following morning, heading directly into the rising sun. I squinted against the bright light and eased into a steady clip beside McGrath. I shouldn't have been surprised that we had so much in common. Seemed that teachers and cops were way more alike than different. And the fact that we had the serious hots for each other didn't hurt. As we ran through the increasing pedestrian traffic, McGrath slowed and motioned for me to move ahead of him. While I understood and appreciated his gallantry, I would have liked to study his fine ass in running shorts. Instead, he studied mine.

We ran a good four miles before I slowed in front of the Golden Arches. Strange as it sounds, I felt a steady comfort in eating there, in repeating the same routine that my late husband had recited to me time and time again. I felt like he was with me, and I needed him today, the day that I would discover the details of his accident. Deep in my heart I recognized that the news might not be so good. The once faithful image of my husband might be forever tarnished today. I didn't want to feel angry and bitter. In any case, knowing the truth would help me gain closure.

McGrath, ever the gentleman, stood in line and ordered our breakfast sandwiches, waters, juices, and coffees while

I used the facilities. I snagged a corner booth. We needed a little privacy to discuss how and when I wanted to view the accident report. I wanted Toshi to drive us to the accident site. Visiting the exact spot where my husband had driven off the road would finally make it real. I prayed for the strength to face that scene.

McGrath set down the tray on the table and passed out the food. I felt suddenly famished and wolfed down my sausage muffin. Silence hummed for at least three minutes while he did the same.

"So? What's the plan?" I finally asked.

"Here's my thinking," he began. "There's a fair chance Stitsill either has or is going to have our hotel room bugged. Once he figures we're staying here, I'm guessing he'll want to know why. We can't talk about anything related to the case when we're there, alright?"

"Agreed," I said.

McGrath held up his index finger and left the table. Puzzled, I watched him saunter up to the counter, stand in line and return less than a minute later with additional sandwiches. He set one in front of me, unwrapped another, and began to eat. After swallowing his first bite, he quipped, "Sorry. Starving."

I nodded and smiled.

He continued right where he'd left off. "I'll sweep the room when we get back, but there's no guarantee I'll find anything. Clearly, this guy's an expert."

"Don't sell yourself short," I said.

"Either way, we must be extremely discreet. We don't want to raise any more suspicion than necessary. What do you think about Stitsill?"

"I'm not sure how much he knows about what I know about him. Does that make sense?"

McGrath nodded and kept right on chewing.

"I don't believe he saw me when I spotted him at Rosie's. I believe he killed Rex and Jon. Somehow, he's onto me. Or after me because of Jon. Then, there was Rosie's death. My house got tossed about a week later and right before the guy showed up in my basement. The guy I shot. The guy we thought was Stitsill. He's got help on the inside. The FBI, maybe even the CIA, or that other group you mentioned as a possibility."

McGrath wadded the sandwich wrapper into a ball as he frowned. "This guy is a major player."

I sighed and nodded. "I know I should walk away. But I need to know what happened to Jon."

"I hear you, but here's the thing. Jon could have been mixed up in something far bigger than we ever imagined. Poking around, especially with an animal like Stitsill glancing over our shoulder, is beyond dangerous. I'm struggling with all of this right now. Not because I'm not up to the challenge, but because I don't want you in harm's way."

"But I want to get this guy. He deserves to be caught and put away, or better yet, he needs someone to snuff out his little candle."

"His candle is hardly flickering," McGrath reminded me. "You have no idea how these guys operate. This snake is above the law. He's received several awards for his crime-stopping activity. Meanwhile, he's the biggest crook of all. Beautiful set up."

"What do you suggest, Detective McGrath?"

"Extreme caution. A heightened state of alertness at all times. And that's just the beginning. We'll need weapons. I'm not sure how to obtain guns in Japan, but we should both be armed."

"I remember how to shoot."

McGrath laughed so hard, his eyes crinkled at the edges and sparkled at me through tears.

"What's so funny?"

"Just remembering being at the range with you the day I taught you how to fire a gun."

"I was so nervous." At the memory, my cheeks flushed. "And confused. I was so attracted to you."

"The feeling was mutual." McGrath squeezed my hand, leaned over the table, and planted his lips atop mine.

Delicious. I moaned a little, then I tore myself away from him, and sat back. "We're getting off track. Not that I don't welcome the distraction," I said, "but we need a plan."

"Here's a suggestion. Let's go back to the room, shower, and dress. I'll have Toshi pick us up."

I scrunched up my face. "Just how much did you pay this guy to be our personal driver?"

McGrath grinned. "Enough."

"Thank you," I said.

McGrath nodded. "Now you're distracting us."

I apologized, and he continued.

"While we're waiting for him to arrive, we'll sit in the lobby. It's open and public. We can read the accident report there. When Toshi shows up, I'll send him across the street to grab us a couple of Cokes. Stitsill's smart and motivated. He may have figured out I've hired the guy to be our driver, and we can't be too careful. I'll check the car for bugs."

My stomach lurched. "The accident site is in the mountains. It's remote. What if Stitsill has someone waiting for us there?"

"We can call off the trip right now. Head back to the States. It's your call." McGrath squeezed my hand, and I locked eyes with him.

"No. I have to see this through."

We tossed our garbage, and headed the short distance to the hotel. Once inside the room we stayed quiet at first, both being careful not to say anything that would incriminate ourselves, but then fell into a comfortable rhythm of conversation. Light-hearted and natural, we spoke of the weather, sight-seeing, restaurants and the like. While we chatted, McGrath scoped out the room for listening devices and cameras. He didn't find anything, but like he said, that didn't necessarily mean there wasn't anything there.

In the midst of all of our preparations, I remembered that it was Jon's stolen passport some ten years ago that had started this entire chain of events. So, I packed my laptop, our passports, and everything personal in my backpack. If we lost our identification, we could end up in serious dung, and at the complete mercy of Stitsill.

With that frightening thought, I made a quick call home, needing confirmation that Ed and the kids were okay before we took off for my day of mourning. At least all was well at home.

In the lobby, seated at a beautifully crafted mahogany coffee table, I finally withdrew the accident report. It was several pages long. My eyes widened as I flipped the sheets, one after the other. The entire thing was in Japanese. How had I not thought of this?

I frowned at McGrath. "We're fucking idiots," I said. And then I handed him the file.

CHAPTER TWENTY-SEVEN

MCGRATH PATTED MY hand and murmured reassurances. "It's not a problem. We have Toshi, remember?"

"But he'll want more money. We hired him as a driver, not as a translator. And if we let him read this, are we putting him in danger? I can't be responsible for another life, damn it."

"Sam." McGrath flashed me a look that said get a grip. So, I did.

"Okay." I nodded for emphasis.

"Let me handle this."

I drew in a deep breath. McGrath was right. I needed to calm down. Didn't I have enough on my plate just visiting the accident site and finding out what had happened? I thanked God McGrath was here to keep me on track.

"Toshi just texted me." McGrath said, and we were out the lobby door.

Toshi agreed to translate the accident report as well as drive us to the site. I hoped the name and address of the passenger who'd accompanied Jon at the time of the crash was listed. McGrath had assured me that if Japanese procedures were anything like the States, the report should bear not just her name, but a valid address and driver's license number. We should be able to locate her, unless she vanished like the woman who'd supposedly been involved with Coswell.

I couldn't put Jon to rest unless I knew every last ugly detail.

Toshi drove to his home. We sat at the kitchen table, spread out all of the reports and drank tea while he went through the business of sorting out details. He pulled out a laptop and located our destination. McGrath explained our interest in Jon's traveling companion, and Toshi plugged her name, Nanami Sato, and address into his computer. He nodded to McGrath when he finished.

We loaded back into the car, me on the verge of hysteria, while McGrath remained my stalwart companion. His fingers rested atop my hand, stroking gently. I tried to even out my breathing in order to relax. Giant fail.

The trip to the mountains took us along narrow roads and winding curves. As Toshi drove, he explained the road we traveled was one of the most picturesque along Kiso Valley. Densely forested with the famous hinoki, the Japanese cypresses which had furnished the wood for many of the castles and shrines, the beauty of my surroundings overcame me, the lush greens and soft browns briefly soothing my spirit. Sun streamed through the clouds overhead, and I felt somewhat swept away by the moment. Maybe everything would be okay. I leaned my head against McGrath's shoulder and prayed.

Then, the startling realization that Jon had probably traveled this same road struck me like a cleaver between the eyes. What had he been thinking on this drive? Was he overwhelmed by the majesty of the mountains, too? We had always enjoyed exploring new worlds together. Had he even thought of me during his trip? Wished I'd been there to share it with him? Or had he been too wrapped up in what's–her–name? A knot formed in my stomach. I swallowed, hoping to keep down my breakfast.

I closed my eyes and wrung my hands. I just wanted to reach the site of Jon's accident. To have it done and over with. Ten minutes later, Toshi pulled into an overlook and instructed us to exit the vehicle for a short walk down the road. Thankfully, the road, both narrow and steep, was lightly traveled. Not a safe place for a pedestrian, which reminded me I had five kids at home who'd already lost one parent.

Toshi stopped and bowed. He then nodded at McGrath, and I understood his gesture. This was the site of Jon's crash. I began to hyperventilate. My stomach knotted. I wanted my husband back. Or I wanted to throw myself over the cliff and join him in the great beyond. I couldn't bear to live without him for one more minute.

Come back to me, Jon. I choked back a sob. Please, come back.

I'd fooled myself for over a year now into thinking he'd simply made a wrong turn and crashed. In reality, he'd been several hundred feet up in the air. When Jon's car had veered right, it had leapt off the side of a cliff. Vomit rose in my throat as I peered over the edge of the embankment.

It had to have taken several seconds before Jon and his passenger hit the valley floor. Wait. No one could have survived this crash. I knew in that moment I'd been duped again. No one had been in the car with Jon. Damn it. I refused to hand over this moment to Stitsill.

This moment belonged to me.

I stepped to the guardrail and peered over. What had Jon thought in his final moments? Had he thought of me? Had he uttered my name? Called for the children? Told us he loved us? Had he seen his life flash before him? Did he have regrets?

Come back, Jon. I'm right here waiting for you.

I couldn't turn off my brain, or my shaking limbs, or the stabbing in my heart.

"I'm so sorry, Jon," I said.

The world began to spin out of control. McGrath came up behind me and wrapped his arms around my waist.

"Deep breaths, Sweetie," he instructed. "Deep breaths."

I tried to follow orders, but I couldn't. Toshi rushed to my side as well. He and McGrath found a place for me to sit. I tucked my head between my knees. My ears rang. My heart raced. In that moment, I thought I might die. And in that moment, I would have welcomed death.

* * *

McGrath waited patiently, his steadying hand atop my shoulder. It took me a good long while, but somehow my respiration evened out and the world came back into focus. A full minute later, I began to hear normal sounds again rather than the white noise of sheer panic. First, the wind rustling through leaves, then McGrath and Toshi's soft murmurings. I inhaled a floral scent. Clean mountain air? Probably. In any case, strength finally returned to my legs again, and with McGrath's aid, I was able to stand.

"Do you wish to return to the hotel?" Toshi asked, his gentle voice weighted with concern.

"Thank you, no," I said. "I'm feeling much better."

He nodded. Jon had often reminded me that the Japanese showed little outward emotion. I suspected my display left Toshi feeling uncomfortable and unsettled. McGrath stood sentry beside me as I gazed out over the expanse below the deadly drop-off. We stood in silence for a long moment. Then, McGrath looked over Toshi's notes and explained the events of Jon's fatal crash to me.

The investigators surmised Jon had become distracted, either by the GPS, his fictitious passenger, or from taking in the sights. The crash had occurred at dusk, a difficult time for clear visibility. Add to that a thick fog which had settled over the mountains early that evening. Any one of those things could have caused Jon to become distracted and miss the sharp turn in the road where he veered off the cliff and into oblivion. Or, someone could have forced him off the road. The message from the back of the newspaper clipping flashed through my mind. "You're next."

My eyes filled with tears. Overcome with a profound sadness, I silently prayed. May God bless your soul, Jon, and may I preserve the best parts of your life and your legacy. For our family's sake. Amen.

McGrath pulled me close to him. I broke down, sobbed into his chest, then blew my nose into the handkerchief he offered me and sighed. I felt like a fish washed ashore. Goosebumps rose on my flesh, despite the smothering heat.

I turned away from the precipice. "Let's go," I whispered.

"There's no rush," McGrath assured me.

"I'm done here."

CHAPTER TWENTY-EIGHT

WE WALKED SLOWLY back to the car, McGrath's firm grasp of my arm supporting me. Exhaustion refused to ease, and as if I'd been sucker-punched and stared down my husband's assailant, I realized that standing at the sight of my husband's death site may not constitute the most difficult moments of my day.

"I'm worried about you," McGrath said. "We've done enough for today. Let's head back to the hotel."

"And do what?" I straightened my shoulders. "Dwell on the fact that I've been lied to and betrayed? I thought you knew me well enough to know that I face my demons head on."

"I do know that about you. But you're scaring me. All the color's drained from your face. If you have a stroke, it won't prove a goddamn thing."

"Toshi," I said. "May I borrow a cigarette, please?"

Toshi looked over the front seat nervously. It was clear that he had no idea how to respond. He looked to McGrath for permission, which pissed me off.

McGrath peered at me, nodded at Toshi, and said, "Pull over, please."

I stepped out of the car. McGrath delivered a cigarette and offered me a light. I inhaled my first puff and felt a strange calm come over me. Right before the lightheadedness and coughing set in.

I threw the butt on the ground and stomped it out.

"Okay," I said. "I feel better."

McGrath looked more worried than I'd ever seen him. With good reason, I suspected.

"I want to go to this woman's house now."

McGrath closed his eyes, inhaled sharply, shook his head.

I locked eyes with him, more determined than ever to have my way.

After a full two minutes, McGrath suggested we arrive unannounced, and I agreed. It didn't make sense to alert the woman. Nor did I wish to give her the opportunity to consult Stitsill if some involvement existed between the two of them.

"I'll take the lead," McGrath said.

I nodded and awaited his instructions, relieved that he'd agreed to visit Jon's companion today. I couldn't face putting off the inevitable any longer. I had to meet her. I had to know.

"Keep in mind, Ms. Sato may not be at home. She may work, which might make sense. How else would Jon have come to know her?" McGrath's gaze held a tenderness reserved for the grieving.

He was right. I was a crumpled, mourning mess. I cringed. I didn't really want to think about the possibilities, but I recognized McGrath's mission. He was bracing me. I waited patiently for further details.

"If she's home, I'm simply going to explain we're from the U.S., and we've come to gather information about Jon's accident. Also, I'll clarify we'd like to understand the particulars surrounding the crash."

"Wait, what makes you think she'll talk to us? Do we tell her who we are?"

"The Japanese are law-abiding citizens. I'll flash my badge. I have no jurisdiction here, but she'll answer my questions. "

Confidence is good, I thought. "So, I needn't speak."

"You could nod as I explain who we are," McGrath said.

I had an absurd flashback. "As I did at countless business dinners with Jon. I'd sit at his side wondering how he understood the Japanese accents. They don't use "r's" so it can be tough to translate once they get going."

McGrath shot me a sympathetic smile. "That a girl. Keep your focus light."

Light. I'd just been to the site where my husband died a horrific death. And we were going to see the woman who could have been his mistress... Sure, I'd keep it light.

"We can always hope." I swallowed over the growing lump in my throat. Did I really want to know if Jon had been involved with this woman? No. Did I need to know? Yes.

McGrath laid his hand over mine, and I fought the urge to pull away. How could I love two men at the same time? How could I lean on McGrath while I grieved for my husband? The love of my life. Overwhelmed by heartache, my stomach clenched, and I stopped breathing for a full sixty seconds. McGrath whispered, "Breathe."

I smiled weakly, rolled down the window, and scanned the terrain. The twisting road was not helping.

Toshi seemed to grasp my anxiety and flipped on the radio. While the restful jazz played, I forced myself to relax. McGrath tapped out a beat on my wrist, which felt like the drumming motion of a massage. By the time we reached the woman's apartment complex, I'd almost settled down. The power of positive thinking — or existing in a trance–like state.

As we exited the back seat, McGrath reminded me of our mission. I nodded. Then, he asked Toshi to accompany us inside, and to act as an interpreter, if necessary. Toshi bowed slightly to indicate his service. My brain took flight. Auto-pilot time.

I promised myself that when this ordeal had ended, I was going to drink until I was numb.

We rode the miniscule elevator to the 4th floor. Toshi led us down a narrow hall where three young children played with interlocking blocks. We dodged them and smiled, then Toshi stopped abruptly and nodded at a door on our right. He stepped aside, and McGrath knocked on the door. Boom, Boom, Boom. The sound reverberated in my head like rounds of a machine gun.

I closed my eyes, saying a quick prayer that this foray into Jon's past would not prove to be a dead end. Yes, I'm a glutton for pain. A bolt slid inside the apartment just before the door opened. A tiny Japanese woman, perhaps thirty to thirty-five years of age, stood before us, looking confused. She weighed ninety pounds at most. Her skin was like porcelain, her hair reminiscent of a cascading bolt of black silk; she reminded me of the traditional dolls with which Jon had gifted the girls. I was startled by her beauty. Her full lips were the color of a ripe watermelon, sans make-up. Holy crap. No wonder she was Jon's companion. She was irresistible. Hell, she took my breath away. An uncommon sense of calm descended upon me. It was the shock.

I stood silent while McGrath explained the reason for our visit, but didn't hear a single word. After a minute or two, she invited us in. I gazed around the tiny apartment. In denial, I began taking inventory. A studio set up. Very neat, very sparse. On the wall farthest from me I viewed the kitchen area, three yellow cupboards with a sink and range. A fridge and tiny table for two. To the right, a double bed, dresser with portable TV on top, and a clock radio. To the left, a modern loveseat and an additional table, IKEA style. Total area of her living space, maybe 600 square feet.

Simple enough. Then, my eyes centered on something. Tucked in the narrow hallway toward the bathroom was a bassinet. A baby's bed.

For the second time that day, I thought I would faint.

McGrath, ever watchful, gripped my arm and led me to the sofa. I sat on the edge, words flowing around me, but

I couldn't make sense of them. Before long, someone set a cup of tea in front of me. I sipped and regained my focus.

I did want to hear what was being said.

Through the Japanese and English mix, this is what I inferred. Nanami Sato worked for the same company as Jon. Currently on maternity leave, her baby had just turned five months old. She must have been newly pregnant at the time of the crash. Although I recognized that another man could have fathered her child, the growing lump in my throat told me otherwise.

Nanami became tearful at the mention of Jon's name; she also glanced over at the bassinet. The answer to the question that had been burning in my heart this past year became clear. My husband had been having an affair. Best guess, he'd fathered this child.

Somehow, I gathered my wits, stood and stepped over to the wicker baby bed.

"Sam," McGrath warned, an edge to his voice.

I waved him away.

When I stopped at the foot of the bassinet, I asked, "Boy?" and waited for Nanami's response. She simply nodded. I reached out my hands and looked into her eyes, seeking her permission.

"Sam." McGrath's voice grew more urgent.

Again she nodded and I reached inside and scooped up the infant who laid on his back, a sleeping cherub. I nuzzled him against my shoulder, and allowed my cheek to rest upon his downy head. As precious as any baby I'd ever held, I lost myself for a moment in the sweetness of his smell and his skin.

I walked back to the sofa, sat down, and moved the baby to my lap where I settled him between my legs and cradled him between my palms, poring over his face.

His mother had moved closer, watched me closely. I was vaguely aware that McGrath had also moved closer.

The baby's round face matched my husband's, but

didn't confirm a single thing. Babies often have round faces. The infant's eyes eased open. My own eyes became slits, searching for any sign that this Asian child had been fathered by my husband. Big green eyes gazed back at me, and a smile formed on the baby's lips. I returned his grin as tears streaked my cheeks. Jon's intelligent green eyes were what drew me to him in the first place. A sudden chill sliced my spine and my surroundings faded. I locked eyes with my husband's child for a long moment. A connection gripped me, as real as if Jon were standing behind me with his hand resting on my shoulder.

I whispered, "He's beautiful, isn't he?" I should have been angry, incensed even, but I couldn't muster up an ounce of hatred. This precious baby, Jon's foreign legacy, would soon leave my arms. I'd walk away from this child, leave this precious piece of my husband behind. One child I had no control over. One I couldn't adopt or take under my wing. I swallowed over the lump in my throat.

Then, I heard McGrath ask, "Where you intimately involved with Jon Stitsill?"

She lowered her head and nodded, then returned her gaze toward the baby.

"His child?" he asked, sympathy in his eyes.

She nodded again. Hearing the words, the anger finally welled inside of me. I wanted to run, to scream, to pound Jon's chest with my fists. But he wasn't there, and I had to hold it together for the safety of this baby. I rose and held out the baby to Nanami. She gathered him into her arms, kissing his silky hair and nuzzling him to her face. Not his fault, this fatherless innocent. I suddenly felt sorry for the woman, and sad for this child.

"How long were you and Jon together?" I asked softly.

"Two years," she said, tears still streaming down her face. McGrath handed her his handkerchief as he glanced at me.

I nodded for him to continue his questions.

"How did you survive the crash?"

She rambled on in Japanese now, even though she spoke perfect English. Toshi interpreted. "She wasn't there. She simply reported him missing when he didn't arrive back at the hotel."

The rage returned and I had to leave. Right that minute.

She had to be part of the set-up. Part of Stitsill's team. My husband had been a pawn in a deadly game. At the moment, I couldn't consider another explanation.

As I walked towards the door, I heard McGrath politely ask Nanami if we could return or call if we had any further questions. Like most Japanese, she became stoic, very gracious, and bowed as he said goodbye. I didn't even turn.

I gripped McGrath's arm, hissing into his ear as we left the complex, "I'm done. Enough. I want to go home…"

CHAPTER TWENTY-NINE

MCGRATH THANKED TOSHI for the ride back to the hotel. I just walked away.

I wept. Blind. Empty.

"Let's get you a drink," McGrath said.

I let him guide me and swiped at my tears. We walked into a bar. He ordered. I drank. One. Two. Three shots. I couldn't bear to leave Jon behind. Not like this. Not with the memories I'd held so dear destroyed.

"How could he have done this?"

McGrath reached out to comfort me, but I pulled away.

I'm so sorry," he said, folding his hands in front of him. "Maybe it's not as it seems."

"Right. Maybe some random Caucasian guy with green eyes impregnated Nanami, had her lie that she was his mistress, and then drove his car off a cliff. Makes perfect sense."

McGrath locked eyes with me, clearly sympathetic and sorry for me.

"Don't pity me," I ordered. "I brought this on myself. I should never have come here."

McGrath shook his head. "You're in a lot of pain right now, but you'll get through this."

It took every bit of restraint I had not to tell him to 'fuck off'. "I get through every shit-crap scrap of my life. I'm sick of it. If I never see another day, it won't hurt my feelings."

I glared at him, challenging him to make me feel better. "I want a beer."

"Maybe we should head upstairs. Sleep will do you good." He removed a credit card from his wallet.

"I want a beer."

"Here's an idea," McGrath said. "Let's get settled upstairs. Pajamas, in between the covers. Then I'll serve you a beer in bed."

"I need to use the restroom."

McGrath nodded, signed our tab, and led me towards the lobby.

"Where are we going?" I asked.

"There's a restroom near the front desk. It's just around the corner."

I wobbled as we wound through the hallway.

"Will you be alright?" he asked as he deposited me at the Ladies Room door.

"Yes. In fact, I'm going to splash some cold water on my face. I need to sober up a bit."

McGrath smiled in agreement. "I'm going to stop off at the front desk while you're inside. Wait for me right here." He pointed to a chair.

I saluted and made my way into the restroom. When I came out, McGrath was already back.

"Ready?" he said.

"Yes. I feel better."

"Good," he said as he led me to the elevator and pressed the 12th floor button.

"Um," I said, "that's the wrong floor."

"We're going to stay in another room tonight. I want you to be able to relax." He poised an index finger over his lips. "If you feel like talking, you can speak freely. Anything you need, I'll be happy to collect from our room. Trust me on this."

At that point, I was talked out. I had nothing more to say about my cheating husband, but I was too sloshed to resist his instructions. It didn't matter where I slept.

McGrath planted me on the bed, removed my shoes, and lay me back on the pillow. Then, he removed my clothing and tucked me under the covers.

"Be right back," he said after leaving a glass of water on the nightstand.

"Where are you going?" I asked, suddenly frightened to be alone.

"Getting you some pajamas. I promise, I'll be right back."

I curled up on my pillow and promptly fell asleep. When I woke some time later, I felt panicked and disoriented. I cried out for Jon.

"Sam," McGrath said. "It's me. Jon isn't here."

"I want him back," I cried. "I want my husband. He loved me. With his whole heart. I want him back. He needs to take care of me and the kids."

I began to sob. My world was crumbling beneath me, and I couldn't find any solid ground on which to stand. McGrath wrapped his arms around me and held me close, but I could no more accept his comfort than inhale a full breath. I pushed him away, dropped my head in my hands and wept. "Why did this have to happen? What did I do wrong? He was lonely. I get that part. But did he have to find someone else? Someone other than me?"

"Shhh," McGrath murmured. "It'll be alright." He laid a hand on my shoulder.

I brushed away his hand. "Alright?" I screamed. "Alright?" I sucked in a ragged breath, "When will it be alright? After I'm dead and I can no longer feel? How do I face my children? Now I have to live a lie with them! Pretend that their father was a hero, when in fact, he was a liar and a cheat…" I dropped to the floor, cocooning myself in my arms.

"I want to die," I cried. "I just want to die."

McGrath sat in front of me. Patient. Kind.

"In time, I suspect you'll be able to hold onto the good

stuff. He did love you. He did love his kids. You're raw right now. It's a fresh, deep wound."

I cried, and sobbed, and blew my nose. Then I wept some more. I could barely breathe. My head felt as if it were loaded with lead. My throat ached and my mouth was parched.

McGrath stood and reached for my water. "Here," he said. "Drink this."

I sipped. The water tasted cool on my throat. I caught my breath and forced a deep inhale, then an exhale.

"Good girl," McGrath said. "You're going to be okay."

I finally looked at him. Held his gaze. I took another breath. I saw kindness in his eyes. And concern. And caring.

"Make love to me."

"No," McGrath held firm. "Not tonight. Let's cuddle up, get some rest, and I'll catch you in the morning."

"I need a cigarette," I said.

"You tried that. It didn't work out all that well," McGrath reminded me. "You don't smoke."

"But if I did, this would be a really good time." A ragged exhale later, I shook off an unexpected chill and leaned back against the bed.

McGrath raised his water glass and clinked it against mine. "Well done," he said.

"Well done?"

"Grieving's hard work." He patted my knee, helped me up and into bed, settled a gentle kiss on my forehead and climbed in beside me. I slept for hours. Deep and dreamless.

* * *

We headed back to our room the next morning, and I stepped into the bathroom to shower. It was then that I noticed my toiletries had been moved. Housekeeping? The hairs on the back of my neck prickled. I felt uneasy. I walked back into the bedroom and studied it. Other items had been moved.

"McGrath," I said, forcing a calm I didn't feel. "Someone's been in our room."

"I was here last night, remember? And housekeeping's been here since we left yesterday," he answered.

I checked under the sink. "No, the backpack. It's gone."

He bolted upright and flew inside the bathroom. He turned, searching and taking inventory as I raced over to our luggage.

"It must be here somewhere."

He looked startled, as if he were still processing my words. "Did we leave it in Toshi's car? No. I remember seeing it in the bathroom. Shit!"

I completed a thorough inventory as he completed his own.

Then, he darted over to the desk and began to write on the notepad.

"What are you doing?" I asked.

He turned and gestured for me to be quiet.

I looked at him, puzzled and dizzy.

He handed me a note. "The room is bugged. Follow my lead."

I nodded and fell onto the side of the bed. Panicked, I grabbed the pad from him and wrote, "Our passports!"

He patted his blazer pocket and shook his head. Empty.

"Shit," I whispered.

"This is a problem," he wrote back, before he sank into a chair.

"We can't get out of the country," I jotted quickly.

"Not without going to the Consulate and reporting our missing passports." McGrath handed me his scribbled note as he scrubbed his face with his hand.

"Stitsill would love that, wouldn't he?" I wrote back.

"I'm sure that's his plan. We have to run, before he kills us." I read the words from over his shoulder and felt my knees turn to rubber.

McGrath reached for the room phone and called the front

desk. "I'd like to report a robbery," he said.

We quickly dressed and waited. Within twenty minutes hotel security knocked on the door and McGrath invited them inside. We described the backpack along with a selective account of its contents. The guys took the report, said they'd look into it, and asked if we wanted the police to be summoned.

We nodded.

The only thing of monetary value in the pack was my computer. I wasn't worried about the actual laptop since the flash drive in my safe deposit box back home contained its entire contents. But by now, Stitsill knew what I knew about him. And now, we were stranded in Japan. If we weren't in danger before, we were now. What had I done?

CHAPTER THIRTY

A S SOON AS the hour was reasonable, I called home. A feeling of impending doom blanketed me like thick fog. I feared for my life and the life of my family. But I couldn't risk sharing that with Ed. My phone was probably bugged. I'd have given anything for a magic wand, so I could transport myself home and huddle with my family, safe and sound in the shelter of my fairy godmother. But that wasn't an option, so I summoned my inner actress and made small talk with each and every one of my children. Safe. Sound. I drew a measured breath, allowing myself to feel a small bit of relief. Nick hinted about a female friend of Ed's, and I couldn't resist asking him about it. When all else fails, pretend everything is normal.

"So, anything new?" I asked.

"No, can't say so," Ed said.

"A little birdie mentioned you might be getting on with your life," I teased.

Ed cleared his throat. "A guy can't get away with anything."

I laughed. "If there's ever something you want to run by me, just let me know."

"I think I have it covered, Sam, but thanks." He chuckled. "Who was it? Who ratted me out?"

"I'll never tell," I replied.

We caught up on the kids. If anything was amiss, Ed

certainly wasn't about to admit it. According to him, the kids were busy with friends at neighboring cottages and with each other. No major catastrophes. No sibling warfare. Miracle of miracles.

Speaking of miracles, McGrath and I could have used one at the moment. Instead, he produced the next best thing — a bottle of bourbon, ice and rock glasses. He poured us both a shot.

"Sometimes, we need to break the rules."

I shook my head before I let it fall to the back of the chair. My shoulders ached with tension. I tried to think of the next best move, but nothing came to mind. Holy Crap.

After we finished our drinks, we showered and dressed for the day, careful to discuss only insignificant matters. McGrath winked at me when he suggested a day of shopping and sight–seeing, and I heartily agreed.

"There's nothing more to be done," he said. "We reported the robbery. The laptop can be replaced. Now, it's time for vacation." We both understood the importance of getting out of the room and finding a private spot where we could speak freely.

Once we exited the room, McGrath motioned me into the elevator and kept the banter light–hearted, discussing souvenirs we hoped to purchase and possible tours we could schedule. We entered the Takashimaya Department Store, and McGrath ushered me into the lingerie section of the store. He wandered to a display of kimonos and began shuffling through the racks like a man on a mission.

"Shop," he commanded. "Find gifts for the kids, Ed, Di. Whatever. Buy yourself a dress to wear to dinner. Just stay focused and very busy. I have matters to attend to."

Worry creased my brow. "Like what?" I didn't want to be alone, and I didn't want him drifting off, from me or without me. "Please don't leave."

"I'm a cop. A good cop."

I locked eyes with him, surprised by his words. "Of

course, you are. I've never thought anything different."

"I need to embrace the cop in me right now, in order to take care of you and your family. I'm asking you to trust me."

"Where are you going? How long will you be gone?"

"I'm not sure, but I'll be safe. I promise. Don't worry. Just do what I've asked, alright?"

I nodded. I trusted this man with my life. I'd do whatever he asked me — without further questions. "Okay. But will you call or text me? Let me know you're safe?"

"I'm going to purchase two cell phones first, one for each of us. Once I do that, I'll text you. But the message will be from my current cell, and it will say, 'meet me in Men's'. That's our signal."

"Our signal that you've secured a phone." I looked at him for confirmation.

"Yes. We'll use our current phones for routine business, like calling home. For everything else, we'll use the new cells. We need unmonitored communication devices. I've seen them for sale on the street."

"Burner phones," I said. "Please be safe." I paused. "You'll text me the same message again when you arrive back here?"

McGrath nodded, kissed my cheek, and disappeared.

I struggled to get a handle on worry, panic, sadness and about a zillion other emotions. I failed, so I forced myself to shop. In my present state, I could not have cared less about the Japanese kimonos for the girls, or the matching brightly colored ornate belts and hair ornaments. But I purchased them anyway. Then, I discovered a rack of CD's of popular teen music. I grabbed several CD's for Nick and then scrounged the electronics section for a game for Will. Ed would be harder. I spent the better part of an hour searching through each and every department, trying to find the appropriate gift. I came up empty.

I located a coffee shop, paid for a tall black blend, and

sat at a table with my packages balanced on a nearby chair, to dissuade anyone from joining me. I felt foolish. Selfish. McGrath and our entire relationship seemed to be based on the Stitsill mystery and my dead husband. I'd pulled him in with little regard for his safety, his wishes, or his life. What did I know about him? Other than the fact that he'd been a cop going on twenty years, other than the fact that he'd been divorced for at least ten years, what else did I know? Not that I suspected he was somehow linked to Stitsill or anything, but I needed to think more about him. Get to know him better. Stop being so wrapped up in my life.

I grimaced. Could be a little difficult considering our current circumstances. I knew this was the biggest mess I'd ever gotten myself into, but I also felt a sense of calm. Misplaced perhaps — kind of like the lull before a treacherous summer storm.

My cell phone buzzed and I pulled it out of my purse. McGrath. Our code message. Meet me in Men's. I breathed a sigh of relief. He had the prepaid phones. Mission accomplished. God only knew how many other items were on McGrath's agenda. I needed to trust he would be safe and return soon. I finished my coffee and left the small shop. My packages were weighing me down, so I considered dropping them off in our room. Hotel security had assured us that they'd be extra vigilant, but I still felt violated and hesitant. Could I trust their expertise? Especially against a guy like Stitsill, clearly an expert in undercover work. Espionage. That's what it was really. The guy was an assassin and a spy. But for whom and why? How far out of my element was I? I wondered how long I had left, for I'd surely be killed. But worse, were my children in danger?

Like it or not, it was imperative that I leave the emotional baggage from yesterday behind me. At least for now. I had to protect myself and my family. I prayed that McGrath didn't get hurt in the fray.

How had my Jon gotten mixed up with Stitsill II? I thought

long and hard about what I knew. Jon had mentioned money problems within the company, and the expectation by higher-ups that he would sort it all out. What the hell had happened? Missing money, Jon had said. Why was it his job to fix it? Was that different than his other duties? Unusual? Yes, I thought. While I recognized with increasing clarity that I didn't know everything about my husband's work, I knew a fair amount about his business dealings. Being connected to the money end of things wasn't out of the norm, but being responsible for missing money or investigating what had happened to extorted funds might have gotten him murdered. That much made sense to me.

I juggled my bags, made my way to the elevator, and stepped inside. After a quick ride upstairs, I set my purchases down and listened carefully for any sound from inside our room before I inserted my card key and pushed open the heavy steel door. I glanced around, making sure the room was empty and looked as it had when we'd last headed downstairs. The bathroom door stood halfway open, at just the angle I'd left it, so I felt safe enough to enter.

There's a moment when you realize that what you now consider "reasonable" is not. It was unreasonable that I expected someone to be in my hotel room…that I expected danger and did not run the other way…that I could not ask the authorities for help.

This was that moment. I was mixed up in a deadly game, and most likely going to die. And because of me, so would McGrath. And maybe my kids. I needed to stop and think things through before I did anything whatsoever. Stop acting on instinct, or worse than that, impulse. Exercise caution with every step. Above all, I vowed to return to my kids in one piece. They deserved at least one living parent.

CHAPTER THIRTY-ONE

I ARRANGED MY souvenirs in my luggage, and headed back downstairs. I had no appetite but grabbed a bite at a noodle shop to keep up my strength, then thought about my next move. I had no idea where McGrath had gone, and I prayed he'd somehow finesse getting us out of the country without passports, but without visiting the Consulate again. From the amount of time it had taken him to acquire the cell phones, I figured it would be a while before he returned. I couldn't just sit there waiting, I needed to do something.

Questions of Jon's final days stuck like cobwebs to my brain. What gets people killed? Power. Sex. Money. What got Jon killed? Jon wasn't about the power. An affair? Maybe. Jon had mentioned missing money in one of our last conversations. He'd been worried. Maybe this was the missing piece.

Knowing what I now knew about my husband, I was disillusioned, and could have fallen apart, given up on my life and all that I held dear. So much had transpired over the past two days. Still, I struggled letting go of the Jon I knew. He was a good man, with a stellar reputation. Caring. A man of integrity. The mere thought of my husband losing his life over something as stupid as money broke my heart all over again. I felt helpless. If I could just find out what really happened, I'd feel better. Although unwise, I searched my cell for one of his employee's phone numbers.

Mark Johnson. Mark was younger than Jon by about five years, but fluent in Japanese and immersed in the culture, having lived in the country for four years after college. One of Jon's most loyal employees, his devastation had been clear when I'd run into him at the office after Jon's death. He'd offered to help me in any way he could. At the time, I couldn't imagine a single thing he could do. Now, however, the situation proved quite the opposite.

Mark could be an asset. He'd been near Jon during those final days. Even though I realized I was calling him from a phone that might be bugged, I dialed his number. I'd be careful to keep the conversation superficial. He answered on the third ring.

"Hi, Mark. Samantha Stitsill." We exchanged pleasantries for several minutes. Then, I decided on a semi-straightforward approach. "Mark, I'm struggling. I just celebrated the first anniversary of Jon's death and I'm trying to get some closure. Is there any chance we could meet in the next few weeks?"

"Sure. I'd love to see you. We could get together when I return from Japan."

Shocked, I felt my neurons fire. "You're in Japan?"

"Yes," he said.

I massaged my temple as I thought. Bad idea, getting someone else involved. But I needed answers...and then I heard my words: "I'm in Japan as well. I'm staying at the Marriott Associa in Nagoya."

"Me too." He sounded surprised, but it made perfect sense to me. Anytime anyone from Jon's company visited the plant or office in Nagoya, they resided at the Marriott.

"Any chance you could meet me?" I asked.

"I'll catch a cab from the office and be there in thirty minutes."

"I'll wait in the lobby. Thanks," I said.

My head spun. Thankful Mark would meet me at the hotel, I hoped McGrath would trust my judgment in calling him. Hell, I wasn't sure I trusted my judgment, yet Mark might be able to provide the information that would finally solve the puzzle. And help me stay alive.

I fidgeted with my handbag strap while I waited, hoping Mark would be up for a drink in the bar. I wondered if he knew about Jon's affair and the baby. And if he knew, would his loyalty to Jon keep him from being truthful with me? My head began to pound. In reality, Mark's knowledge of Jon's indiscretions was the least of my concerns. More than ever, I needed to stay focused on business concerns and their link to Stitsill and my Jon. Nothing more, or I might risk what little sanity I still possessed.

For the time being, I counted Caucasians as they passed through the lobby. Then I guessed whether their visits to Japan were intended for business or pleasure. It seemed like an eternity passed before I spotted Mark heading towards me. He looked the same as the last time I'd seen him. About 6' tall and thin as a reed, his pale brown eyes shadowed—a look I'd witnessed on my late husband too many times to count. Falls under the heading of too much travel through too many time zones. Mark smiled as he approached. I stood and we hugged. It felt oddly soothing to be in the company of one of Jon's friends. Almost reassuring.

"Can I buy you a beer?" I asked.

"I never turn down the offer of an adult beverage." Mark offered me his arm, guiding me with swift determination, as if a sense of urgency existed. I felt nervous and confused. Something was up. Once we arrived inside the Estmare lounge, he spoke Japanese to the hostess, who escorted us to a small table at the rear of the bar. Flanked by overstuffed leather chairs beneath a low light, Mark huddled next to me after ordering our drinks.

"I can't believe you're here. What an amazing coincidence. You look great, Sam. How are you? How are the kids? I've wanted to call, but I also didn't want to intrude. I can't tell you how much I miss Jon, how the entire company misses him. His was the voice of reason with these people, and they can't seem to pull their heads out of their asses since his death."

Mark's voice carried and he gestured emphatically as he spoke. I smiled at him. He was as ADHD as the day was long…but warning bells went off. I knew I'd become paranoid, but I'm the ADHD expert, and his agitation seemed to come from a deeper place. His eyes darted back and forth. He kept looking over his shoulder. Did he feel he was being watched?

I patted his hand, then held it, oddly feeling Jon's presence between us, tying us and connecting us like a magnetic force, full of strength and healing.

"Everything's fine, Mark." I locked eyes with him, then continued. "But I need your help. Before Jon's accident, he spoke of missing money, even hinted at the possible extortion of funds. Do you know anything about that?"

Mark lowered his voice, pulling out a cigarette and leaving it unlit between his lips. He peered at me over his wire-rimmed glasses. "I know everything about it." He pulled the cigarette away from his mouth and rolled it between his fingers. "Why do you want to know?"

"I met Jon's mistress and child yesterday. It's possible Jon was killed because of them, or because he had an affair with a colleague, but I can't help but wonder if something more happened. I'm convinced he was forced off that cliff. Maybe something to do with work."

Mark became even more pensive. "Listen," he said, "if you're looking into his death, you're in over your head. Jon was in over his head, too. Jon kept his personal life close to the vest, so I'm not sure about that, but I will tell you about something I do know about."

"Why tell me now? Why not earlier?"

"Look, Jon took good care of me. He saved my ass more than once. I owe him. But I'll tell you once, then we'll never speak of it again. If you ask me about it later, I'll deny this conversation ever took place. Two American employees have driven off cliffs." He shook his head. "It's bullshit. I don't want to be the third."

My stomach knotted as I waited for him to explain.

"Somebody at the top found out about the boss' purchase of Russian missile sites. At least that's what I think."

My eyes widened. "Russian missile sites?"

"Watanabe-san's crazy. He spends other people's money like it's leftover rice. He decided to purchase these sites— sorry, not sites. Silos. And he used the company's money. They were expensive. I'm talking about an unbelievable amount of money."

"What does any of this have to do with Jon?"

"Jon knew about it. He tried to dissuade Watanabe-san, but you know the boss. He's an outlaw from the Wild West. All that ego. All that power. I'm pretty sure he ordered Jon to hide the expenditure, and Jon would have done the best he could, but once the quarterly report came out, I heard one of the auditors saw through it and Jon got shoved under the bus." Mark clamped his hand over his mouth. "I didn't mean that the way it sounded, Sam. I'm sorry."

"Wait," I said, staring him down. "This makes no sense. Silos?"

Mark's voice hushed. "The silos' walls were lined with valuable metals. I don't know the science, but lining them provided radiation shielding of some kind. Platinum, tungsten, gold, silver. You name it. The idea was to mine the metals and make even more money on the initial investment."

"Seems right from what I know about Watanabe-san," I observed.

Mark paused. I could tell there was more, but he double-clutched. It was important not to speak. He needed space. I waited.

"I believe Watanabe implicated Jon." Mark hung his head.

I held my breath. "Why? And why didn't anyone say anything after Jon's death?"

"Internally, it was whispered about, but there's an unspoken code. The company line—show your loyalty at all times. You know that. There is no one, nothing more important than the company. Once Jon died, the issue was considered closed. I'm not in the inner circle, but I can tell you this. They hired new auditors. Brought in money from who–knows–where to cover the losses. Paid people off. Everyone was busy saving their own ass at that point. It proved too risky for anyone to speak up, to question Jon's death. Again, I don't know any of this for sure, but I'm as smart as the next guy. I can add."

I wished they'd have paid Jon off, too, rather than sending him off a cliff. But no, that wasn't Jon's style. He would never have accepted a bribe. "Didn't the shareholders or auditors try to recover the missing funds? If they blamed Jon, why didn't they come after his accounts? You'd think they'd have investigated our finances. I never heard a word about this." I could hardly contain my fury, but I kept my voice low, sure that by now that Mark and I were probably being watched by one of Stitsill's minions.

"Don't you get it? Everyone knew what was going on. Everyone. And that means nobody knew. No one did or said anything because they feared for their lives. No one came after you because everyone knew the truth. Their heads were down. Between their knees. Kissing their own asses. Hoping they weren't next. I'm risking my skin telling you this. Leave it alone, Sam. Let it lie. For your own good. Hell, you could get killed. History says these guys will stop at nothing if they fear you're onto them. Cast suspicion on them, and you're next."

You're next. Holy shit. I'd seen that message before. I inhaled a ragged breath before continuing. "Hold on. Who was selling the silos?"

"Former KGB. Bad Russians. Dangerous guys with too

much knowledge. Undercover lunacy."

"Silos." I thought for a long moment. "Governments would never allow that. It had to be black market." Was this real?

"It was secret. Jon had covered several million of Watanabe's spending within the six months prior to his accident. At the time he died, an additional eighty million dollars had gone missing."

"Eighty million? That's crazy! How could anyone possibly cover it up?"

Mark dropped his hand on mine, checking his wristwatch. Then nodded. "Two minutes. I've already said too much." He shook his head with regret.

"Two minutes? I don't understand...But, there's more to this, isn't there?" Jon had shared the bare minimum with me about this. I felt guilty. I should have paid more attention to him at the time, asked more questions, helped him to work his way out from under this.

Mark nodded, then paused. He was weighing what to tell me, weighing if he would tell me. His guilt seemed heavy. I knew enough to hold my tongue and wait. But I had so many questions. How would I ever make sense of this?

"I think Jon knew way more than he wanted to. Watanabe traveled to Russia on more than one occasion. Rumor has it, Jon guessed the money had been laundered through Swiss bank accounts or the like. The dealings were totally illicit. In Japan. In the States. Everywhere. Highly risky. A huge embarrassment. It put the whole company in danger." Mark lowered his voice even more. "The silos were supposedly outside of St. Petersburg. Extremely remote, reachable only by car."

"Let me get this straight. Watanabe used company funds to invest in Russian missile silos with the intent of making a profit by purchasing the structures, stripping the interiors, and cashing in on the metals."

"Thousands of silos, Sam. As you said, all very black

market. Jon made an offhand comment once. He thought Watanabe was making bad decisions and had no idea how dangerous Russian thugs can be. He worried Wantanabe-san would wind up dead. Frigging naive Asian."

I needed a minute to collect my thoughts. But I didn't have a minute, and Mark just kept talking. He locked eyes with me. "I think Jon may have been about to blow the whistle. I'm not sure in what way or with whom, but gossip is that Jon had uncovered some scary stuff."

"Scarier than missile silos?" I had raised my voice, and Mark looked around, clearly alarmed.

My insides were rocking and rolling. I forced myself to assume a calm demeanor I did not feel.

"Jon intimated that some of the warheads were still active. Who knows? When they dug up these things, they could have found missiles, too."

"What?" My voice was too loud. Mark crushed my hand under his to warn me. But I just felt more agitated. I locked eyes with him

My voice calmed, because this is what it all came down to, and I already knew the answer. "Jon was killed because he knew too much."

Mark's eyes filled with tears as he reached for my hand and turned it over. He tapped my palm with his index finger. I grabbed it and held on tight.

"Tell me," I demanded in a whisper.

Mark squeezed my hand. "I think he posed a threat."

"What about you, Mark? Are you safe?"

"So far. Jon took good care of me. He protected all of his employees. But let's do this in case someone is watching us. Burst into tears, and we'll hug it out, and then leave like old friends."

I nodded and squeezed shut my eyes. My breath stuck to my lungs. I could neither inhale nor exhale. Finally, I drew in air. Then, I began to weep. The tears were honest. I wasn't play-acting. I was sad, and furious, and scared.

"I hate what you've been through," Mark said. "I'm sorry there's nothing more I can do for you."

"Thank you. You've helped more than you know. I'm going to be here a while longer. Let's touch base before I leave."

He looked at me warily, then shook his head.

I understood and nodded.

He pulled me into his arms. A sweet, friendly embrace, and then he whispered so softly that I struggled to hear. "There's a guy Jon was in touch with before his death. I think Jon trusted him. I'm not sure, but he might be CIA, stationed here in Japan. His name is Lucas Sweeney. He phoned me at the office yesterday and asked if I'd been in touch with you."

I wrapped my arms around him and shook with fear. I was still crying, but my brain cranked into overdrive. What? Who?

Mark whispered, "I'm not sure what he's after. He just asked how you were. Maybe he can help."

I nodded slightly, and our embrace softened, both of us wiping our eyes. I took a moment. Lucas Sweeney. The name rattled some distant memory. Why did this name sound familiar?

Mark glanced at his watch again and pushed himself up to his feet. "I'm late. I have a meeting at the office." He dug inside his pocket and withdrew a wad of bills, tossing several onto the table. "This will cover our drinks," he added.

I stood and embraced Mark one last time, the remaining link to my husband and his death. For some strange reason I didn't want to let go. He'd confirmed my worst fears. Jon had been at least peripherally involved in some kind of mob connection, which most likely included Stitsill, and it had gotten him killed. Maybe McGrath and I could bring down Stitsill once and for all. And maybe this guy that Jon had reached out to could help us.

Mark leaned forward one last time, taking my hand firmly and staring into my eyes. Encouraging, strong. A friend. As he pulled away I felt the paper he'd placed inside it. I clenched my hand around the note, then slipped it into my pocket for a tissue where I dropped the paper for safe-keeping.

CHAPTER THIRTY-TWO

THE STRAIN OF the past two days wore on me. By the time McGrath texted me that he'd arrived back at the Marriot, I was two beers in.

On top of everything else, my late husband Jon had been at least superficially involved in some kind of dealings with the Russian mob. I had cause to feel both exhausted and ready to puke my guts out. Meanwhile, McGrath had gone who–knows–where to do who–knows–what. I hoped he didn't have more bad news to add to my overly full plate. I couldn't handle it. Sadly, the beer was not helping.

When he located me in the bar, I stood and held onto him for a full sixty seconds. Not one of those happy–to–see–you embraces, but rather an "I'm–never–going–to–let–you–out–of–my–sight–again" clinging vine hugs. I'd never been so happy to see anyone in my entire life.

"I could use a change of venue," I said.

"How about the rooftop bar?" McGrath suggested. "There's a great view, and it's private."

At the moment, I guessed I knew way more than McGrath about the necessity for privacy. And the fact remained, if we were being watched, it would happen anywhere we went. I told McGrath to stop off in the restroom and check himself for bugs or wires. I had no idea if someone could have dropped a bug in his pocket without him knowing, but I excused myself as well, dumped my purse out on a chair in the Ladies Room and looked for foreign objects. I found nothing.

When I met McGrath in the hall, he nodded, indicating the 'all clear' and we stepped on the elevator and rode to the roof.

"How are you?" McGrath asked, after we'd settled at a table near the rear of the restaurant and ordered drinks.

"I'm numb. None of this seems real, so I'm doing what I always do when life gets too damned difficult. I'm focusing on things I can control." I smiled faintly as McGrath patted my hand. "In any case, I have some news to share once you tell me about your day." I offered him a weak smile.

"I'm here for you. Whatever you need." He squeezed my shoulder and clinked his glass with mine.

I explained how I'd come across Mark Johnson, his association with Jon, and the news he shared. Every bit of it.

McGrath sank back in his chair, air gusting out of him. Then, he shook his head and turned parchment pale. "Sam," he said in a hushed voice, his eyes darting around the room, "do you know what this means? This is much bigger than I ever considered, or we wouldn't be here right now." He paused. "I have to get you out of here. Hopefully, some of the steps I took today will help to keep you safe, but I'm not sure anymore. This is too big…"

I'd never seen McGrath so distraught. He downed his bourbon and waved for another.

"I know," I agreed. We were in too deep.

"I purchased two cell phones. And two guns. Don't ask me how or where." He patted the inside pocket of his sports coat to indicate their location. "Then, I called Toshi. We need him."

I nodded.

"We rented a car. In his name. I drove it and parked it in a public garage. Toshi will drive his car and park it there, then switch vehicles when we need him. We can't leave any kind of a paper trail. I'm convinced Stitsill is watching us. I didn't spot a tail when I was out today, and hopefully, I eluded him by leaving you behind, but I'm not foolish enough to believe I was successful."

"You drove here? You have to have an International Drivers Permit to drive here. You could wind up in jail."

McGrath shook his head, disgusted with me. "I'm a cop, remember? I took care of the license before we left the States."

"But you have to drive on the right side of the car and the left side of the road. Jon said it's confusing..."

"Enough about Jon. Please."

I teared up.

"It's just driving, Sam. People do it all the time. Face it, driving is the least of our problems."

I blinked, fighting unsuccessfully to dry my tears.

"Your news about the warheads raises the bar." McGrath sounded as if he were in a squad room. I let him continue without interruption. "Do you know the history, Sam?"

I bit my lip. A sudden surge of anger erupted, but it was better than sadness. I'm a teacher, for God's sake. Yes, I know my history. Instead of being a smart ass though, I simply nodded before adding, "Yes, the Cold War. Both Russia and the U.S. agreed to destroy all of our nuclear weapons. I read an article about ten years ago, maybe fifteen. I'm not sure why I remember it, but this silver haired fox, some U.S. ambassador, discussed a program in which the U.S. had invaded Russia in a covert operation in order to locate and disable their weapons. He was a frigging diplomat. Like Stitsill."

McGrath raised his eyebrows and frowned. "Thing is, there's no way the Russians didn't know what we were up to. They had their own teams, hiding weapons, falsifying documents. This goes way back, before the Internet, before computers. Old–fashioned spies with Mafioso ties. Russian mob. When the Soviet Union fell, the KGB no longer had jobs. Many of those guys sold themselves to the highest bidder, and they raised their offspring to do the same."

"Shit."

"Exactly." McGrath tossed back a gulp of whiskey.

A bright light flashed in my memory. "I just thought of something."

"What?" McGrath stared at me.

"Maybe this Lucas Sweeney works for Japanese Intelligence, or the CIA, or better yet, both. I checked the paper Mark handed to me when I was in the bathroom. There's a phone number. We should contact him." I fumbled in my purse for my cell.

"We have no idea if we can trust him," McGrath said.

"I agree. But we need help." I stopped fumbling and looked at McGrath with total focus. "Do you have a better idea?"

"No." McGrath looked resigned.

"Then I think we need to call him," I said, grabbing my cell from my purse.

"Don't use that phone. Do it later. Privately. After I give you the phone I purchased."

I felt like an idiot. Of course I couldn't use my regular phone. I was so glad he was there to think of the things I didn't, helping to keep me safe. I just hoped I could keep him safe as well.

I shook off a sudden chill, then nodded and shared more of what I knew with McGrath. "Here's what I'm thinking. Mark suggested a lot of what he knew was rumor. Jon kept information close, to protect others, including Mark. On the other hand, Mark is smart, and I'm sure he speculated on some details on his own. He's the product of a strict Mormon upbringing, and a very straight-shooter. I know Jon trusted him. I trust him. We need serious help. Remember, Lucas Sweeney had been in touch with Jon."

McGrath thought for a moment before speaking. "Having Stitsill out of the way will make it easier to get home."

"I don't know if this Sweeney guy is Japanese intelligence

or CIA or what. But this is a matter of international security. Nuclear proliferation is way bigger than you and me. If Sweeney can infiltrate Stitsill's circle, once and for all, we might be okay. Stitsill's a serious threat. Now, more than ever." I reached out and gripped McGrath's hand.

"He wouldn't think twice about taking us out. Plus, there must be other mob out there, too, ready and willing to 'off' anyone who compromises their enterprise. Shit, Sweeney could be mob!"

I shuddered. I knew McGrath was right, but I couldn't bring myself to verbalize it.

McGrath's worried expression said it all. "Look," he said, "if this guy can help us, and if you feel reasonably sure we can trust him, you're right. We should give him a call. We need help. We've run out of options."

I had no idea what to do. But I knew McGrath was right. We had little to no reason to trust this guy, but maybe... "I'll call him. Try to set up a meeting in a public place. Maybe he can tell us something official. Who he works for."

"Unlikely. These guys don't give up their creds. We can ask, but I'll tell you right now. Not gonna happen."

"What should I do?"

"Call him," McGrath said.

I glanced at my watch. Close to five o'clock. We ordered a quick meal and while we waited for our food to arrive, I stood, kissed McGrath and held on to him while he dropped one of the cell phones he'd purchased into my bag. I slipped into the Ladies Room, past the separate sitting room, and checked each stall. When I felt sure I was alone, I dialed Sweeney's number. As I waited for him to answer I replayed his name in my head. Sweeney. Where had I heard that name? For the life of me, I couldn't recall.

When he answered, I explained who I was, and told him that I needed to speak with him privately about my husband's death. Sweeney agreed to meet us in a little noodle shop in the basement of the hotel around seven. I told him I was scared and I didn't know who I could trust. Perhaps I was making myself too vulnerable, but we needed help.

"I'm afraid I'm being watched," I added.

"You are," he said. "By Stitsill's people. And mine."

"Yours?"

"We can talk more about this when we meet."

Maybe I could trust this guy.

Ninety minutes. McGrath and I made small talk and tried to distract ourselves. We decided that an appearance at the room might be a good idea. The best defense is a good offense. Once in our room, we each showered and dressed in fresh clothing and chatted about the city sights, faking arrangements for a castle tour the following day.

McGrath kissed me, signaling me that it would be a great way to throw a listener off track. What a way to fuel a romance.

CHAPTER THIRTY-THREE

THERE ARE TIMES in life when there's no turning back. A little voice tells me I'm about to do something that will change the course of my future. This was one of those moments. A defining moment. I could feel it. Probably because that little voice was no longer whispering, but screaming a warning at me. Flashing a red stop light in front of my eyes, lowering the unmovable bars of steel at the railroad crossing. Don't drive on the tracks. Stay off the tracks.

I hesitated for a long moment before McGrath and I stepped out of our room. I inventoried my luggage, my toiletries on the counter, and the few familiar things which still remained in my possession. I texted a loving message to Ed and the kids. Then, I took a deep breath and headed to the noodle shop. Head first, off the cliff.

The tiny shop reminded me of a diner in the U.S., except the food looked mostly indistinguishable. Since McGrath and I had already eaten, he ordered a few different dishes, unconcerned about their contents. We spoke of inconsequential things, both restless and anxious for the moment when Lucas Sweeney would walk through the door.

When the Caucasian entered the shop, I figured it was Lucas. He looked vaguely familiar, something in the eyes, but I couldn't place where or when I'd seen him. I guessed him as close to forty, but it was hard to tell, his angular features and wise brown eyes suggested he'd been around the block more than once. Good spy, I thought. I would never have any idea of his profession if I'd encountered him on the street. Neatly bearded and long haired, he looked more like a computer geek who spent his life in some dark, secluded basement. Lucas repositioned his backpack on his shoulders, spoke with the proprietor and was directed to the table next to us. He settled into a chair, placed a laptop on his table, and spoke quietly, "Look at your friend and tell the story."

"Can you show us some ID?" McGrath asked.

"I can't. I understand your concern, but the less you know the better."

"Please understand," I pleaded. "We don't know anything about you. Talking could be suicide."

Sweeney sat, deciding, for a full minute. "I know about Rosie. The tritiated water. I attended her funeral. And about your dog. I'm sorry I couldn't have helped you sooner."

The funeral. That's where I'd seen him.

I nodded at McGrath, and he perked up, then nodded for me to continue.

As naive as I mostly am, a different feeling settled over me. It wasn't just my normally trusting nature that kicked in, but the fact that he knew the history. Things that no one else would have known. A quick look into the man's eyes told me that he'd experienced pain, deep pain that had been with him a long time. I recognized the look. I saw it on my face whenever I looked in the mirror. This guy was for real. And if he wasn't, I'd wind up dead anyway. He was our only hope.

Although it felt awkward, I did as instructed, starting with the letter from Botswana some ten years ago, finishing with Jon's involvement with the Russian missile silos, his mistress, and baby. McGrath filled in the gaps. I felt like we talked for hours, periodically calling for drink refills. Lucas never looked up. He recorded copious notes on a pad of paper while keeping his gaze fixed on the computer screen. I guessed he didn't want this information on his hard drive.

After an hour, we stopped talking. McGrath and I both felt fairly satisfied that we'd imparted as much information as we knew.

Lucas nodded when we finished and then spoke quietly as he looked straight ahead.

"While I'm not at liberty to tell you who I work for, I can tell you that Jon and I met a few years back. I have the advantage of knowing a lot about this case. I have contacts in both Japan and the U.S. I want to help you."

This man knew my husband. He knew about "the case". Which case? My case? Jon's Russian missile silos? Both of them? Focus, I told myself. He'd said he'd help us.

I hadn't even realized I'd been holding my breath. But when I exhaled, it felt as if I'd been storing a week's worth of oxygen in my lungs. Along with that exhalation came a huge sense of relief. Whether well-founded or not, I couldn't be sure. But my gut felt good about this guy, and I needed to trust my gut.

I glanced in his direction. When he didn't look my way, I remembered the gravity of our situation and averted my gaze.

"I have your phone number," he said. "I'll be in contact tomorrow morning. We'll find a safe house for you until we can secure passports and fly you out of the country."

"I don't know how to thank you," I said.

"Don't thank me yet," Sweeney said. "I'll get you out of Japan, but I have limited assets here. Considering the magnitude of this affair, it will be tricky assuring you safe travel and arrival back in the States. Once you return there, you may still be in danger."

I squeezed shut my eyes, feeling relieved, terrified, and sad at the same time. Not only would McGrath and I require protection for the remainder of our stay in Japan, safe return home would be negligible, and our lives and my kid's lives would still be in danger once we arrived stateside.

What I knew of witness protection programs danced in my head. How could this be happening? There must be another way. I feared for mine and McGrath's lives, but even more for my children's and Ed's lives.

Anger welled inside of me. How could Jon have done this to us? In that moment, I felt hate for my dead husband for the first time in my life. Not disappointment. Not anger. Not rage. Hate. God damn my very dead husband.

Lost in thought, I practically cringed when McGrath reached out to touch me. I blinked and brought him into focus. He was friend, not foe. When I squeezed shut my eyes for another long moment and attempted to regain my bearings, he spoke my name.

"Sam. You okay?" he asked.

I glanced at the table where Lucas had been seated. He'd disappeared while I struggled to fight my way back from the shock and hatred.

"Past pissed." I shook my head, cleared my throat, and pushed myself up from my chair. "Do you think there's any chance we'll live through the night?"

"Not really," McGrath said. "But let's give it a shot."

I bordered on hysteria for a few seconds longer and then spoke sternly to myself. Get your shit together, woman. You've got five kids at home. They're depending on you.

McGrath grasped my hand and led me out of the shop. His arm circled my shoulder as he guided me to the elevator. We rode to the lobby floor, stepped off, and headed for the Zenith Sky Lounge where he secured a table near a window which looked out over the city. Bright lights illuminated the now dark metropolis. A live band played jazz in the background—a taste of Americana for those travelers thousands of miles from home.

McGrath ordered a nightcap and brought his chair up next to mine.

I sat, frozen in disbelief.

"There's nothing more to be done tonight," he said. "We'll be alright. Lucas already has people watching us."

"Great. MORE people watching us." Yet, I knew it had to be a good thing. "You think we can trust him?"

"I've been around a lot of bad guys and good guys. I can never be 100% sure, but my gut says this guy's alright."

I struggled to relax, to take in McGrath's words, and to let go of my fury.

I lifted my Bailey's to my lips and sipped. "Lucas said he couldn't tell us who he works for," I said. "Does that make sense?"

"Total sense. He can't blow his cover." McGrath leaned forward in his chair. "Here's my thinking. It wouldn't surprise me if the CIA planted a guy in the State Department, or even within Japanese Intelligence. That way, the guy can be assigned an embassy job, and perform that role while fulfilling a covert mission on behalf of the CIA," McGrath said. "But he'll never admit it."

"He could have shown us some kind of ID. Hell, he could have shown us a fake ID and we would have bought it."

"Yes," McGrath said, nodding his head. He sat back in his chair and sighed. "I'm more comfortable that he didn't.

I nodded.

"I know it feels impossible," he said. "Try to let it go."

I agreed, then slowed my respiration. McGrath was right. I clamored for control over a situation much bigger and far more dangerous than anything I'd encountered in my entire lifetime. I needed to allow him, and Lucas, and whomever else I could find and hold onto, to help me. It would pose a terrific challenge, letting others pave my way. I found it hard to trust when I felt so hurt and violated by a man in whom I'd put all of my faith.

Jon.

Maybe one day I'd be able to forgive him. To understand what he'd done and why. Not tonight. Or tomorrow.

CHAPTER THIRTY-FOUR

I LET MCGRATH take care of me. Escort me to the room after I'd had a bit too much to drink. Undress me. Have his way with me.

I lost myself in him that night, and gave myself to him in ways that I'd never done with another man. Maybe it was the fact that our lives were hanging in the balance. Maybe it was the alcohol. Maybe it was that I was scared out of my wits and desperate to be closer to another human being than I'd ever been in my life. I just know, in the instant when we joined our bodies, our souls became entwined like the threads of the finest woven silk. Beautifully perfect. Magnificently strong. Blessedly shielding.

I said prayers before falling asleep, begging God to keep my father–in–law and children safe until I saw them again. I prayed that we'd live to see another day. And I prayed that if we survived, McGrath's and my love would endure this crisis and chaos.

I slept fitfully, trapped in bizarre dreams of being lost in an underground world, falling down an elevator shaft, being chased through the jungle. Somehow, I incorporated the ringing of the phone into my dream, searching for my phone in the brush. McGrath had to shake me for a full ten seconds to wake me.

"What?" I asked. "What is it?"

"Your phone," he said as he handed it to me.

"Hello?" Still groggy and unsure of time and place, I heard Lizzie's voice on the line and bolted upright. "Mommy?"

"Hi, Sweetie," I said. "How's my girl?"

"I miss you, Mommy. I wish you were coming home soon."

"It won't be long now," I lied. I had no idea how long it would be, but I closed my eyes and hoped beyond hope that I'd see all of my kids soon. My heart felt as if it was being clutched from my chest. "What's new?" I asked, hoping to distract her.

Within a minute, her voice grounded me. I spoke to each of my children for as long as they liked. It didn't seem important to worry about things like international minute overages any longer. It just felt damned good to be rooted in my family and all the goodness they represented.

After I ended the call, I kissed a sleeping McGrath, got up from the bed, and sat in the dark. My life had taken me to such unexpected places. I recalled marrying Jon some twelve years ago. How we'd planned our wedding around the kids' naps. Nick had snored so loudly throughout the ceremony, our guests clutched their stomachs to control their laughter. I remembered sweet Lizzie's birth and how it had cemented our brand new family. Once Jon and I had loved each other, brought out the best in each other, were better together than apart. We'd built a strong foundation for our kids. That foundation still existed. Maybe in spite of him right now. But it still existed. I needed to hold on to that with all my might.

I climbed back into bed and spooned up next to McGrath and counted my blessings. This man loved me in spite of the fact that I still wrestled with my past. He threw his arm over me. I let myself relax into his warmth, matched my breathing to his, and fell back to sleep. Somehow, someway, this would all work out. It had to.

* * *

The sun awakened us early. We showered and made small talk, pretending to embark on a normal day, not one full of fear and uncertainty. Without words, we packed our bags and moved about the room, checking drawers and closets for forgotten items. McGrath brewed coffee with the machine in the room. Running down to the lobby for coffee seemed out of the question. We were both too frightened to leave one another alone, even for a few minutes.

We sat and waited. Sipping our tasteless coffee helped a little. In truth, patience had flown out the window as soon as we'd zipped our bags shut, but we had no choice but to wait for further instructions from Lucas. He said he'd call in the morning. It was morning. McGrath and I locked eyes and shook our heads, the wait interminable. What was taking Sweeney so long?

I suddenly panicked. If our room had been bugged as we suspected, it could prove risky to accept the call. I reminded myself we could offer short answers and receive instructions, but had to be careful not to say anything incriminating aloud. My heart thrummed. I prayed I wouldn't unravel under the pressure.

McGrath must have read the look of terror on my face. He reached out and patted my knee. I welcomed his touch, but couldn't manage to relax. Two seconds later, he reached inside his pocket and pulled out the vibrating cell phone he'd purchased. He nodded in my direction and held up the text display, which said, "Go downstairs in five minutes and wait for my call."

In that moment, I could have slapped myself. Lucas really was a professional. He knew what he was doing. I snatched a pair of earphones from my luggage then gestured to McGrath. We stood silently and left the room.

Once we were outside, I took a steadying breath. "Ready?" I asked.

McGrath patted his waistband, where he'd holstered his recently acquired gun, and grinned, a serious intensity in his eyes that I'd only witnessed once before—after I'd shot Stitsill's lackey.

It felt unreal, as if we were Bonnie and Clyde. Or as if I were Julia Stiles following close on Matt Damon's heels in the Bourne Supremacy. I did what any other hunted woman would do. I put one foot in front of the other and trailed McGrath. We rode the elevator to the lobby.

After we located an empty loveseat in the expansive corridor, I plugged the earphones into the cell phone so we could listen to Lucas' instructions simultaneously. I figured that between the two of us, we could keep his directions straight. I nearly jumped out of my skin when the phone vibrated in my hand. McGrath inserted an ear bud into his ear, gesturing for me to do the same. He rested a calming hand on my knee as he answered the call.

"Hello, McGrath," Lucas said.

"Sam's on the line, too," McGrath said.

"Let me explain a few things before we get started," Lucas continued. "Mr. Drummond, the man you know as Stitsill, is a free agent who's worked for any number of governments, including ours, carrying out the dirty jobs. He's into a lot of other stuff, too. Thanks in part to your husband, Sam, I've been on to him for a while now."

"Alright," I said. Considering Stitsill's contacts in Canada, Botswana, Mexico, the States, and Japan, along with all of the fake passports McGrath and I had discovered in the lock box Rosie had sent to me, it made perfect sense.

"I'm aware of many of his connections. In light of that, it's unadvisable to use normal channels to get you out of the country. We'll do our best to throw Stitsill off track."

I swallowed hard.

"First, catch the JR train to Maibara, but disguise yourselves. I'll put out a team or two of look–a–likes, but you still need to be extremely careful."

"I've hired a driver," McGrath offered. "I'll have him take us on a short sight–seeing trip. That way we can spot a tail if there is one."

"No," Lucas said. "I'll have your driver pick up one of the decoy teams. You get to the Shinkansan station entrance. Before you go, buy new bags and some clothing unlike what you usually wear. Stick your hair under a cap, Sam. Then, head out the rear exit of the hotel, behind the basement shopping area and into the parking garage. A cab will pick you up there. The driver will carry a sign that says "Smith". When you reach the JR Shinkansan station entrance, go to the ticket office. There will be a package of tickets waiting for you. Board the 12:16 p.m. bullet train to the Shin–Osaka station. From there, change trains to the regular JR and travel north to the city of Maibara. A ticket for that train will also be included in the envelope. The trains run every thirty minutes."

McGrath jotted notes furiously. "I have cash," he said. "No paper trail."

My feet felt as if they'd been planted in wet cement. No way. I couldn't do this. I kicked myself in the pants. Listen. Follow directions. Move.

I looked to McGrath for strength. He nodded at me as he jotted more notes in his pocket spiral. Thank God for McGrath and his foresight. I'd brought the earphones. He'd brought brains and everything else we needed.

Lucas continued. "Do not check out of the hotel. Your doubles will take it from there. The agents at the ticket booths speak English. Pick up the tickets for the Smith party. Board the train. When you arrive in Maibara, come out of the platform exit. Straight ahead, you'll spot the west exit out of the terminal. Go through it. You'll see a parking structure directly across the street. Ride the elevator to the third floor. A white Corolla with tinted windows will be parked to your right as you exit the elevator. The keys will be in the ignition. When you start the vehicle, you'll find the GPS has been preset for your destination."

"Got it," McGrath said. He reached over and squeezed my hand, offering me a faint smile.

"You'll drive from Maibara to Fukui. Do you feel equipped to drive?"

McGrath answered with a confident yes. I had my doubts.

Sweeney continued. "Fukui is an isolated resort village in the Fukui Prefecture. The inn was once used as a safe house. We no longer use it, but it will be the perfect spot for you now. There are only six guest rooms. It sits on the top of a cliff. Very remote. Very safe. The owner, Momoko Suzuki, is someone I trust, and she will be at your service. She speaks limited English, but do not be shy. Tell her what you need in terms of food and housekeeping as you would when you stay at any hotel. She's accustomed to American guests."

"How long will the drive take?" McGrath asked.

I immediately began to consider food. Guess it's the mom in me. In my world, car trips meant hunger and boredom. We'd need snacks and scheduled pit stops. Hopefully, McGrath had some experience driving on the wrong side of the road, because all I could picture if I were at the wheel was my vomit splattered on the pavement, or splashed on the windshield, or pooled in my lap. Especially if we'd be expected to negotiate narrow mountain roads like the one Jon had driven when he'd been killed.

Lucas said, "Plan on three hours. It's slow through the mountains."

I sighed. No need to panic about food. Nevertheless, with five kids, I'd learned to plan for every eventuality. I'd grab some sandwiches, Cokes and candy bars from the hotel snack shop before we left. Between the train and the car ride, we'd require sustenance. And I required control over something.

"Any questions?" Lucas asked.

"No," McGrath said. "But we can call if we run into a problem, right?"

"You can try, but I can't guarantee phone service once you're in the mountains. If you think of something, call me before you leave Maibara. Be alert for a tail, or for Stitsill. My guess is that this matter has become personal for him. From what you've told me, he will view you as a threat. You know too much. He probably won't send a hired hand this time. He'll most likely want to take care of you himself so the job's done right. It's what I'd do."

Goosebumps rose on my flesh. I began nodding involuntarily, as if reassuring myself I could see this through. Don't think, I told myself. Just do.

"Once you arrive at the inn, hang tight. I'll be delivering appropriate documentation along with airline tickets so that you may safely return to the States. In the meantime, I'll also try to fix it with Stitsill so that he no longer poses a threat to you."

I wasn't sure exactly what Lucas meant by that, but I felt fairly sure I didn't want or need to know. I just wanted Stitsill out of my life. Once and for all.

I managed a quick 'thank you' before McGrath clicked off the cell. I removed the ear bud and tried to quell the knots in my stomach. McGrath drew close and held on.

"It's okay, Sam," he said. "Everything's going to be alright."

No other choice but to believe him.

CHAPTER THIRTY-FIVE

I BOUGHT SOME sweats, a ball cap and a collapsible duffle, blended in with more souvenirs for the kids, then ran upstairs. I shoved my hair under the cap, donned the sloppy sweats and a pair of flip–flops, then packed my other belongings inside the bag. I glanced in the mirror. While my disguise might not throw off a tail, it threw me off. McGrath dressed in a t-shirt, jeans and some athletic shoes and stuffed his blazer and his other items inside a bag he'd purchased. He slipped into the bathroom a few minutes later. I heard his electric razor buzz, and when he stepped out I clamped my hand over my mouth. His head was bare.

I had a momentary desire to see our doubles. Where did they find two Caucasians in Japan? But then I quashed it. Not my problem.

Whether our feeble attempt at disguises would work or not, we headed downstairs with our bags and out the rear basement exit. We spotted our driver right away.

As he pulled out of the garage, I thought about Toshi, and wished I'd had the chance to say goodbye. I'd grown fond of him. I looked back at the Marriot with sadness. All told, my dead husband had spent several years at this place. It felt like another goodbye.

When we arrived at the station, we grabbed our bags and headed inside. It all seemed so surreal, and every time

I glanced at McGrath, I did a double-take. His bald head would take some getting used to.

I stared at the arriving train, which reminded me of a duck-billed platypus. Sporting a long nose, its headlights resembled nostrils. I followed McGrath to the ticket office, kept my head down and my sunglasses plastered to my face while he collected the ticket envelope. Hard to appear invisible when you're the only Caucasians in the terminal.

McGrath's voice broke my thoughts. "We've got a Green Car seat."

"Sorry?" I stared at him, perplexed.

"See the car with the cloverleaf?" He pointed to my left.

I nodded.

"It's first class. Sweeney must have decided it would be safer."

"We can only hope." I followed McGrath to our reserved seats.

"We've got a ninety minute ride ahead of us," McGrath reported.

I nodded, trying to convince myself we'd be safe for that time, nestled into this comfortable first class car. At least I'd die in style. I settled in and let my eyes drift to the passing landscape. My gaze settled on the rows and rows of bicycles parked near the track. We passed a few miles of small homes cramped together, almost like traveling through a Lego town, electricity towers rising above them into feathery grey clouds. It struck me as odd. There were few trees or other vegetation in the areas where the people lived, and I was momentarily stabbed with a pang of longing for my peaceful front porch and my serenely statuesque oak trees with their canopies of protective leaves.

The further we traveled from the city, the more mountainous and beautiful the scenery became. I rested my head on McGrath's shoulder and his sideways glance and his ease as he shifted so that my head naturally curved into the hollow between his neck and shoulder spoke volumes.

It all seemed out of body. What had I gotten us into? Would I have been safer had I stayed in the States and left well enough alone? How would what I'd learned about my husband and our marriage bring me closure?

A sudden wave of nausea rolled over me that couldn't be attributed to the train's 170mph speed. I rifled a banana from the food bag and ate it.

"You okay?" McGrath asked.

I nodded, wound my banana peel around itself and deposited it back into the bag.

He patted my knee. "Everything's going to work out. I promise."

I settled into him once again and focused on the passing mountains. I'm always struck by the fact that tranquility holds hands with chaos. My life hung in the balance and yet here I was, traveling in a majestic foreign country with the man I loved. The man who loved me more than life itself. How could these totally polar opposite events occur simultaneously?

McGrath must have been reading my thoughts. "This will all be in the past someday," he said. Then he leaned over and kissed my temple, squeezed my hand, and offered me all the reassurance I needed.

"I love you," he added.

"I love you, too." I managed a smile.

"Where should we get married?" he asked.

My heart fluttered. "Married?" I asked. "Is that a proposal?"

McGrath turned in his seat and faced me. He smiled. As his dimples creased his cheeks, it made his eyes twinkle. Heaven sat behind those eyes, and I grinned back at him.

"That came from somewhere deep." He laughed. "I have plans for a grand gesture. You know, getting down on one knee and all. Presenting you with a velvet covered box, satin-lined and holding a large stone on a platinum band inside. All of it. You deserve that, and so much more."

"Nice job distracting me from the threat of dying and all." I bracketed his strong face with my hands and planted a huge kiss on his lips. "You're my light," I said. "It seems like forever since life was easy. Then again, it's never been easy for the two of us."

"C'mon now. I seem to remember some pretty special moments in the not so distant past."

"You're right, I suppose. But wouldn't it be cool to have a normal life? Like other people. You know, coffee on the front porch in the morning. Quick kisses goodbye as we run off to work. Suggestive text messages. Dinner on the deck."

McGrath laughed. "You are dreaming. Have you forgotten your five kids?"

I laughed, too. "No, I haven't forgotten." I frowned then, worried that the kids would be an issue for him. "If you're proposing, you must be thinking you can adapt to a large family. How would that work?"

"Stop worrying. We'll sort out the details later."

I kissed him then, long and hard.

"Is there a sleeping berth on this train?" he joked.

"I wish." I weaved my fingers with his and gazed out the window, pointing at a lake off in the distance. "Look, beauty is all around us."

McGrath looked from the lake back to me. "Beauty is looking at me right now."

"Aw, shucks." I smiled at him and my heart tripped to a new and contented rhythm. It seemed odd to think of a future right now. But I wanted one with this man. I'd do whatever it took to make it happen.

* * *

Thirty minutes later, the train pulled into the Shin–Osaka station. I immediately panicked. Would I remember to collect all of my belongings? Would we find our way? I'd become a head case. McGrath erased my jitters by ushering me off the train and over to our connecting rail, the local JR to Maibara. Again, he impressed me with his confidence and skill. When you're in a pickle, I thought, it's good to enlist a cop as a traveling companion.

I peered through the car windows of the JR train as we walked. Much different from the Shinkansen locomotive we had just debarked, it appeared to be more like a commuter train back home, its seats lining the windows like the Amtrack. Evidently, we weren't boarding one of those cars though. Somehow, McGrath knew enough to lead me to the car where our reserved seats were located. Not nearly as plush as the Shinkansen, but comfortable enough.

We arranged our bags and took our seats. Compared to our previous train, this one poked along at a mere 60 miles per hour. And unlike the four stops the Shinkansen had made, we seemed to stop at every little town along the way. There were no announcements at the stops, and I freaked out when I noticed the signs were only in Japanese. I asked a fellow passenger how far to the Maibara stop, and she held up seven fingers. Seven more stops. While McGrath and I ate lunch, we joked about being the only two Caucasians in the entire country. If we didn't stick out like sore thumbs, I didn't know who did. So much for disguises.

I briefly wondered how our lack of anonymity would affect our stay in Fukui, pleading with God to grant us safe travel back to the States. Even though Sweeney said we'd be safe there, could he really be sure? What if the proprietor told someone we were visiting? He'd said the place had been a safe house years ago. Was it still safe? I knew it wouldn't serve any useful purpose for me to dwell on plaguing thoughts like living till tomorrow, or living long enough to see my kids again, or living long enough to live happily ever after with McGrath, but the thoughts crept in just the same.

I reminded myself to stay alert, counting each stop. When

the seventh stop occurred, I asked the same passenger again, and she nodded, indicating we'd arrived.

By the time we stepped off the train in Maibara, I felt somewhat calmer owing to the momentary dream of a future. I helped McGrath with the luggage. We followed Lucas' instructions, heading to the west exit and locating the parking structure just across the street. I noticed McGrath glancing over his shoulder. He seemed satisfied we weren't being tailed. That bothered me a little, because I remembered that Lucas had said he'd have someone keeping an eye on us. I didn't see any sign of anyone who looked like a bodyguard, which spiked my alarm, but I guessed I needed to trust that Lucas had dependable allies capable enough to keep us out of harm's way and not sell us to the highest bidder.

McGrath and I rode the elevator to the third floor. We discovered the White Corolla parked exactly where Lucas had indicated. As he'd specified, we found keys in the ignition. We loaded the luggage into the trunk and drove to the car elevator where we were transported to ground level. I'd never ridden on a car lift before, and I was briefly entertained, like a kid on an amusement park ride. McGrath fired up the GPS as we left the structure. We were directed, in English, out of town and onto a narrow two lane highway, barely wide enough for two vehicles. I could hear my late husband's voice, "The roads were built eight hundred years ago. Wide enough for carts, not cars." I wondered if I'd hear his voice on each leg of this trip.

As we'd been advised, the GPS indicated our arrival time would be approximately three hours from now. Before leaving Maibara, McGrath negotiated a stop at yet another McDonald's. We used the facilities, purchased two Big Macs and large drinks.

Rows of houses appeared along the flats during the first hour of our trip. McGrath's knuckles turned an unnatural shade of white, and he'd slowed his speed to twenty miles an hour. We didn't speak, fearful that even a scrap of conversation would break his concentration.

Then, we began to ascend the mountains. The flats had been a dream compared to this. McGrath had been drifting over to the right far before we hit this steep road, but his control wavered even more as we climbed. No shoulders. No bail outs. Only mistakes. Add heavy traffic to the mix and he forced breath out through his teeth, practically hyperventilating, his eyes becoming mere slits as he attempted to negotiate the slender track of pavement.

I attempted looking out the window. If I hadn't been gripping the roll bar for dear life, leaning toward the center of the vehicle for some sense of false security, and fighting the urge to scream, I might have noticed the beautiful scenery. Instead, I closed my eyes and prayed. If Stitsill didn't kill us, this drive might.

I thought about how beautiful driving through tunnels, winding on curved roads surrounded by spectacular mountains and blue skies, and in and out of cozy hillside villages would be if one knew how to drive in Japan. But their splendor stood in striking contrast to razor–sharp bends in the highway. Four foot mirrors had been placed roadside to warn of approaching vehicles. I swallowed hard. This was like the road Jon had died on, and the Jon I knew would never have driven on a mountain road like this. He'd told me countless times how it scared the wits out of him just thinking about it. Jon didn't frighten easily. But when he did, he'd avoid revisiting the event like a visit to the dentist. Now that I knew about the missile silos and his involvement, I was pretty sure that his "accident" had been a homicide. I tossed around scenarios. Someone had forced him behind the wheel. Lured him into driving. What would have been incentive enough? I couldn't imagine. I recalled the accident scene. Jon had been driving on the left. He'd had to have crossed the road to drive off the cliff. Why hadn't that thought occurred to me until now? What distracted him? Could it really have just been an accident? I stopped breathing for a full sixty seconds, struggling to keep down my lunch.

The sound of a blaring horn startled me from the shock. Then, the sharp jerk of the car, and a muttered foul word from McGrath.

I inhaled sharply to stifle a scream, relaxed momentarily when McGrath managed to position the car in the center of the narrow lane, then glanced at the GPS. We had another two and a half hours ahead of us. How we would arrive at our destination in one piece, I hadn't a clue.

It seemed advisable to keep my eyes open and try to coach McGrath, somehow help him. I glanced behind us. A black town car followed a quarter mile back. I'd noticed the same vehicle earlier. It could be Sweeney's assigned chaperone. It could be our enemy. It could be no one. Nothing to be done about it now.

McGrath jerked the wheel again. His erratic driving prompted my stomach's contents to flip. Jon had told me that the inclination to stay to the right side of the road was instinctual. Obviously, McGrath had discovered the same to be true. Plus the fact that every two hundred yards or so, a new switchback appeared. Even though a steel guardrail sat to my left, it didn't seem like much protection next to the sheer cliff it separated us from. I gripped the side of my seat with both hands, terrified, and closed my eyes again.

McGrath slowed his speed, sputtering one foul word after the other. Horns continued to blare. He'd drifted over again, no doubt.

I opened my eyes to check, looked at McGrath, focused on the road in front of him, and turned my thoughts back to assisting him and offering support as he drove.

"Nice driving," I whispered.

He sighed. "Shit," he said. "I'm going to need a stiff drink once we reach Fukui."

I patted his knee and smiled. "You're doing great."

"Thanks," he said, his eyes plastered on the asphalt in front of him. He approached a small town and made a left hand turn. Problem was, he reflexively veered into the right hand lane as he completed the turn, and headed directly into oncoming traffic.

"Damn it!" he muttered amidst blaring horns, and pulled the wheel sharp.

We drove in silence for the next hour or so. I popped open a can of soda and handed it to McGrath. He plucked the drink from my hand without allowing his eyes to leave the road, took a sip and handed it back to me. I was in a fix. I didn't want to distract him by talking, didn't want to turn on the radio, couldn't look over the edge of the cliff at the scenery, and couldn't allow my thoughts to wander. So, I opened a Milky Way bar instead and munched on that. Every so often, I broke off a bite and popped it into McGrath's mouth. Luckily, it made him smile and I felt useful again. Any port in a storm.

CHAPTER THIRTY-SIX

A FTER WHAT FELT like an eternity, we finally descended the mountains into the most breathtaking view. We arrived in the postage stamp–sized town of Fukui close to dinnertime. McGrath drove slowly through town. The seashore appeared directly in front of us, waves crashing on the shore, and water the color of sparkling sapphires, the deepest blue I had ever seen. Mountains of volcanic rock grew up around us, cliffs jutting out over the sea. Fishing boats dotted the seascape, and men rode bicycles with fishing poles strapped to their backs.

McGrath glanced at the navi and announced, "Two more miles," and wound the car around another twisted curve as we ascended the mountains once again. Spectacular.

Finally, McGrath pulled into a squat driveway and parked. Directly in front of us was a quaint building, built to resemble a small temple with a front canopy over the doorway, a simple and delicate sculpture. I helped him hoist the bags from the trunk and drank in our surroundings, all the while glancing over my shoulder. It had been over an hour since I'd spotted the car which had seemed to be tailing us through the mountains. No sign of it. I sighed in relief, and then reminded myself this might be the false sense of calm before disaster struck.

I turned toward the inn then, nestled amongst towering trees and surrounded by beautiful grounds and the gardens which provided a verdant blanket. A sweet fragrance filled the air — jasmine — and I heard the sound of trickling water. I spotted a small fountain running over some rocks. The sound soothed and cradled me. Again, I accepted the fleeting peace.

As I entered the lobby, I swiveled around to view a small reception desk which stood to our right. A desk bell sat on its counter. As we got our bearings, I rang the bell, telling the jitters in my stomach to still, and waited silently with McGrath for Momoko-san to appear.

She entered through a beaded curtain from behind the reception desk, a tiny woman with petite features to match. Wearing a traditional kimono, brightly colored in shades of teals and emerald green and belted with a contrasting cherry sash, she wore her gray hair pulled into a tight bun. Her lips turned up in the gentlest of grins, and she bowed slightly.

"Momoko-san," McGrath said as he returned her bow. "It's a pleasure to meet you."

"Smith-san," she answered simply.

I recalled Lucas using the name for our tickets at the railway station, and assumed he gave her that name as well. Hereby, McGrath and I would be known as Mr. and Mrs. Smith. Momoko-san stepped around the desk and began to recite instructions in Japanese.

"I'm not hearing much English." I smiled and said to McGrath.

She then nodded and gestured us over to a mat where several pairs of slippers sat neatly arranged. When we looked confused, she pulled two pair from the row and motioned for us to remove our shoes and don the odd footwear. The sandals were slip-ons, wooden shoes with the strangest sole I had ever seen. Triangular in shape, I rocked back and forth after sliding my foot inside. My balance wavered. These shoes were accidents waiting to happen. I struggled to follow Momoko-san as I dragged along my bag. McGrath looked even more flummoxed. The shoes were way too short for his feet, and he grabbed my arm to keep from tumbling head over heels. Somehow, we made it across the linoleum floor to the narrow staircase where Momoko–san indicated that we remove the shoes and assume a different pair, evidently made to wear on the carpet. Great. I had to worry about my stupid shoes in the midst of trying to stay alive.

It suddenly occurred to me that we must be in a Ryoken. Jon had stayed in one of these houses once on a side trip. He had told me that Ryoken's were traditional Japanese inns with legendary hospitality, supposedly rich in the culture of the country. Perfect.

McGrath looked relieved to lose the rocking shoes, and he donned the new slippers with a sigh of relief. In spite of myself, I squelched a chuckle. Momoko–san pointed out the kitchen and dining room to our left, and a small business office with a desk and computer, all the while yammering in Japanese. The rooms were exquisitely ordered and clean. In the dining room, I noticed the traditional low table and cushions. Without allowing us time to wander, Momoko then led us up the stairs. McGrath fought to manage the suitcases on the narrow staircase.

Once we arrived upstairs, she pointed to a sliding door. I slid open the paper–thin entry. She put her hand out to stop me, directing me to remove my shoes once again. Then, she leaned down after I removed them and placed them onto another mat which sat outside the door. Next, she gestured me inside the room. The floor was covered with a tatami mat and I remembered Jon had shared with me that these floors were only meant to be walked on in stocking feet. I stopped, unzipped the front of my bag and pulled out a pair of white running socks, placed them on my feet, then entered the room. McGrath followed my lead a few moments later. Between the two of us, I hoped we'd be able to remember which foot coverings to wear and when to wear them.

I whispered to McGrath, "This seems impossible."

"Enjoy your final days," McGrath advised.

"Funny."

Two twin futons or sleeping quilts were arranged on the floor with a low table between them. McGrath set our luggage inside where Momoko-san instructed, and then she continued to jabber, leading us back into the hall and directing us to open another door. Inside sat a porcelain pit, one of those traditional toilets we had avoided in our travels since it required a squat and straddle approach along with an extremely accurate aim. It was also wedged in so tightly between the four tiny walls, I could scarcely imagine McGrath fitting inside with his wide shoulders. Sort of like sticking the Jolly Green Giant inside a phone booth.

A surprised expression clouded his face, and I patted his arm. Together, we'd figure this out. Everything happens for a reason. Make lemonade.

Next, Momoko-san handed us each a white robe. Jon had mentioned these housecoats years ago, along with the fact that they were hardly long enough to cover his family jewels.

I smiled at all 6'4" of McGrath, sure that he had no idea of the look he'd be sporting soon. "I can't wait to see you in your robe," I teased. He pinched my behind and I jumped. "Behave yourself," I added. "Mama-san is watching."

"Bath," Momoto-san said, leading us down the hall to the rear of the building. She opened a sliding door to reveal a magnificent view of volcanic mountains, seashore and clear blue skies. Once we stepped outside, we realized our inn rested on a hundred foot cliff, its terrace dangling out over the sea. On either side of it were sheer drop-offs, then other peninsulas like ours, poking out into the water. Inns such as ours sat on each cliff, extending above the raging waters far below. To the right of the terrace, a pool, or hot spring, lay fenced in by a lava outcropping. Mama-san used her own sign language to let me know we were to remove our clothing and wash inside the wooden closet, which was equipped with a short stool, a hand-held shower, and soap.

I tried to keep my eyes from popping out of my head, then gestured to her that Mr. Smith and I would return after we had changed into our robes. With no idea whether she'd be standing guard or not, I wanted to be sure to cover myself and somehow insist on privacy for McGrath and me.

"C'mon," I whispered to McGrath. "Let's go change."

McGrath looked uneasy. He shot Momoko-san a sideways glance, like she'd somehow lost her mind.

"Adventure," I recommended. "Think adventure."

McGrath inched close to me and whispered, "Weird."

I shoved his robe at him. "Trust me, it's going to get weirder. But as angry as I am at Jon, I have to thank him now. I understand where we are and what the procedure is because of his stories. Let's make it fun, because it's certainly going to be different."

"How so?"

"It's traditional to bathe before dinner. According to Jon's report of a trip to a similar inn, one must change into their very skimpy robe, go to the public bath, bathe in the nude, and dry off with a towel the size of a washcloth. Thankfully, we have a private bath."

"Wait a minute," McGrath said. "That bath is a hot spring, right?"

"Yep," I answered. "About 120 degrees. I say in and out. It's going to be scorching."

"Can we bring wine?"

"I think we can bring whatever we want. Other than Mama-san, we have the place to ourselves."

"Not exactly, Sam." McGrath shook his head and frowned.

I panicked. Not alone? Holy crap. We had been followed.

"I spotted someone on the roof of the neighboring inn. It's probably one of Lucas' guys."

"Wait," I said, "what's he look like? How do we know

he's one of the good guys?"

"Cuz he didn't shoot us. Think about it. Stitsill isn't going to wait for just the right moment. The guy kills for a living. He has no conscience. If it was him or one of his minions, we'd be goners by now."

"Lucas said he'd have someone keep an eye on us." My eyes darted from rooftop to rooftop. "I'm freaking out now. We need a plan."

McGrath led me inside, up the stairs, and into our room. "I've put your gun inside this bag. Keep it with you at all times. You know how to use it." McGrath pointed to a small tote bag.

I lifted a few items from my suitcase, then stuffed my book and magazines on top so I could use it like a beach bag. "Where's your gun?" I asked.

McGrath patted his waist, wrapped his arms around me and pulled me close. "Relax. Our job is to act like a married couple. Mr. and Mrs. Smith, remember? Lucas will take care of the rest." He nuzzled my neck.

"Seriously, Detective. I wish I could pretend we were on vacation and make wild, passionate love with you, but I can hardly breathe right now. Practice patience, would you?" I pushed him away, slipped off my blouse and slacks, and slid on my robe.

"I lack that virtue," McGrath teased.

"Put on your robe. I'm not sure how much time we have until dinner, and you're going to want to change before we eat. If you sit Indian style on the floor cushion, you're going to give Mama-san a free show."

"Yes, ma'am." He saluted for good measure.

McGrath shed his clothes and donned his robe. He'd stopped to grab a bottle of wine, glasses and a corkscrew, but managed to stay right on my tail in spite of his mission.

When we arrived outside, we discovered Momoko-san had disappeared. We walked along the path to the patio, then over to the edge of the hot spring pool. As I'd guessed,

Momoko–san had left us two washcloths, no towels. Before I removed my robe, I looked to the roof of the nearby inn, checking for our bodyguard. Maybe he was on a dinner break, or he felt we were safe enough that he didn't need to be watchful 24–7.

I slipped my robe off my shoulders, dipped my toe into the steaming hot water, eased myself along the edge of the pool and sank into its heat. The water startlingly hot, it took a moment or two to adjust to the temperature. When I turned to look at McGrath, I saw that he too had checked for our sentry before removing his robe. He handed me a glass of red wine.

"I've decided to follow orders," he said. "But that won't keep me from sharing my desires. If I could, I'd seduce you right now. Skinny dipping sex holds a ton of appeal. Once this is over, it's going on our bucket list."

I offered him a wary smile and nodded. "You got it."

CHAPTER THIRTY-SEVEN

AFTER A MEAL of snow crab, delectable vegetables and steamed rice, McGrath and I wandered down the path to the edge of the cliff to watch the sunset. It was a clear evening, warm but not hot, and the sound of the waves crashing below us provided the strains of a lullaby. Still, I couldn't shake the chills. We pulled together two wooden chairs on the stone patio, clinked glasses, and held hands.

"I can't wait to marry you," I said, a sudden rush of emotion gripping me. "We have to survive this mess."

"We will." McGrath lifted my hand to his lips and kissed it.

My brain took an abrupt detour, and I frowned at him. "So," I said, "how do you think this is all going to go down?"

McGrath locked eyes with mine. "Take the night off."

"I'm trying, but it feels impossible."

McGrath nodded.

"I might be having a mini-meltdown." A tear slipped down my cheek.

McGrath turned to me, set aside our glasses, and took both of my hands. "Tell me," he said.

"I don't know how to say this." I hesitated.

"Just say it," McGrath said, his gaze telling me it would be okay.

"As you've noticed, I've thought about Jon a fair amount on this trip. I feel awful. I'm not being fair to you."

McGrath grasped my hand. "I snapped at you earlier and I'm sorry. It's been hard living in Jon's shadow on this trip. Hell, I feel like I'm competing with a ghost. A ghost we now know let you down. I'm jealous, and I'm angry with him for what he did to you. You didn't deserve that."

I nodded.

McGrath drew in a deep breath. "This trip has been about finding the truth. About helping you gain closure. I want you to be able to move on. With me. I understand you and Jon shared a good life, and that you have fond memories. I want you to hold onto them. I want you to take the time you need to finish grieving for him. Share your thoughts with me or not. But please don't shut me out or turn me away. That year we were apart was sheer agony for me. I never want to be without you again."

"It's unfair of me…to be grieving for my husband when we're together."

"Wouldn't it be nice if life were that simple?"

"I hate life sometimes. It's too damned difficult."

McGrath's smile said it all. "I've got baggage too. It'll come up from time to time." He squeezed my hand. "But we'll go through life together. All of what came before brought us to where we are now. It's all good, kiddo."

I climbed into McGrath's lap and tucked my face into his shoulder. "Thank you," I said.

"For what?" he asked.

"For loving me. For taking care of me."

With a dimpled smile, he said, "It's my pleasure."

CHAPTER THIRTY-EIGHT

I WOKE EARLY, slipped on the appropriate shoes, left McGrath asleep on the floor, and wandered downstairs. Mama–san had left a pot of coffee on the counter with two mugs beside it. Sweeney was right. She was used to Americans. I filled a cup and headed outside to the terrace. I glanced next door and noticed my sentry on the neighboring rooftop. I sighed, recognizing that I should be grateful for his steady sentinel, rather than feeling like a caged animal. I positioned a chair close to the railing and sipped my coffee.

As I sat and listened to the pounding waves, I lingered on the gulls swooping over the sea. Then I grabbed a pair of binoculars, peered through them, and spotted a circle of humpback whales bubble feeding in the distance. By the time McGrath showed up with his own cup of coffee, I felt momentarily at peace. He kissed me, then settled in beside me.

"Good morning," I said. "Sleep okay?"

"Like a baby until 3 a.m.," he replied. "But the crab kicked up and I wound up in the bathroom, which, by the way, leaves a little to be desired."

I laughed. "I bet. How'd that work out for you?"

"Like a skit from Saturday Night Live." He clasped my free hand. "Hopefully, I won't need to use the facilities too often."

I laughed. "Stand is the operative word." My mood took a serious turn. "What do we do now?"

McGrath smiled and patted my hand. "Sit tight. We've got great scenery, a hot spring to play in, and great food, courtesy of Mama–san. We can always amuse ourselves in the bedroom if we get bored."

"I hate this waiting. I want to go home. See Ed and the kids. Get my life back on track."

McGrath patted my leg. "Call home. It might help."

"Am I too much to handle?"

"Absolutely not," he said. "But we need to take care of ourselves and each other so we can get home safely. I'm like you. I like to control what I can. Prevent, rather than react. But sometimes, like now, things are out of our hands and we have to rely on others to do their jobs and protect us. Go, call the kids."

I checked my watch. Eight in the evening back home, a perfect time to call. I ran upstairs and dialed, waited anxiously for the call to connect, and reminded myself that I couldn't allow myself to become emotional when I spoke with the kids.

Nick picked up on the fourth ring. "Mom!" he said.

"Hey, Bud, I miss you," I choked out. A single tear trickled down my cheek. So much for keeping it together.

"Yeah, me too," he said, blowing me off like any typical teenage boy. "Guess what?" His voice carried a wave of excitement.

"Um, you caught a huge bass. Or you bought a huge bass," I joked.

"No, but if you want to buy me a bass when you get home, I can help you pick one out."

"Haha," I said. "Not likely. So, tell me, what's up."

"Grandpa has a girlfriend! She's awesome. I told you about her last time, remember? At first, she dropped by a couple of times and brought us homemade cookies and stuff, but last night, she and Grandpa made us barbecued chicken and fresh corn, like they're officially a couple, then they took us to play miniature golf."

"So, you like her because she brings food and plays games."

"Yeah, so when you get home, you can introduce us to your boyfriend and we can all hang out together."

"What makes you think I have a boyfriend?" Damn kid. He has laser-like ESP when it comes to his mother.

"Mom," he said, "I'm not stupid."

"No, you're not. Is there any other news?" I asked by way of distraction.

"Marie and Annie are hanging out with boys, too." He began to sing Love is in the Air, the song I always sang as a way of teasing the girls when they entertained boys at the house.

I laughed. "Okay, dude," I said, "now put your brother and sisters on the phone. I need to catch up with everyone."

"Sure, Mom," he said. "Love you."

I spoke with each one of my kids, telling them I loved them and that I'd see them in August. Hedging my bets. I felt better after hearing their voices, and then again after Ed reassured me that all was well.

"You alright, Sam?" Ed asked.

I paused for a moment and thought this over. "It's been a difficult trip, Dad. But yes, I'm well. Right now, my plan is to spend a few more weeks here, maybe take some side trips. But as soon as I firm up my return, I'll let you know."

"Take your time," he said. "We're great."

"That's what I hear," I teased.

After I ended the call, I refilled my coffee mug and strolled back to the terrace. I spotted our guard, just barely. The bill of his cap peeked over the rooftop next door.

I pulled out a pencil and a pad of paper from my pocket and jotted down a rush of thoughts:

STITSILL.
- Confirmed, calculating killer. Accomplished and well-traveled hit man with serious connections.

- Killed people to fake his own death. Twice?
- Killed for hire/vocation.
- Poisoned his wife, Rosie, and made it look like an illness.
- Lots of lethal skills and no conscience.
- He may want to make this personal. I know too much. He sent a lackey to kill me last summer. I'd killed him instead. He'd might as well do the job himself this time and make sure it's done right.
- I may not be safe once I returned to the States. Will the Witness Protection Program accept me? And my kids? And Ed? And McGrath?
- Plan wedding???

McGrath arrived and peered over my shoulder. "What's this?"

"Just organizing my life," I joked. "How 'bout you?"

"My quads and gluts are killing me. I haven't squatted that long in my entire life. The pain in my backside makes my stomach problems the least of my concerns."

I laughed. "Now you know what we girls go through in public restrooms."

"But at least you fit inside the stall. I'm a contortionist in there."

I laughed, just imagining.

"It's not funny." McGrath frowned and shook his head.

"I'm keeping a lookout for our friend on the roof. I can see him if I squint really hard," I said.

"That's good. We want him to blend right in." McGrath shot a sideways glance at the neighboring rooftop, then raised his eyebrows and nodded.

"Sitting on a roof in a polo shirt and shorts with a pair of binoculars strapped to your eyes works well in these parts." I laughed, fidgeted briefly, then said, "I remember spotting a computer inside."

"Why? What's up?" McGrath narrowed his eyes at me.

"Just want to Google something."

"You've been in Google withdrawal since losing your computer, haven't you?"

"I didn't lose my computer. It was stolen! By Stitsill, I might add. I can't wait to be rid of him. Once and for all."

McGrath chuckled. "He's been around for a long time. The guy's infiltrated several countries as a hired gun, a thief, a philanderer, and he also indiscriminately impregnates women and then disappears. He's not going to be easy to take out." McGrath squeezed my shoulder. "Now what is it you're about to Google?"

"I'll let you know when I'm finished."

McGrath's face changed. His voice became serious. "Don't Google his name, or any of their names, or the Embassy, or the Consulate. None of that. It could compromise our position."

I shook off a sudden chill. It wasn't what I intended to do, but I made a note of it. I stood, hurried inside, and located a desktop computer complete with an English keyboard tucked behind the tiny reception desk. With Momoko-san nowhere in sight, I sat down and Googled the Witness Protection Program. Sweeney hadn't mentioned it, but I'd watched enough Dateline to know the score. Stitsill had lots of connections. Each breath brought worry for me and my family. If I did make it back to the States in one piece, could we live our lives safely? If not, where would we go? I'd probably be unable to teach, my life's blood pumping in some unfamiliar direction. How would I deal with that? Would I wind up as a greeter at some warehouse store? What about my kids and their lives? Could they start over? I wanted to feel furious with my late husband in that moment, blame him, but I couldn't summon the energy.

As the cursor whirled, I drummed my fingers on the desk. I clicked on several different links. What I uncovered did not make me happy. The OWP (Office of Witness Protection) worked in conjunction with Interpol and numerous other countries, including Japan. Stitsill remained my priority. Certainly, he had access to all of this information—who was in the program, where they were living, and the like. I didn't imagine Lucas would decide the Witness Protection Program was a safe haven for me and my kids, because we'd never be safe from Stitsill. There was only one way out. Stitsill needed to be…neutralized, for lack of a more derisive term.

My stomach knotted. I recognized that I should follow McGrath's lead. He seemed so calm. "Let the professionals do their job," he had said. I struggled with that. Relying on others had always proved a stretch for me. Could I really trust anyone else? I guess this experience would serve as a true test of my ability to do just that.

My thoughts rambled. I'd been a fighter as long as I could remember. Independent, headstrong, albeit impulsive. I knew it had a lot to do with my childhood. Losing my parents had shaped me in countless ways. It was the deciding reason I'd become a special education teacher. I picked up strays. Not cats. Children. Since I knew I could count on myself for anything I needed, I could take care of others and protect them from the kind of pain I'd endured as an orphaned teenager.

I thought then about my emotionally impaired students. Jack had often said that I understood them in ways no one else would. He also said no one would have spent the time with them that I did. He was busy writing kids off before they ever entered his classroom, and I was always busy trying to convince him that there were justifiable reasons that these poor kids acted in the bizarre fashion that they did. I frequently reminded him it was our job to mold their little psyches by supplying the love and support they so deserved. I thought, mistakenly sometimes, that every heartache could be cured with enough love and guidance, forgetting sometimes that these kids had to go back home each and every night, to endure the same insanity that had made them so nutso in the first place.

This might be a good opportunity to get a handle on my need to take care of every living thing, settle down, and let McGrath take care of me. Right! All I could envision was gunning down Stitsill. All by myself. Giving him a piece of my mind before I shot his miserable ass. Guess that meant I was getting past my issues, didn't it?

I shook my head. I'd turned into a cold, heartless bitch. But Stitsill had given me reason, hadn't he?

I recognized that my emotions had more to do with the need to protect my family than anything else. For a moment, though, it seemed as if the fine line between my conscience and my wrath had blurred. I just wanted this man gone from my life. Forever.

My thoughts drifted. How had Stitsill grown up? As a misunderstood kid? Raised by a dysfunctional parent? Abused? Forgotten? Jack had been right. None of it mattered if Stitsill spent his life hurting other people. As far as I could tell, he'd already hurt way more than his fair share.

What the hell was wrong with me? I didn't have time to worry about his psyche. I had one, and only one, concern. His permanent departure from my life.

CHAPTER THIRTY-NINE

STIR CRAZY AFTER my Google search, the absence of answers, and my own conflicted thoughts, I wandered through the first floor of the inn. Momoko-san had vanished, so I had free reign. The common rooms of the hotel were spotless and sparse. A chair here, a plant there, but for the most part, the decorating emphasized simplicity and cleanliness. Surely a life lesson existed in there somewhere, but I couldn't focus on it. I climbed the stairs to our room and discovered McGrath, showered, dressed, and speaking on the phone.

He waved me away, which surprised me. Before I left the room, I did a double-take. He looked worried and disturbed, not a great combination for the guy I considered my ballast. With that, I grabbed the beach bag with my books and the gun McGrath had warned me to keep nearby at all times. I quietly closed the door behind me and stood in the hallway to eavesdrop. McGrath had forgotten that the walls here were paper thin, and I could hear each whispered word.

"How?" he asked.

I listened with rising anxiety, unable to discern what McGrath's words meant or whom he spoke with. He probably suspected I stood just outside the door, and used his words cautiously, either to keep from alarming me, or to keep me in the dark until he decided how he wanted to handle the news in the call.

I decided it was best to leave him alone, so I walked outside. I noticed a workman on the rooftop of the inn to the other side of ours. So, Lucas had guys planted on both sides of us. Did that mean trouble lurked even closer than it had before? Was that what McGrath was talking about with the unknown caller? Or was I overreacting again? I should feel even safer with two guys watching over me, shouldn't I?

What little patience I possessed escaped me. I needed a distraction, and I needed one now. I rifled a magazine from the bag and leafed through it. I read about nail shellac, outfits I could purchase for under $100, and tips on parenting a difficult teen before I settled on a short story about a woman who had been assaulted many times throughout her life as a journalist. I sipped cold coffee and became engrossed in the compelling story.

Then, like a flash of lightening, a realization struck me. If Jon had left behind a message, something explaining what had happened or how he felt about me and the kids, I would have felt closure much sooner. It made sense to write the kids a letter. Pronto. I dug inside my bag and discovered my travel journal, still full of blank pages. I opened it to the first sheet and began to write.

My dearest children,

I came to Japan to find answers about your dad and his final days. While I didn't discover all I had hoped, I've learned some serious life lessons and I need to share them with you.

There is nothing more important than family. Loving each other, encouraging and supporting each other through life's ups and downs are the greatest gifts you can give one other. Spend time with each other. Laugh, cry, even argue with each other. In the end, it's best to know that you have loved each other completely and well.

When the time comes for you to choose a soul mate, look for someone who brings out the best in you, celebrates who you are, laughs with you (and sometimes at you). Find someone who is willing to go the distance.

As your mother, I know your special gifts. Annie, you have the determination of an Olympian. Make it work for you. Stomp your feet all you want. Demand what you deserve. But forgive others for not being as smart as you are. Marie, let your sweetness light the world. Demand that others appreciate it. Don't let people take advantage of you, and don't use your kindness to take advantage of them. Nick, your intuition is spot on. Trust it. Encourage others to discover their own ability to be watchful and perceptive. Believe in yourself. You're way more capable than you're willing to admit. Will, your loyalty will reap many rewards. Don't be afraid to tune in to your abilities. Accept them and the people in your life. Don't turn others away if they aren't quite like you. Branch out. Love the world. And Lizzie, your loving nature and patience will bring you much love in return. Your happiness is contagious. I don't know why I'm telling you this now, but I want you to be strong. Maybe because you're such a bit of a thing...or maybe because I won't be around to see you grow up.

None of us are perfect. That's a good thing...

I stopped and reread my words, the page now blotted with tears. My heart overflowed with emotion. No mother could love her children more. In that moment, I realized that it didn't much matter which words I had chosen for my children, but that I'd left something of myself behind. Something tangible.

I heard footsteps approaching and leaned back my head, pursing my lips in anticipation of McGrath's arrival. As the approaching figure halted, the hair on my arms prickled, and nausea rose in my throat.

"Samantha," the voice said, confident, commanding.

I turned to face my fiercest opponent. Jon Stitsill, my

husband's impostor.

"Mr. Stitsill," I said, shoring up every ounce of strength within me. "I've been expecting you."

He took the chair next to mine, as if he was nothing more than a fellow traveler intent on joining me for a simple chat.

"We do have matters to discuss, don't we?" His smile, sly, slick, and well-practiced, said it all.

I sat back then, like a mere observer, and took stock.

He looked very business-like, dressed in an expensive suit and tie. He'd forgotten that I understood him. Knew him. I'd seen him move in the shadows. Feeling a bit surprised that he seemed as comfortable approaching me in broad daylight as he had been hounding me in the middle of the night, I reminded myself it wasn't Stitsill who'd shown up at my house a little over a year ago. It had been one of his lackeys. Correction — one of his very dead lackeys.

My eyes darted from rooftop to rooftop. I tried to keep my breath even and my thoughts calm, but my heart raced and my pulse points throbbed.

"I've taken care of your friends, Samantha," Stitsill said, his green eyes piercing like razors. "All of them. It's just you and me now."

My heart rose and jammed my throat shut. Did he mean McGrath, too? McGrath was smart and savvy. No way would he have let this guy kill him. More than that, I needed him alive. He had to save me.

"What is it that you and I should discuss?" I asked. I summoned every ounce of courage I ever possessed, imagining him as one of my most challenging students. Never give in. Never give up. Never let them see you sweat. Speak calmly. Continue to breathe.

"On second thought," he said. "There isn't much left for us to talk about." He smirked, seeming quite satisfied with himself.

I swallowed hard, praying with all my might that McGrath was still alive. "I do have a couple of questions, if you don't mind." I needed to buy some time.

He sat back, his long forearms resting peacefully on the arms of the Adirondack–style chair. "By all means," he said.

I studied him. So relaxed. I knew this guy was crazy, but I'd never personally witnessed, up close and personal, the calm, cool exterior of a sociopath. It scared the hell out of me.

"Why my husband?" I asked. "Did he get too close?"

"Funny," Stitsill said, "it all began innocently enough. I came by your husband's identity through an associate. Then, after I began to use his credentials and people began looking for me through him, I guess he got curious."

"Bredel from Botswana," I told him. "You're aware you fathered Suzanne's child, right? Anne is her name, I believe."

Stitsill shrugged.

I nodded as I raised my brows. His lack of concern seemed spot on.

"I still don't understand why you had to kill my husband. Why stage it to look like an accident? How did you persuade the authorities that the woman was in the car with him? Clearly, she wouldn't have survived the crash."

Stitsill locked eyes with mine and chuckled. "There are many people who listen to me. Many people, much wiser than you and your husband, who know enough to follow instructions and keep their mouths shut. Neither you nor your late husband seem to possess that kind of wisdom." Stitsill steepled his fingers, tapping his fingertips together in a slow–steady rhythm.

"So, you have connections to government agencies here and in the States, and they're willing to lie for you."

He locked eyes with me. A confirmation.

"Did Jon find out something about you? Was he close to blowing your cover?"

Finally Stitsill sighed as he made a decision to speak. "Your husband was a nuisance. He found out about the Russian missile silos. He connected the dots from Botswana to Mexico, and then from the States to Japan."

So, I thought, Jon had sorted out Stitsill's involvement. Jon had knowledge of his company's shady dealings, and must have fit the pieces together between his boss's illicit purchases and Stitsill. Meanwhile, I'd been on Stitsill's trail as he'd been poisoning Rosie. I guessed Jon lied about the Botswana calls so I wouldn't worry at the same time I'd been trying to shield him. We were both attempting to figure out the entire situation, and also trying to protect each other and the kids from harm. Then, he'd been killed. Further evidence that fewer than six degrees of separation exist. Unbelievable.

Stitsill had staged the accident, or…maybe Jon's company had done that…made it look like my Jon had driven off the road.

"Why did you kill Rosie? She didn't deserve that. How did she pose a threat?"

"My, my, Samantha. You have a knack for solving puzzles. A schoolteacher with a bit of a brain. Surprising." Stitsill smiled snidely and chuckled. "Rosita was a stupid woman. She should never have contacted you. But you were stupid too. You let her suck you in."

Great. Rosie had put me on his radar. He'd seen me enter his house. Probably saw me watching him walk down the street. He was right. I was stupid.

If he hadn't pissed me off before, he'd succeeded in doing that now. I'd use that anger to fuel my survival instincts.

"You're quite the little Nancy Drew, aren't you? Solving her death." He patted my hand.

"Don't patronize me." I glared at him.

"I've been impressed. You had enough guts to kill one of my men. In cold blood, no less. You didn't flinch, did you?"

I ignored him and directed the conversation back to Rosie's death. "Rosie could have hurt you, if she hadn't been so afraid of you," I said.

Stitsill nodded at me, studied me. "I respect you. You're

tenacious."

I could hardly thank the bastard for the compliment. But I could compliment him instead. Tell him that I admired his ability to get to Rosie, to Jon and me. Sociopaths appreciated praise.

"I admire you, too. You're quite accomplished. I respect your focus."

His eyes drifted to the sky. I could tell he was thinking, deciding what he wanted to say. "Your husband remained focused as well. He refused to become involved with Nanami, but she didn't mind accepting a bribe to lie about her involvement with him, nor did she balk about conceiving a child with a green-eyed Caucasian."

My breath caught in my throat. Jon hadn't betrayed me. Stitsill had set him up. Set me up. Made it appear that Jon had been involved with another woman, engaged Nanami in some kind of sick cover up. All this time, I'd doubted Jon, yet I knew now that he'd been a faithful husband. Tears clogged my throat, and outrage burned beneath my skin, but I wasn't about to let Stitsill see me cry. And I needed to keep my wits about me, so I shelved my rage. There wasn't time to assimilate all this now. That would have to come later. After I'd survived this meeting with the devil.

"You're going to disappear. It's easier than if someone were to find your body, don't you agree?" Stitsill studied me. "Where is the strong box she mailed to you?"

I laughed this time. "I burned the contents long ago. So, I don't know nearly as much as you think I do."

"Regardless, I can't let you live," he said as if he were ordering a sandwich with wheat bread instead of white.

Him or me. I swallowed hard. No question about it. He intended to kill me. Bottom line…I wouldn't go easily. I'd never give up without a fight. I began to think about the gun. If I could just wiggle my nose and have it appear in my hand. Think, Sam. Find a way, damn it. My mind took flight. What was he planning to do to me? Where was my bodyguard? Where was McGrath? Had Stitsill really killed them? Focus, damn it. Keep Stitsill talking.

"Your boys are in trouble," I said. "The family that took them in after Rosie's death isn't able to care for them any longer. Are you truly so heartless that you don't care about your own flesh and blood?" I knew the answer to that, but I was desperate to keep Stitsill distracted, and to stay alive for as long as possible.

A far–away look appeared in his eyes. He drifted off, as if he were bored. Clearly, he wasn't interested in the topic of Joey and Emilio. Try something else, Samantha.

"A young woman called Jon from Canada some years back, looking for you, I believe. Rosie mentioned that you had four daughters in Canada. Could that have been one of your girls who called? The same girl in the wedding photographs?"

"It's possible," he answered, almost as if he was musing about an acquaintance from the distant past.

"Does anyone matter to you?" I asked.

He shrugged. "Stand up."

I had no choice but to do as instructed. Where the hell was McGrath? Where were Lucas' men? I refused to believe they were dead.

"What do you have in mind?" I asked calmly, my knees knocking as I stood before him.

He stood then, too, and pulled out a gun from beneath his suit coat. It had a long nose on it, like some I'd seen on television. I guessed it was a silencer, and I could no longer keep my tears at bay. My kids' faces flashed through my mind. I'd be damned if I would let this sociopath murder my children's only living parent.

I summoned information from the deep recesses of my brain. What had I learned about sociopaths in my years of training with emotionally impaired children? I formed a mental list:

- Sociopaths are charming.
- They are master manipulators with only one goal... getting what they want.
- Sociopaths feel entitled.
- They're pathological liars, so good, in fact, they've been known to manipulate lie detectors.
- Sociopaths don't feel guilt, remorse, or shame. Ever.
- They lack empathy.
- Sociopaths don't accept responsibility for their actions.
- They tend to be vagabonds.

So far, Stitsill met the bill on all counts. I also remembered that sociopaths don't form lasting, loving relationships. Stitsill demonstrated that element of his illness as well.

My thoughts flashed to successful interventions. What worked with sociopaths when they felt desperate to protect themselves? Wait a minute, Stitsill never considered a situation dangerous. He felt invincible. I suddenly remembered my colleague Jack's advice. "Save yourself, woman," he'd always say. "These kids will take you down if you let them."

Stitsill wants to win, I told myself. *He needs his ego stroked. How do I let him win, yet stay alive?* I studied him. He had to be close to sixty, but in amazingly good shape for a guy his age. He had a good eight inches on me, too.

"I have copies of everything you found in my backpack," I said. "If I disappear, the government will come after you. And the media will love this story."

"Go ahead," he said. "Have your fun."

Shit, shit, SHIT! Nothing was working. I decided to forget about letting him win, and concentrate on saving my skin.

"Stupid woman," he muttered. Then, he wound a rope around my wrists. "We're going inside," he instructed. "You can say goodbye to your boyfriend there." My head began to throb. Dusk settled to dark before my very eyes. Help me, God.

I didn't know if I'd find McGrath dead or alive. I only knew that Stitsill had given me the gift of time. I prayed with all my might that I would use it wisely. At this point, God was my only hope. Stitsill and I had been outside long enough. If Lucas' guys were still breathing, they'd have rescued me by now.

I stopped dead in my tracks. "I have one more question," I said. I didn't give Stitsill a chance to respond. "How did you find me?"

Stitsill tossed his head back and laughed. "You called home, Samantha. I had a lock on the kids' phone. The cell tower signaled your location. Small potatoes for a guy like me."

With each passing second, I became increasingly aware of his power. I walked slowly, buying every second possible. Once we entered the inn, I searched for traces of Momoko-san, hoping that Stitsill hadn't killed her along with Lucas' men. An eerie quiet met our arrival.

I winced as Stitsill's voice turned to a creepy whisper. "Now, go upstairs and we'll find your lover boy. Then, I'm going to watch while you kill him."

Time had run out. C'mon, God. It's your big chance. Save me.

I slowly climbed the stairs, my hands still bound behind me. Stitsill had the gun on me, but I couldn't change the course of my thinking. He's gonna kill me. I have to do something. With as much might as I could muster, I launched myself backwards and head-butted him. We hurtled backwards down the stairs. I landed at the bottom, startled, choking on the blood dripping down my throat. When I looked up, coughing and sputtering, I spotted Stitsill tangled in the railing, his arm dangling at an impossible angle, like that of a ragdoll. I couldn't see the gun. If my hands were free, I'd have searched for it and grabbed it. Not an option.

I screamed bloody murder, hoping to warn McGrath. "Stitstill's here. He's on the stairs. Run!"

I scrambled to the wall, pushing myself up, and dashed outside. Tears obstructed my vision. I slammed into Sweeney.

"He's inside!" I screamed.

Lucas turned me around, undid the bindings from my wrists, and pushed me toward a panel truck parked just beyond the end of the driveway. "Get inside," he ordered. "Stay in the back. Secure the latch and wait. Don't get in the cab. You could be spotted there. I'll tap on the rear door twice after I finish up with Stitsill. If after fifteen minutes you don't hear from me..." he paused for a millisecond, "move to the cab and drive away. Do not look back. There are passports and cash in the van. Get to an airport and board the first plane to the States."

My eyes pleaded with him. To be careful. To rescue McGrath and bring him to me in one piece. "I escaped from Stitsill in the back of the inn," I whispered.

"Go," he commanded as he tore for the inn. I hurried around the curve of the driveway to the truck, then stumbled to an abrupt stop. Momoko-san's hand appeared from behind the pond. As I stepped closer, I saw her. She lay dead at my feet. Nausea filled my throat, and I swallowed. Hurry, I told myself. Get away while you still can. Don't leave your children.

I heaved open the rear door of the truck and scuttled inside. Finding the interior of the cargo area pitch black, I fumbled in the dark, finally registering the glint of a door handle. A small door opened from the back of the truck into the driver's cab. Lucas had said to stay in the back and sit tight for fifteen minutes, but I didn't have a watch and I figured it would be easier to get away if I were in the driver's seat. I reasoned it out. Only seconds had passed. Stitsill was still inside, as were Lucas and McGrath. On the other hand, if I snuck back inside, maybe I could help. I clambered into the rear of the truck, located the overhead light and rifled the rear bed until I located a tire iron. It didn't have the quick firepower of a loaded weapon, but it couldn't hurt to be armed.

As I opened the rear door of the truck, I heard a shot. That paralyzed me for a good ten seconds. Stitsill had a silencer on his weapon. Please God, let him be the one who'd been shot. Not just shot, killed. I hurried past Momoko-san, cringing at the sight of her vacant eyes. How I wished I could change all this. So many people had died because of this man. I raced to the entrance of the inn, then thought better of speeding inside. It made more sense to find a safe place, listen, and size up matters before making any more rash moves.

I hid behind the fountain wall near the doorway and held my breath. I heard the sound of the water trickling over the rocks. Nothing else. Next, I heard the squeak of the heavy entrance door. From my hiding place, I stared as a wounded Stitsill stumbled outside. He dropped headfirst to the ground just a few feet in front of me. I lingered, hopeful that McGrath or Lucas Sweeney would appear, ready to finish the job. No one came.

My breathing became ragged. I slowly inched forward, keeping my eyes fixed on Stitsill and waiting for him to make any sudden moves. He lay motionless. I approached him from behind as quietly as I could, the tire iron positioned for a vicious strike if the need arose. Blood oozed from a hole in his back. I watched for signs of life, but there were none. I hit him anyway...just in case. It connected with his head, making a sickening sound. A softened metal-hitting-skull sound.

It was viscerally satisfying. I raised the bar to hit him again. I had to be sure he was dead. But Lucas and McGrath rushed out the door and grabbed my arm. McGrath removed the tire iron from my hands and tried to lead me to a nearby bench.

"No, I want to see his face. I want to feel his pulse. I need proof that he's dead. I want his head in a fucking JAR!" I yelled, building up steam. McGrath stepped back and let me through.

After I checked Stitsill, no pulse, no breathing, no more blood pulsing out of the wound, I checked his face, just to be sure. Definitely him this time. From the stench, his bowels had also let go. Good. Death was messy, and this guy deserved every indignity.   McGrath led me to a bench. I sat there, utterly stunned. Lucas made a series of calls. Emergency personnel soon arrived. Déjà vu. A year ago, I'd killed a man. A man I'd thought was Jon Stitsill, my husband's impostor. Today, we finished him off, the true impostor.

CHAPTER FORTY

MCGRATH AND SWEENEY huddled in front of me as I struggled to regain my bearings. I dabbed the blood still flowing from my nose with McGrath's handkerchief, coughing up the last of the mucus which hung in my throat. Magically, Sweeney delivered a cup of water. I thanked him and managed a sip, even though my hands shook uncontrollably.

Lucas explained to McGrath that once he had sent me to the truck, he'd entered the inn. Stitsill had evidently righted himself, because Sweeney had discovered McGrath and Stitsill at the top of the stairs. Stitsill's back faced Sweeney, and Lucas yelled, hoping to distract him. But instead, Stitsill lunged at McGrath.

McGrath broke in, "I'd been stuck in the fucking can. When I heard Sam yell, I crept into the hall. Stitsill was crazy. His arm looked broken, and he didn't have his gun. He kept coming at me. Screaming some crazy shit about having won. He must have thought he could kill me with his bare hands. I shot him."

Sweeney slapped McGrath on the back. "Can't think of anyone who deserved it more."

"I have no regrets," McGrath said, through a hooded brow.

He had a heart, even with the bad guys. It's what made him a good cop. It's what made me love him.

McGrath had shot him at point blank range. Still, the guy had managed to stumble out of the inn and cross my path before he collapsed. Another shocking chapter in my life had come to a close.

After McGrath regained his bearings, he excused himself. I guessed he wanted to wash the dirt off his hands. It's what I would have done.

Lucas pulled me aside. "I need to explain a few things to you, Samantha," he said.

I nodded. As I turned to face him, I suddenly remembered where I'd seen his name before. On the back of the letter I'd received from Rosie, after she'd died. Scribbled. Just the name. No explanation.

"I witnessed Stitsill kill an innocent man years ago. In a parked car. He got the guy drunk, shot his head off, and walked away. I didn't realize it at the time, but I came to discover that Stitsill had staged his own death."

My eyes widened in shock, remembering Rosie's words. She'd never seen her husband's body after his death. He'd been identified though the belongings investigators found on his person.

"I was a different man then," Lucas admitted. "An alcoholic, in fact. That drunk he killed could easily have been me."

I looked into Sweeney's clear brown eyes. "Doesn't seem possible." Still, I listened intently, driven by the need to understand this man, wondering if he was the attorney Rosie had mentioned before her death.

"I'd recently lost my wife and baby in a fatal car accident. My slope was steep and slippery. Nothing mattered after their deaths. Just my next drink. I'd lost my law practice, my family. Everything." Lucas covered his face with his hands, took a measured breath, and then continued. "I'm not proud of those days. I'd witnessed Stitsill kill another man and did nothing. But it did kill my desire to drink. It took a few years for me to get a life back, and that was with an agency. I reached out to Stitsill's wife, Rosita. Because of her terror, I made a vow to her and to myself — to find him and never to rest until I was able to bring him to justice."

"I believe we accomplished that today," I said, locking my gaze with his.

"It's important that you understand that your husband loved you," he added.

I'm sure I looked surprised. These connections seemed impossible. Yet, their existence couldn't be denied. Tears spilled down my face.

"Jon and I became friends during the course of an investigation," he continued.

"The Russian missile silos…"

"Precisely," Lucas answered.

I rested my hand on Lucas' arm. "I'm sorry for the loss of your wife and child," I said. "And Momoko-san. She didn't deserve this."

"It's not your fault."

"My sadness runs so deep. So many people have lost their lives. Good people. I hate what's happened. I'm guessing my understanding will grow with time, but I'm not there yet."

Lucas nodded and took my hand. "I can't tell you how sorry I am that I couldn't have prevented your husband's death. Jon and I worked together once he became aware of his boss' dealings with the missile silos. He fed me information. Jon wanted to do the right thing, but keep his employees and his family safe at the same time. His courage impressed me, as well as his devotion to you and the kids. We were friends."

I could only shake my head. None of this seemed real.

"I can only imagine how confusing all of this has been for you." Sweeney's eyes reflected a pain similar to my own.

"Do you know what really happened to my husband? How did he really die?"

"He was run off the road. No one ever believed a woman

had been in the car with him, but she appeared at the accident scene claiming to have somehow escaped the crash. I don't have enough evidence to confirm my suspicions, but there's every chance Jon's company was involved in the crime. Stitsill had company connections too. My guess is as their hired hand. It's as ugly as it gets."

I felt as if my heart would arrest. My poor husband. What went through his mind as he hurtled over that cliff? I'm sorry, Jon, for ever doubting you. Please forgive me.

Lucas squeezed my hand. I buried my head in his chest and sobbed. Several long minutes later, when my tears finally subsided, he spoke.

"Jon made me promise to keep an eye on you. He knew if anything happened to him, you'd get involved. I phoned you after his death. Several times."

I lifted my eyes. "I stopped answering calls. Stopped listening to voicemails. It became too difficult. I had no idea what had happened to my husband. I'm not just talking about the accident, but for many reasons, I ceased trusting him. I regret that now. More than I can say."

"Things happen," Lucas said. "Things we can't always understand. But know this. Your husband loved you and your kids more than life itself."

"I need a few minutes," I told Lucas. I closed my eyes. After several moments, I was able to take in air.

"Please, may I stay in touch?" he asked.

"Of course," I answered, grabbing his hand and clinging to him.

"I have matters to attend to." With that, he patted my hand, stood, and re-entered the inn. I sat alone in the quiet darkness, drinking in the possibility that I might now be safe and able to carry on with my life. Return to normal. A new normal, at least.

For sure there'd be more fallout. I'd be forced to reorder my life once again. In the meantime, I counted my blessings. McGrath and I were safe. Stitsill was dead. Out of my life.

Forever.

McGrath stepped toward me. I rose and held onto him, asking, "How did Sweeney manage this all by himself?"

McGrath held me at arm's length. "I'm not sure, but I'm guessing he had some amount of backing, probably asked his people to allow him to come in first. For him, as for Stitsill, this had become personal."

"He said he promised Rosie that he'd take care of her husband."

"I've seen it before," McGrath said. "Hell, I've done it before."

* * *

Before our flight departed, I called Ed and the kids, letting them know I'd see them in ten days. First, I planned to return home and make sure the reconstruction effort had been completed. And I wanted time to regroup and settle back into my life before I headed to the cottage. So much had changed.

McGrath and I occupied First Class on a direct flight from Nagoya to New York. We decided to rent a car and drive the eight hours home once we reached the States. Debriefing time and all. Lucas had assured us of safe travel without the aid of false passports, and McGrath joked that he'd rather we traveled as Mr. and Mrs. Smith than as ourselves.

Perhaps this entire insane episode was finally over.

"Why was Sweeney the Lone Ranger?" I asked McGrath. "Why didn't he have more help? You'd think he'd have had an army behind him."

"He's on foreign soil, Sam. We will never know what really happened, or Sweeney's role, official or unofficial. It's an intricate web Stitsill wove, and it won't be undone in any way that we'll ever know about. It would just endanger us more. Sweeney did what he had to do in the way he had to do it. We can't question him. Only thank him."

I gazed out the window as I fought to put this nightmare behind me.

McGrath laid a hand on my knee. "How's your nose?" he asked.

"It's the bruising that bothers me the most." I winced as I touched my cheek. "And my shoulder still aches." I tried stretching my arms over my head. Not quite yet.

"I say we take Nick's advice and you bring me along when you drive up to the cottage. If the kids are used to Ed's new woman, they should take to me like a duck to water."

"Nice diversion. Now who's living in la–la land?" I joked.

I settled my head into the crook of his shoulder and slept. When I awoke, McGrath and I decided important matters like where we would stay that night and what wine we would drink with dinner.

My cell rang as soon as we touched down in New York. I answered before checking the caller ID. It was Di.

"Sam, where have you been? I've been trying to reach you. I was getting worried."

I sighed and chuckled. "It was a great trip. I'm feeling better. I'll tell you all about it when I see you. What's up with you?"

"Great news! I finally took your advice and Chris and I went away for the weekend. All it took was some hot sex, and he agreed to adopt the boys."

Another member of the La–La Land Club, I decided.

"Really? Just hot sex? Certainly, it couldn't have been that simple."

"Chris has a big heart," Di insisted. "He's always wanted a son, and since he's getting older, he was an easy sell. This way, he doesn't have to wait through the baby and toddler years to play ball with his boys."

"I'm happy for you, Di," I said, "and those boys are very lucky to have you and Chris as parents. I'll be home in a week or so. We'll talk then, alright?"

"I can't wait to help you get the house settled. I walked

by there yesterday. Julie was outside checking on the crew, and she let me peek inside. It looks just like it did before the fire. You're going to be happy. Are you sure you're okay? The trip had to be hard on you." Di hadn't changed a bit in my absence, and I felt certain she'd be happy to line my refrigerator shelves with paper towels. I loved her and realized I couldn't wait to see her.

"Everything's great, Di. Honest."

I remembered the day Di and I had canoed on the river. She'd told me then that Chris was the one. The look of possibility had made her eyes sparkle. I glanced over at McGrath, and imagined I held that same look in my own eyes in that instant.

After I ended the call, McGrath tipped my face toward his.

"I love you, Sam," he said.

I hesitated, suddenly overwhelmed by the reality of what I'd learned from Stitsill and Sweeney at the inn. "In those final moments," I admitted, "I learned some things about Jon. Stitsill had set up the entire thing: the mistress, the accident, the baby. I'm sorry I didn't tell you sooner, but it changes my grief, knowing that Jon had been faithful. I need some time to sort it all out."

His brows knit. "What are you saying?"

"I might be sad sometimes."

"I'm here for you. I'm not letting go. In good times and bad. In sickness and in health."

A lump formed in my throat. Bottom line, Jon would have wanted this for me.

I then pressed my lips to McGrath's, asking God to free me from the past, and whisk me like a gentle breeze, into the future.

–END–